REVOLUTION OF THE SPECIES

The Terrifying Environmental Thriller

By

Simon Holder

This is a work of fiction. Names, characters, businesses, organisations, places, events and incidents either are the product of the author's imagination or are used fictitiously. Any resemblance to actual persons, living or dead, events, or locales is entirely coincidental.

Dear Reader,
If you enjoyed this novel, I would be grateful if you could kindly give me a 4 or 5 star rating on Amazon.com or Amazon.co.uk. This would really help me - thanks in anticipation.
Simon.

BY THE SAME AUTHOR

For The Love of a Life - an unusual international love story.

It's All In The Script! - a dastardly humorous thriller involving a present-day TV soap opera set in the 18th century.

A Cultured Pearl and other stories of Love, Longing, Mystique and Hope…

To Abby -
Best wishes,
Simon

THE REVOLUTION OF THE SPECIES was originally written and published in 2006; revised and updated 2023. This edition is dedicated to the hundreds of friends and well-wishers who have pleaded with me to revise and update this work; although it is fiction, its main premise has become perilously close to being partly true as some elements happened after its first publication; it is this that makes them believe that this novel is so environmentally important and a 'ripping good yarn' to boot! Anyone with a concern for our planet's future should enjoy and empathise with this tale…

CONTENTS

BOOK ONE

In The Beginning...

Chapter 1

The air was fresh, with a dash of rain; below the hanger, an occasional stream was starting to swell, becoming more perceptible by the moment. Above, an escarpment sheared away like a scimitar, and sparse, small dark clusters of trees gave an alien, unnatural feel to the predominantly brackened landscape. To most eyes, this was the quintessence of an English fell: open, hostile, wild, barren but savagely serene under its vast sky. Apart from a wretched grass, only mosses, lichens and weeds clung to the skin of earth that was forever in danger of slipping off its rocky foundations, both of which were doused incessantly; this continuous movement of water, falling relentlessly from iron skies, made any permanency impossible. Clumps of sod, bracken and gorse - even orphaned trees - were frequently found at lower levels than at which they started out, the water causing an inexorable decline to the base of this cleft slope. Then the cycle started at the top again, with green young sprigs straining hopefully towards the big but murky light.

Shepherd Scar - for such was its name - was a hostile place for man or beast and, in normal circumstances, would not have entertained the former very often: indeed, even surefooted sheep were sometimes found lifeless at the base of its sheer side. Formed by a landslip many thousands of years ago, its immense curve stretched for nearly two miles, although in several places this was broken by jagged outcrops that reached out to scratch into the rain and mist. Below this gash, though, was a more sheltered terrain, where vegetation had evolved with a more varied provenance, twisting itself into the heavy atmosphere and clawing at life through the thin, slippery soil.

But Shepherd Scar had another claim to the second part of its name. Just above and behind it, the ground fell away sharply: this sheer drop then became a small plain which, behind and below the summit, formed an isolated expanse surrounded by tall crags on all sides, jutting irregularly upwards and resembling the ruined foundations of a Norman keep. These were not large or majestic but stolid and unforgiving - the perfect place behind which to hide something sinister, remote, camouflaged and difficult to find. Indeed, these conditions had been deliberately adopted because these outcrops - colluding with the mist - cloaked a series of low, grey, shed-like structures that vied with the sky for dank dullness. Birds would have noticed the first four letters of the alphabet distributed severally on each roof of these hideous testaments to humanity: each of the four long huts had a corridor protruding from one of its short sides where the ends were closest to each other, and these were all joined together by their meeting at a smaller hut that made one room in the middle of them all. Here, there was a main entrance, announced ignominiously by a slab of seeping concrete which served as a car-park, stretching flatly between the two easternmost blocks. From this, a poorly-maintained asphalt track crunched its way off the plain, squeezing through two furrowed black boulders and down to the outside world. The four quadrangles looked as though they had been constructed in a hurry in case the weather broke before completion - or their location became known. They had been built as a secret but stood out so blankly against the surrounding green that even the carefully-planted but distressed and anaemic trees were never up to their job of concealment. As if to accentuate this, at the ends of the two westernmost buildings there were six open squares extending further into the drizzle, built into a slight downward slope that made them lower than the buildings: they were holding-pools and the first pair, bridged by two rusting pipes across the gap between the huts, was higher than the subsequent one. Then the next was a little lower still, so that sediment within the waste liquid emanating from the buildings sank to the bottom but the cleaner water oozed over the edge into the next, until the final pool, whereupon it trickled over the edge and into the environment as supposedly clean fell water...

The complex had been constructed when the environment held no votes and the pools were wide open to any creature that did not understand the otherwise compelling signs to keep out. But as the first twitchings of green politics had started in the seventies, so state-of-the-art sensors had been installed, so that when the first two pools became a rank, foul, viscous mess, these sensors alerted the authorities. A crack team would then empty the sludge into a tanker, whereupon it was disposed of 'in the proper manner': in other words, it was surreptitiously dumped at sea. However, successive government cutbacks, lack of interest - and the fact that fewer and fewer people knew the site was there at all - meant that a conspiracy of apathy and desuetude had rendered the sensors useless: and even if they had worked, there was now no-one there to do anything about it. And so, more and more frequently, it was a toxic fluid that seeped over the final edge...

The pools had all but evaporated over a drier than usual two months; but now, as the rain intensified, so they were slowly, inexorably filling again as the downpour complemented the waste within them. Scar Brook was growing again, too: starting from the top of the crags as a trickle, it dropped two hundred feet to their base, then flowed past these holding-pools where it mingled with whatever was being disgorged. It then became a small, murky marsh and subsequently disappeared underground, eventually re-emerging on the other side of Shepherd Scar as a small waterfall which propelled itself in a torrent down Scar Fell. It was a pure, bright stream, which had flowed for thousands of years on its course down to Bracken Mere.

The Shepherd Scar Research Centre was both an enigma and a lie: successive governments had always pretended not to acknowledge its existence, which meant that it could theoretically be used for any type of secret research according to the whims of the time - which it always was. Initially, it was built for germ warfare; then, in the seventies, it became a base for nuclear research; in the eighties, it was for neutron annihilation; now, it was part of a project to research the capabilities of genetically-modified intelligence through DNA. But whatever its purpose, the spartan rows of research equipment within were as anonymous and banal as ever, the dispiriting scene lit by awkward metal windows that had occasionally rusted shut. To complete the picture, the rooms were bathed in the cold glare of fluorescent light.

Thus, the Shepherd Scar Research Centre had never quite been allowed to be forgotten - an excuse looking for a sinister answer. And so it had continued to exist. But time had not been kind to this place: it would soon be unkinder still.

This was the environment in which Doug Sprake worked - a pasty, puffy, pallid man who reflected his surroundings. He inhabited hut D, where his own brand of DNA-changing research took place; it was being pursued at Shepherd Scar Research Centre because it was on the borders of legality - where sanctioned government projects had sinister ramifications attached to them, for whatever reason, just in case they were ever needed: a sort of dossier on deformation. He had worked at Shepherd Scar for most of his adult life and had accepted the changes in its evil emphasis without demur; he was one of life's acquiescents: but along the way he had used what experience he gained there to complement his fine university grades in physics, biology and chemistry. He had graduated with distinction in all three and had been taken on at Shepherd Scar when it was realised his ethical commitment was negligible. He had been the perfect, willing civil servant, ready to accept the beckoning of any and the remorse of none. Having taken the easy route, though, he had become as unseen as the projects he was involved with, a reason - or, perhaps, an excuse - for ministers to pursue enlightenment within a dark void of secrecy. This was his world, and he knew no other.

He shuffled into hut D. The creatures there - those that were still alive in any sense of the word - were of many types, though mostly mice; some had huge heads or limbs, or ghastly weals on their skins; one had two heads, and others had a variety of abominations that would make a freak-show look like a tea-party, such as human ears growing on their backs, eyes four times normal size, rabbits with six legs and others very obese or skeletally thin; there were those lacking various limbs, genetic attributes or normal senses - or had had them grotesquely enhanced. There was no hierarchy: fish in murky aquaria, dogs, cats, rats, mice, pigs and chickens had all been equally abused at some stage as the unwitting players in this earthly vision of hell.

Ignoring all this silent suffering, Doug systematically and dispassionately unloaded another dozen mice into a large perspex container. He shut the lid down, and wandered off to the canteen for breakfast in 'A' block: there was not too much to do today, as always - just inject a few more creatures with inoxyphenalimine, record and compare the results and go home. But as this unshaven, overweight fifty-year-old passed his few colleagues and several cases of suffering creation, he was vexed: not at their potential demise - any sense of caring had evaporated years ago - but for his research, which was not progressing well; he needed a spurt of inspiration if he was to create some breakthrough. For what was uppermost in his mind - and had been gathering momentum for some months - was to create something at government expense that he could then sell on in the open market: his sense of ethics would certainly never be tested from a loyalty point of view. Not that he would have been loyal at all, of course: working on secret projects was fine in its own way - indeed, he enjoyed the anonymity and the fact that he answered to no-one except his ultimate research superior and then a distant minister - but he increasingly felt the need for recognition. But he was only a guilty secret. As a result, his isolation and the covert nature of his work had slowly caused resentment and, even if it meant exposing all that Shepherd Scar Research Centre stood for, he would profit from it if he could: that was fine by him. He could then live his life as a millionaire in the sun, far away from Shepherd Scar and the ashen inmates within its asbestos walls - the human ones as well.

Two teas, bacon, eggs, toast and marmalade safely inside him, he dropped his head into his pudgy hands, belched quietly and thought deeply. A colleague on a nearby table who worked in hut 'B' tried to attract his attention but was instantly aware that Doug did not want to converse. Even the very simple crossword in the open newspaper in front of him appeared more difficult than usual. He was not good at them at the best of times, but a few solved clues were often useful filling in the long hours waiting for experiments to show results. The muffled thud and whine of a songstress on the canteen radio was a distraction, too, but he nevertheless found himself troubled by the words of the refrain, distantly understood, that kept permeating his mind. "Give-a-little-bit-more, baby, Gimme-another-drop..." It went round and round. Suddenly, he was aware of it. He grunted, then, about to get up, paused. "Give a little bit more, baby, Gimme another drop." Instantly, he knew what he was going to do. Inspired, he bought a chocolate bar from the vending machine on the way back to his lab, determined to ignore his research findings and live dangerously. This meant going against regulations because he had decided to indulge this sudden whim for himself - no-one else would know about it: it was going to be off the record. It was his turn for the good life, and he was going to do it, come hell or high water - and there was plenty of both at Shepherd Scar.

Chapter 2

Jessie Scott was by no means a true beauty, but with a cheeky, sly grin and a superb figure - as well as a wicked sense of humour - she usually got what she wanted. The latest object of this ability was still asleep in her bed, but she had been up early, surfing the internet for information on government deception. Since the Freedom of Information Act had been passed, though, this had become even more difficult to find, as all important files had, under government authority, been decimated, expunged, or re-filed under 'State Secret' - which she felt only put things back to where they had been before. As a tricksy but committed freelance journalist, she had made a name for herself as a feisty, objective, bloody-minded reporter with no political affiliations and a strong sense of duty; and although she had joined the currently governing party, it was not for ideology but for the sole purpose of being able to rub shoulders with ruling ministers. After a few revelations, though, the government now hated her and she had received several bullying, threatening missives from the communications director; but determined to continue exposing political indiscretions and lies, she had been expelled from the party and so now had to live on her wits. It was a situation that gave her the freedom she wanted but made her life difficult, occasionally dangerous - and very exciting. She would not now have it any other way.

She sighed as she got yet another 'information unavailable' pane on her computer. 'If only I was a hacker', she mused. She was trying to discover a new angle on anything that she could berate the government for and had a feeling that it might be her day today: her rising star had been unvocally supported by many in the Opposition and by a host of TV companies, although the BBC had been reluctant to use her officially because, being under intense political scrutiny by the government for 'bias' and concerned about their licence money, she was political dynamite. As far as she was concerned, though, 'truth' was her bias, even though the government liked it not a bit unless it was slanted in their direction. It was that which fired her up, and continued to do so.

She typed 'UK government cover-ups' into her search window and pressed 'enter'. As she did so, a hand started to caress her hair from behind. "Hello, Dan," she said absent-mindedly, watching a whole page of links appear on the screen.

The hand withdrew. "It's not Dan, it's Jason," a croaky, tired voice replied. "Looks as though it's time I left."

"Ah," she said, turning to him. "Sorry."

Jason, unkempt, bleary-eyed and still not a little worse for wear through excessive alcohol consumption the night before, turned away disconsolately but without emotion. "I thought you were like that," he murmured. "Still, it was fun."

As Jessie had turned to him, though, she had seen something on the screen out of the corner of her eye that demanded attention. "Sorry, Jason. Pressure of work," she added towards the space behind her, her focus now fully on the word that had jumped up to arrest her. "I'll be with you in a minute, though - and it was fun..."

Her response was met by the slam of the front door. But she did not mind. What she had seen looked far more interesting...

She had stumbled across a whole set of government links that led her to areas she had never seen before. Confronted with a surfeit of choice, she prodded her mouse on the words 'unofficial drugs' and waited a moment. What came up surprised her: she saw a list of incomprehensibly-impossible names to pronounce that had been supposedly proscribed by the government but which had nonetheless continued in production. The list went back several years, but what intrigued her was the fact that they had slipped through the Freedom of Information bonfire of government-incriminating documents and were there not only to be seen but to be researched into. She chuckled with glee. Jason was an even more distant memory now. As was Dan, whoever he was...

As she searched further, she saw that some of the drugs had been developed secretly in Britain as part of the Americans' Afghanistan war effort: some were of a more domestic nature and some were difficult to assess what on earth they were for - or ever had been. But the bottom line was that someone had spent a lot of time - and put themselves into not a little danger - in order to ensure that these documents had not been silenced... She made a few notes and started cross-referencing some of the drugs' names that she saw. Arriving at a file named 'Top Secret', she was surprised when she managed to get into it. Before her eyes was a long list of drugs - two hundred and seventy-three of them - which were under the heading 'What the government doesn't want you to know'. Astonished at the paradox of the openness and yet intended secrecy, she began to look at them in more detail. What she found confusing was the fact that, after each name, there was a set of initials, most of which were 'SS'. Knowing that it could not be a throwback to the Second World War - all the drugs were far too recent for any Nazi connection - it made her wonder.

She clicked on a drug: its ingredients and intended purpose were displayed. But after some of them - particularly after the ones with these appended initials - there was frequently an added note, often misspelt, which gave a more chilling view of what it was to be used for unofficially. For example, after a drug called anthicin, the supposedly official purpose for its creation was 'the suppression of nausea in post-operative environments', to inhibit vomiting by patients following hospital operations. But after this had been added: 'Also to cause acute nervous paralysis except for speech in post-battlefield operations to extract information without potential for aggressive body movement. Highly dangerous and volatile. Subsequent survival unlikely'. At each of these, Jessie's disbelief became more palpable. And she had the strong feeling that she had barely seen the beginning of it...

Back in his area, Doug looked at his rows of chemicals: "Give a little bit more, baby"; the song went through his mind again. He selected a hypodermic and filled it with the regulation amount of inoxyphenalimine from a glass phial. Then, he added another random amount and, looking along his death row of possible ingredients, picked out another phial in which was a substance called parlazine. 'This should be interesting', he thought: a mixture of a brain stimulant and a substance that was being perfected in another part of the establishment, officially to help stroke sufferers with speech. Unofficially, it was to make those withholding information from the government to talk - without ever remembering that they had done so. As an afterthought, he added another chemical to the hypodermic, a substance called manganese tripuride, which was something he had developed himself to restrict the ageing process: that was the official line, anyway. In fact, it was to ensure that people subjected to torture or acute trauma in military situations would not be scarred mentally: it had a reverse effect to the others on their DNA - and he wanted his subjects to survive if he was to observe the long-term effects of what he was doing.

He regarded the potent mix in his hand, picked up a fresh mouse, injected the liquid into its neck, put it into its own perspex container - away from the others - and sat back to watch...

Chapter 3

The liquid level in the final pair of draining-pools at Shepherd Scar was drawing level with the farthest edge and would soon start trickling over the side...

Scar Brook was full, too, as it continued its course past the research centre, flowed underneath the crags and then on to Bracken Mere, a small lake that was home to a variety of freshwater fish. It then coursed out at the other end into the Hildaburna where, in spring, salmon would risk their lives getting up to this inland lake and then, after spawning, would make the same perilous journey back to the sea. For those people that could make the effort to get there, Bracken Mere offered the rich experience of a perfect ecosystem. Virtually no pollution - except that brought by winds mostly cleansed of their vile industrial content after crossing miles of open fell - offered an unusually pristine environment in this barren place, despite its proximity to Shepherd Scar. In turn, the Hildaburna was a tributary of the Fellrigg River which then joined the Mersey and, growing in importance and power, swept past Liverpool to the open sea, its force of nature, its spate of life, incessant and unstoppable.

At Shepherd Scar Research Centre, the swelling

level of liquid in pool D3 went unremarked upon, as usual. Inside, Doug was watching his mouse closely: it was less agitated than normal after its very large dose of inoxyphenalimine. So what was making the difference? The larger dose or its subsequent reaction with the parlazine? Or the manganese tripuride? It was calmly but cogently looking around as if trying to find something outside its glass case, with a studied expression of comprehension that Doug had never seen before. Suddenly, it fixed its small red eyes onto something behind Doug, its whiskers bristling fervently, and started a high-pitched squeaking. Doug turned to where the mouse was looking, and was startled to see that all the mice in the holding case next to it, rather than sniffing about as usual, were all looking towards their fellow being. Doug's heartbeat quickened a little: he had never experienced this before. He looked around and noticed to his surprise that even the rabbits were quietly observing him: and the other creatures, too. Normally, they were all oblivious to one another, except when mating, and that was only fleetingly. No, this time, there seemed to be a real intent on all their faces, whatever their species, and some were pricking their ears up; but all were intent on the noise coming from the container. Suddenly, the noise ceased, but the rodent onlookers kept their attention fixed: the mouse then let out a plangent cry that was so loud it echoed around the room. The others, in the adjacent cases, all started to screech too, in different volumes, intensities and pitches. But why? He had not given any of these creatures the same drugs, and some were on completely different experiments and not in any way connected with his research on the solitary mouse. And different animals usually required different intensities; yet they all seemed equally affected. Then Doug heard something else: despite the noise, he was suddenly aware of barking and sighing from the beagle-house next door. That in itself was not unusual: what was strange was that it was a different cadence to normal and it seemed more ordered, measured and intelligent.

His interest aroused, Doug shifted his weight and, quite immediately, the noise stopped - first his charges and then, a moment later, the dogs' barking. "Now, here's something interesting," he thought. Then he noticed that all the eyes were on him, following him as he lolled from the first container to the second. The silence continued as Doug decided to try the same experiment on another mouse, but perhaps with a larger dose of parlazine: he was sure it was this that had made the difference and, picking up the sharp, went to his row of deadly ingredients once more. As he did so, the solitary mouse began to screech again, and Doug saw that the others seemed to be listening intently. He filled the hypodermic with the three ingredients from the phials - but with a very much larger dose of each. His actions were accompanied the whole time by the mouse's protestations: as he approached the full container, he noticed that all the eyes were now on him again, and the solitary mouse was still screeching. He lifted the lid, just as the mouse screamed even louder and more violently, as if shouting a warning: he thrust his hand in, which usually resulted in the creatures running in as many different directions as possible. This time, though, they all lunged at it as one, as if they had been instructed to do so: two ran up his arm, and the others bit his hand so hard that the blood flowed instantly from half a dozen wounds. As he recoiled, he dropped the hypodermic from his other hand, which fell into the container; the animals were onto it immediately and drinking from the leaking needle. At the same time, as he recoiled he had knocked the three phials off the bench, which smashed on the concrete floor, their contents spilling outwards with a sputtering sound: he just managed to get the two mice back in the case, and slammed the lid down. He was too astonished to swear, which he would have done normally, and not a little frightened. What had happened? He looked back at the solitary mouse, and saw what he was sure was a look of quiet, subdued contentment on its face. The others, too, were now silent - and each was surveying him...

He perfunctorily wiped his bleeding hand with his other one and went to the first-aid cabinet, taking out some antiseptic, plasters and a couple of gauzes. Noticing some of the liquid mingling with the blood on his wounds, he wiped it off and then wrapped the medicaments around his various bites. His domain was suddenly different, almost alien, despite his years there. He glanced at the floor and noticed that the liquids, which had fallen just by a drain, were winding their way into it... An eerie silence had descended, and he had never in his life felt so observed.

Outside, the wind was lashing the rain into a frenzy of conflicting directions, and the liquid in pool D3 started to drip over the edge: drop by drop, it ran down the side and onto the ground. It then conjoined with Scar Brook and flowed out into the wild...

Doug was now on the phone to a colleague. Mick was a thin, lively, hyperactive sort of man, who never got fat whatever he ate or drank: however, his scrawniness made him look older than his forty-five years. Doug was guardedly trying to ascertain if Mick had done any experiments on his beagles with inoxyphenalimine or parlazine: not wanting to give any of his own research away - and his actions were against the rules anyway - he had to be careful so did not mention the manganese tripuride. Mick, though, was more open and replied to Doug's question that, a day or two before, whilst passing through the fresh dogs' compound - those next for research - he had inadvertently dropped a large bottle of parlazine: the glass had broken and much of the liquid had been lapped up.

"Have they been acting strangely since?", enquired Doug. There was a pause, then: "Yes, I suppose they have."

The words seemed to reach him with a slightly detached echo, as if coming from the far reaches of space.

"How?" he enquired after a moment.

"Well, the ones who aren't actually partaking in the

tests..."

"Yes?"

"Well, they suddenly started howling a few minutes ago... But it was unusual: it wasn't random barking, it was more ... focussed..."

"A bit as if they were actually conversing?"

There was a moment of silence, then: "Yes, I suppose it was. But to whom, or why, I don't know."

A frisson ran through Doug's body: whether of fear or excitement, he wasn't sure. After a pause, he said, "What are they doing now?"

"They're sort of, looking at me." Then Mick added, "With a hungry look."

Doug turned around and noticed that his mice were doing exactly the same thing to him, with the exception of two that seemed to be conferring with each other: but it was not random, it was almost like a conversation.

"What did you do after you'd dropped the parlazine?"

"Er, well, there wasn't a lot left after the dogs had drunk it, but when I got in and pushed them away I flushed it away with a hose down the drain."

"Did you drop anything else that they might have ingested?"

"Erm, possibly".

"Can you remember what?"

"No, but there was something..."

"What?" Doug barked at him.

"I can't remember now. Oh, wait... It might have been inoxyphenalimine." Doug was breathing more heavily, now. "Or was it something else...? But I don't know whether anything was taken in, either way. I mean, I hosed it away very quickly".

"Into the holding pools."

"Well, yes, I suppose so; Doug, why all the questions?"

Doug paused, as if wondering whether to pursue this further. Then a compulsion came over him: "Fancy a pint tonight?" he enquired.

"Well, I'd love to, but I'm -"

"I think you should," Doug snapped, then added, "Mick, I think this might be serious."

"Oh."

"We might've just altered the course of the planet." The hollow laugh at the other end made Doug realise that Mick had completely misunderstood the gravity of what he had witnessed.

"Well, I'll have a quick drink with you after work, but I can't stay long. OK?"

Doug assented, put the phone down, and looked back at his charges, all of whom were eyeing him intently.

The parlazine that had drained out had, indeed, gone into one of the holding pools. As had all the other substances, whether in minute or larger amounts. And as the rain intensified, whatever cocktail was there would soon be freely coursing over the sides of D3 and into Scar Brook, then Bracken Mere. Diluted it may have been, but its effects would be nothing of the sort...

Chapter 4

Jessie's eyes bulged at what she saw... on the screen in front of her was yet another list. This one, though, was even more sinister than the previous she had seen. These were headed by a title which read: 'If you are reading this then you are foul of the Freedom of Information Act, 2004. I have put these into the public domain as the government is misusing this research for unethical purposes. I might not be here when you read this. Remember other government cover-ups.'

Jessie presumed that this person was alluding to the government scientist who had apparently committed suicide after allegedly revealing evidence embarrassing to his administration. Perhaps there was a concern that the same fate might happen to this person, whoever it was: if it had not already. For there was no date: even when she went to the root of the file, it had somehow been expunged. Whoever this was knew how to cover his or her tracks. All she saw at the end of the list were the initials 'MD'. Ministry of Defence? Unlikely: too specific yet too wide. No, it must be the person's initials, yet how many 'MDs' were there in government research? Then again, she wondered, perhaps it wasn't a government researcher who was imparting this information: perhaps it was someone who had a grudge against either the government or the status quo? Or who had worked in private research and had been hounded out of the country, perhaps by animal rights campaigners? She instinctively felt sure that there must be animals involved - the research was so conclusive. And then, she thought, it must be a government department: how else could they still be operating? But then, perhaps they weren't: after all, there were no dates to check. She mulled the thoughts over in her mind. Everything seemed to conflict... and yet she could not help thinking that it must be - or have been - a government institution. It smacked so much of officialdom, somehow. It was only a hunch, but her experience made her believe that this must be so. 'MD... who are you?' she wondered. She stared at the list and shook her head as she reflected on the effort and time - not to mention money - that must have been spent to justify the results of what she was reading. And, probably, the animal suffering. For she noticed that the word 'serum' was the most prominent noun featured: and also the adjective 'deadly'. She wondered whether there were any humans who had been part of the research, or had it been just animals? And if so, would they work as well on one species as another? She suddenly jolted herself back into reality and reflected that she was beginning to think like those she was trying to fathom. But then again, that was her job and her expertise - putting herself in other peoples' positions. She had exposed many a cover-up like that.

She had an appointment later on - one that would entail working away from home for the rest of the day - and decided that she needed to go for a walk first, which would clear her head and help her to think through what she had seen. She printed off a number of pages, then carefully went back through each link one by one, saving them all under 'favourites', so that she could re-trace her research... She then put the computer off, had a shower, and left.

When she returned that night, she was too tired to research further and decided to leave it until the morning after a good night's sleep. She would soon regret that decision.

Chapter 5

The next morning, the rain had given way to an uneasy truce with the clouds. The sun even tried to drive a wedge between them, but it was a lukewarm attempt. High on Shepherd Scar, the birds soared and the wind breathed: everything seemed normal. On the ground, though, there was an almost imperceptible difference: for, outside D3, the insects on and under the ground, rather than ignoring their own and other species with the ususal sublime indifference, had abruptly become more aware of each other, regarding themselves as fellow beings rather than different species. When a predator came near, instead of running in all directions as usual, they formed an intimidatory line, which occasionally saw off the still-hungry animal. It was as if they had found the means of communicating, the ability, until now found only in humans, of taking a joint decision based on experience. A sense of humanity was pervading the natural world. But it was not natural.

Sir Digby Crichton, an under-secretary in the Home Office, looked anxious. His aristocratic bearing, topped by a silver lushness of hair, was tempered by the conundrum in front of him. He had been in at work early to prepare some answers for ministers on a debate in the Commons later that day. But although he was tired, something had just happened which had jolted his brain into a state of heightened tension and alertness: he had received a disturbing e-mail from an anonymous source. He knew it was anonymous because he had tried to reply but it had come back as undeliverable - which had vexed him. Or, more accurately, it would not so much vex him as rock the government if the contents were true - or, at least, verifiable. His usually serene looks - tanned and square-jawed with dazzling blue eyes - had become drawn and pallid. Despite years of work as a career Civil Servant - which had given him an uncanny ability to simultaneously assume several levels of thought at once from any political perspective - this was a tricky one; but he would get to the bottom of it. He always did, which was why he had gained his reputation for being the master of every argument yet the servant of none. He had skirted the abyss of every type of government crisis across a succession of administrations, yet always sorted them out whilst staying out of the limelight. In short, despite his flamboyant nature, he was a safe pair of hands. As a result, he had effectively become a government adviser without being specifically beholden to any political party, and although he appeared to be close to the current administration, he nonetheless appeared to be outside politics completely. This was a situation that suited him and his masters admirably. In fact, the only difference between him and an adviser was that he would ultimately receive a guaranteed pension on retirement.

The person who had sent the e-mail - direct to his inbox, not the office - obviously knew who to target, and probably knew him as well. So it troubled him further knowing that he was known but did not know the sender. One name had dawned on him, but he had dismissed it: that person would not do a thing like this; there was too much at stake. Whoever it was, though, obviously knew what he or she was talking about: the arrow had hit the bull's-eye.

When he had a problem, he went into a kind of semi-vacant state while he worked out all the angles and answers. Except that this one was different: there *were* no obvious answers, and no-one he could turn to for help. It was his baby. He had been officially given unofficial government research stations to look after - those that the government did not want to admit to knowing about, and less still have anything to do with. And the one referred to in the e-mail definitely fell into that category.

He read the e-mail again. Basically, it said that sensitive, officially secret government research notes from the Shepherd Scar Research Centre had been posted on the internet. By whom, he was unsure, but when he clicked on the attached link, he was horrified to see that it was more than sensitive: it was political dynamite. He also realised that he had to shut it down instantly before anyone found it. If the press got hold of it, he was dead - and so was the government. The nature of the research pointed to one person after all - the one he originally thought it was, as many of the allusions were known to him only. Then he saw the initials - MD. It was him. And he knew exactly what he had to do...

Doug's meeting with Mick had not gone well the night before: Mick had appeared aware of what Doug was saying without seeming to comprehend the gravity of what they had each witnessed - least of all from an ethical point of view. In fact, Mick had seemed more interested in getting home to his usual evening on the internet. So as Doug came into his laboratory that morning, he was feeling somewhat apprehensive at what he might find.

He was not disappointed: the lab had an eerie, unusual calm about it. Normally, there were the sounds of scurrying, some squeaks, the odd bark - even gnawing and scratching as the inmates tried to get out. But this morning was different. Very different. He got far enough into the room to realise that all the rats, mice and rabbits, rather than being at polarised points in their prisons, were in huddles, as if conferring: becoming aware of him, they all turned to look at him. Feeling uneasy, he nonetheless went around the lab and stared at his charges in a systematic, accusatory sort of way. For their part, they responded with vengeful, vindictive eyes. If either party felt more nervous or isolated, it was certainly Doug. He decided it was time for breakfast and left quickly.

In the canteen, Doug attacked his sausages with vigour. Despite the weather and his feeling of concern at the mystery of what was happening in his lab, he felt more alert than the day before. The open paper in front of him was still a jumble as his thoughts crowded across the text: but he was also aware that when he turned a page he had nonetheless taken everything in. So much so, in fact, that he turned back a couple of times to see if he had, in fact, read it correctly - which he had. But the importance of what his brain was slowly beginning to realise only became apparent as the crossword fell open in front of him: suddenly, without really glancing at the clues, he felt he knew all the answers. Surely, he thought, as he began to study them more closely, it was just an even simpler crossword than usual? But no; if anything, it was more difficult. He fell into the back of his chair, his bulk bending the supports to the limit. What was going on? He thought back to the last day's events... the animals, their stares, the doses of parlazine, manganese tripuride, inoxyphenalimine. Inoxyphenalimine ... he tapped his fingers on the table - and it came to him: he had been bitten by the mice. Surely... could the saliva in their bites have passed on a biological change to his body? Or had some of the fluid gone undiluted into his wounds? Either way, the result was the same: it could affect his DNA. He went cold with the thought. He got out a pen and started to do the simple crossword but, finding the clues too easy, he turned to the long cryptic one - and had finished it within seven minutes.

"Christ," he wheezed. A couple of colleagues saw him sitting there with an astonished look on his face and enquired after him: he nodded impetuously and kept his gaze in front, his mind working furiously. He was known as a loner and not an easy person to deal with, so this behaviour was not particularly unusual: but he was a well-respected researcher, even if he was the way that he unfortunately was. Here, that was all that mattered.

Aware that he was being observed - by humans this time - Doug got up and disappeared back to his lab, where he found he was placed under the same intense surveillance: as the door opened, all the inmates turned and stared at him. He was beginning to get an idea of what he might have done - and how he could profit from it - ethically or unethically. But the main question that burned in his mind was: how might his DNA have been changed? Was it permanent? Would it alter him or, worse, kill him? Had he broken any serious laws by doing what he had done? Was it his research or the government's? And how could he be sure of keeping any money he might make? At last, he felt he could see a way out of here: and the idea of spending the rest of his life on a desert island surrounded by adoring dusky beauties was also uppermost in his thoughts...

He went to his notes and searched for the dosages he had injected into the mouse, which was observing him with a stare that bored right into his skull. Then he remembered that they had been random doses... he mentally kicked himself for being so sloppy. Now he would have to try and gauge the amounts and, if the results were different, try again until they were similar. But what if he could not ascertain the amount, or if the extent of the doses made little or no difference? Could a trace have as much effect as a barrelful? A mild panic swept over him: then he realised that all the creatures in the lab were studiously dividing their attention between the one mouse that he had injected with the random dose and himself, as if awaiting instructions. The hypodermic that had fallen out of his hand into the container was still there but empty, drained of its contents by the mice that had bitten him. He was not going to risk picking it up... Then the thought struck him: what if, somehow, some traces of parlazine - or the other two compounds - had been transmitted to the others before he had injected the first mouse? That would at least explain their complicity. But this sudden apparent understanding? How? Was it just heightened perception, transmitted mentally? The ones that had ingested his potion seemed neither more nor less alert than the others, yet their gaze was more vindictive... Wasn't it?

The possibilities exercised his mind for a few seconds whilst he observed the mice observing him. He suddenly felt like a turkey at Christmas, being eyed up for slaughter at the choicest moment. Yes, their looks were hostile, he concluded, as he nervously left the room. He stood outside his lab, his thoughts banging around his head in competition with the rain beating on the iron roof. Another call to Mick confirmed that he had actually omitted to hose down his boots after his spillage of parlazine in the dog area: and it *was* inoxyphenalimine that he had also spilled.

Worse, Mick had left these boots on the floor overnight. So, had minute amounts of the drugs been transported around the laboratories by the insects that inhabited them? The old building was full of holes, quite large enough for all manner of insects to gain entry. If that was the case, then once ingested by them, had the mouse somehow been able to converse with them and get them to pass traces of it on to the other specimens? Or just waited for them to enter the perspex boxes? The lids were never airtight and, anyway, the airholes were quite large enough for most insects to pass through. Or had they just been induced inside by the mammals, then devoured, so passing the drug further into the food-chain? But the enormity of his thoughts was eclipsed by the sudden realisation that the mouse was squeaking at him, and his blood ran cold as he felt he understood exactly what it was saying...

Sir Digby Crichton put the phone down and sat back. He glanced at his watch. He felt a little more relaxed now as he had done what he had to do and was sure that there would be nothing to indict him now from other government departments, ministers or the Opposition. Or the media. But despite this, he was still twitchy. Why had this person done what he had? Why had he just not given him a call to discuss it? Why go public? The answers would be known by early the next morning when this person would receive an early, unexpected visit. He felt it was better that way than to alert them to it - a quiet and firm word out of the blue was always best. Then it would not happen again: he could ensure that, at least...

He called his assistant and, being that time of day, requested a cup of coffee and a couple of gingernut biscuits. That would make him feel better. A few hours later, having checked once again that all was well in cyberspace, he went home early. The next day might just be tricky and an evening listening to Berlioz' 'Damnation of Faust' would set him up well for any turbulence.

Chapter 6

That night, Doug did not sleep. Quite apart from being anxious, he did not feel right: he was more alert, and his brain was coursing through its processes at a huge speed, which was perhaps fatiguing him in one sense but keeping him awake in another. But it was a faint throbbing in his head and a mild nausea that really troubled him. He was minded, too, to tell his superiors about what had happened but was worried that they would quietly kick him out of the service for breach of protocol; unless, of course, he could impress upon them it was vital research that would be good for the country or the military, or... whatever. He could not finalise that one. And if this all got out, the secrecy of Shepherd Scar would be blown, for, officially, it did not exist, hence its remote location. What he had understood from the mouse was chilling him permanently as well, and he wondered whether he could ask Mick if he was experiencing the same sensations. But if he did, then Mick might want some of the kudos from his research and, quite honestly, the man was a lowlier specimen than him: Doug felt that Mick would rather hold onto his job than rock the boat but, if he did, would not care whether Doug had a job there or not. But if he wanted to come with Doug, he would be more of a hindrance than a help. So, who should he go to? Or should he steal some of the manganese tripuride that he had created, as well as the other compounds, and set up his own small laboratory on the expected proceeds? That would keep Shepherd Scar out of the equation... But then, would the government want to suppress him - even eliminate him? No, he thought: that was too far-fetched - too many science-fiction novels and spy thrillers. That never happened in real life... did it?

He eventually fell into a fitful sleep, with the mouse's warnings taunting his consciousness. Although he had not understood the specifics of what it was saying, he clearly felt he realised its intent: it seemed instinctive, innate. No sooner had he fallen asleep, though, then the alarm suddenly went off. Cursing, he switched it off, but it kept on ringing. Then, he realised that it was only five o'clock in the morning, and it was the telephone.

It was a very anxious Mick. After opening hostilities about the time he was calling, Doug had to listen. "Have you looked in the mirror this morning?" Mick enquired. Doug scoffed - of course he hadn't, it was too early. "Then do so", urged Mick, his strained voice even more so due to the poor quality of the receiver. Doug put the light on and shuffled to the mirror. He looked closely at himself. Yes, that was definitely him. And yet...

"Well?" screeched Mick down the phone.

"What am I looking for?" he grumbled.

"Do you look different?"

Doug paused, and looked again, turning his shaving light onto his face, so making him look even more grotesque than usual. "Not really," he replied.

"Christ."

"What?"

"I look terrible."

"How?"

"I've aged about ten years since yesterday. My hair's gone white - what's left of it; most of it's fallen out. And my skin..." He broke off, and Doug, suddenly concerned for himself, looked more closely in the mirror. He looked at his eyes first; were those small wrinkles bigger than yesterday? Or were they less prominent? His hair was certainly still intact, but, if anything, it was a sandier shade of grey than he thought it had been. He felt more agile, too... In fact, despite his nausea and the throbbing pain that had subsided but not disappeared, he surmised that he felt better and looked younger than before. Aware of Mick sobbing down the phone, he put the receiver to his ear once more.

"No, if anything, I think I look younger."

A silence greeted this observation. Then: "It must be because I've been experimenting with another drug."

"What other drug?"

"One I've researched and developed myself. But don't tell anyone."

Doug felt suddenly indignant that Mick had been doing stuff without telling him, despite doing the same himself.

"You won't, will you," Mick pleaded.

"No, of course not." He paused. "What was the drug for?"

"It's a nerve serum, for use by the intelligence services. I was approached a couple of years ago, but officially I haven't been doing anything. If I say something, they'll deny it and... well, I'd be dead meat, probably."

Doug, despite his possibly newly-younger appearance, saw the blood drain from his face. Is that what would happen to him? And his research was not official at all, even unofficially. Then he wondered if the two drugs were related: perhaps Mick's nerve serum had become involved with the parlazine? Mick's dogs and his mice? Had the two experiments become unintentionally linked?

"It's possible," Mick rejoined when asked.

"Are you going in to work today?" Doug enquired.

"I'll try - that's if security recognise me and let me in. I look nothing like my photo, now."

"When are you going?"

"Immediately."

"I'll see you there."

"OK."

Each put their respective phones down. Doug stood there for a second, unable to move. Then his phone was ringing once more. It was Mick again.

"Look, if I don't make it, my unofficial notes - not the ones our boss thinks I'm working on - are on my computer under 'Personal'. My password's 'deadlyserum'."

A chill ran down Doug's spine. "I'll see you in forty minutes."

They rang off again. The suddenness and severity of it all were deeply disturbing, not least because of the impact on himself, however selfish that was. He proceeded to shave and got dressed. Then he left.

The sun was trying to break through the thick early mist. In Bracken Mere, the amphibians' sense of being one species - rather than millions of disparate beings - was becoming apparent. As a result of the deluge the day before, the contamination from the Shepherd Scar holding-pools that had been flushed down Scar Brook and into the Mere was causing creatures' instincts - without their understanding why - to suddenly help each other survive, alerting others of their kind to attack from the aerial onslaught of birds. It was not so much an intended communication as an innate transmitted comprehension - like an instinct sharpened over millions of years being acquired in a relative instant. When a bird did catch its prey, though, it carried away and ingested the traces of the compounds and spread their influence far away. Likewise, fish were starting to assimilate the chemicals as well - both through their gills and by what they ate. The moles, badgers, rabbits and sheep that used the pool for drinking, too, had become unwitting carriers and disseminators of the liquid. And in time, the contaminants would pass down the Hildaburna to the sea.

Bracken Mere had become the crucible of what

would take place - a microcosm of the catastrophe to come....

As Doug's excuse for a car got to the top of Scar Fell, the road dropped away before him, stretching into the distance, a parody of the road to nowhere. Unlike his life, though, he would not be travelling all the way along it, but would turn off down a virtually unmade road at the bottom adorned with decrepit 'No Through Road' signs - all part of the government subterfuge. As he started the steep descent, something glinted at the turn-off far below; it was too soon to say what this was, but he had never noticed it before. As he got closer, though, it was obvious that it was a car, a silver car. Mick had a silver car, he thought. As he neared it, he could see that it was parked haphazardly, partially across the road at an angle. One corner was lower than the rest of it, too... He pulled up, and could see the reason why: the driver's side front wheel was just into the border ditch. Fearing the worst, he got out. In the driver's seat was a man, his head thrown back against the head-rest. His pace quickened and he tore open the door. He peered at the face: its gaunt, emaciated representation was just discernible as the man he had once known so well: it was Mick. And at once he could see that he was dead.

Less than half a mile away on Shepherd Scar itself, a hill farmer walked briskly in the fresh breeze towards Bracken Mere. His dog raced on ahead, looking forward, as usual, to barking his will on the sheep: he was to drive them out of a barn into which they had been herded for overnight protection and into some pens for marking. Although overnight protection was unusual, a number of lambs had been taken recently and the farmer could not afford to lose many more. He had managed to build his barn across a part of Scar Brook, so the ewes and lambs were always guaranteed fresh water, whatever the time of night and whatever the season. It had been a good decision: he had not lost one lamb since it was built.

When he surmounted a rise, however, he saw that his flock below were already out of the barn and drinking much further down around Bracken Mere. Looking to the barn, he observed that the moveable piece of fencing stood open, as if it had been carefully placed aside: there was no sign of it having been trampled down.

He scratched his head at this unexpected sight and wondered how the sheep had got out. "Bloody ramblers, I'll be bound," he thought to himself, and stood to watch as his dog raced ahead. He whistled a couple of times and the dog started to chase, surrounding the laggards, crouching, nipping and pushing the sheep in the direction of the barn a half-mile away. He watched, whistled... but then abruptly became aware that his dog was not responding to his calls.

"Damn Spiff," he mumbled, and started to walk briskly towards him. As he did so, he noticed that the lambs and sheep, rather than being herded by Spiff, were actually chasing the dog. Spiff was yelping, unused to this sort of treatment, and howling with indignation and fear as he was surrounded. The farmer shouted and swore at the sheep: one or two looked at him and then turned back to the dog, who was slowly being edged in upon. Then, as the farmer got near to the throng of sheep, his heart pounding, a half-dozen or so detached themselves and started to run towards him: it was is if they were as one, and seemed to be charged with a hostile intent. He stopped, falling back onto his palms; then, as he heard his dog screech in pain as a whole number of sheep attacked, he got to his feet again, turned and ran, the yelps and whines of his dog becoming more distant as he receded - but no less terrifying. Then all was silent, with the exception of his boots squishing the peat, his clothes chafing and his heart banging like an overstretched drum. After a hundred yards he turned around, panting heavily, to see that the sheep had stopped chasing him but were just watching to ensure he did not return, occasionally casting a glance towards the carnage that had been his faithful sheepdog. It was as if they were making a point to him - a point that was all too apparent. He turned and fled.

Back at Mick's car, Doug, shaking, carefully went through Mick's briefcase. It was strangely empty. No notes, no magazines, no computer discs: nothing except a bar of chocolate and a few odds and ends. And no identity badge, either. That was very unusual. Mobile phones worked inside the research centre, where there was a transmitter, but not for miles away from it, which was fortuitous: he would have to report the death at the research centre. But only after he had relieved Mick's computer of its files - he didn't want any one else to see them. And he desperately wanted to know the name of the drug that Mick had developed before anyone else got hold of it.

He put the briefcase back, then took a picture with his mobile phone camera. Gruesome, perhaps, but he wanted proof of Mick's death in case he needed it later. Governments had strange ways of twisting the truth... He sat for a moment in his car, then realised that he would have to move fast, for if anyone saw him he would be implicated. But if he went to the research centre, he'd be implicated anyway, for this was the only way in or out of the place. Well, he would have to get the files and get home, then come back again. No, security was 24 hours a day, there - they would know he had been in early and would have passed Mick's body. Ah, but they wouldn't know at what time Mick had arrived at this point, and suffered this condition. So, then... he'd go in, get the files, supposedly come home again but find Mick's car on the way, then go back and report it. Yes, that was the plan - but speed was essential.

Doug was unaware that he was being watched from high above: still shaking with fear at his colleague's death, he started his car and drove the last mile, up past the crags, to Shepherd Scar Research Centre. After he had disappeared from view, the observer turned away and walked down the escarpment towards a four-wheel-drive vehicle. As he did so, he noticed, a little further on, a seemingly terrified farmer blundering in a terrified and frantic fashion down a solitary road towards a distant small white cottage perched far below on the hillside...

Security waved Doug through. He opened up his lab - he was used to the intense interest the animals showed him now - to make it look normal. Then he realised that the animals were making strange noises, as if they were all privy to some knowledge and were laughing inwardly at him. 'Nonsense', he thought, and quietly went across to Mick's lab, carefully closing all the doors behind him: where he put on lights, he then put them off again. It was getting quite light now as he switched on Mick's computer: he wanted to find, copy and then delete all the files he could from it before telling anyone of Mick's death. Mick's charges seemed to look at him with an intent air; one dog started to bark in the next lab, but when the others did not join in - preferring to watch Doug's movements - it forlornly went quiet again. Perhaps it came from a lab apart from the others and had not ingested anything, Doug thought. He slightly opened a window in the corner of Mick's office and loosely closed the handle: like that, it appeared locked shut to a casual eye but a long screwdriver could open it from the outside.

The computer had booted up now, so he went through the files as Doug had instructed and found the relevant information. He plugged in a memory stick and started to download. When it was finished, he put it purposefully into his bag and did it again;

and then again onto a disc. All the while, the animals observed him quietly through the windows of the lab between them and Mick's office. Then he deleted the files on the computer, again as instructed, and left.

He passed through security again, making the excuse that he had forgotten something and would be back soon, got into his car and drove down the long road back to the junction. When he got there, he stopped in shock. Not because there was any traffic, but because Mick and all traces of his car had vanished completely.

A new dawn had broken - in more ways than one.

Chapter 7

Jessie, as often was the case, had got up very early. She was freshest in the morning and was keen to get back to the research she had postponed after her late return the night before. She switched on her computer. It was an old machine which had been given her by a friend who recycled computers for the government; as such, its unique code made it look as though she was a state employee, which not only gave her anonymity but allowed her occasionally into classified websites with little fuss - invaluable for a journalist. While it cranked up, she made herself a coffee and, when it was ready, looked at the screen and typed in the first link she had noted down the day before.

But she was to be disappointed. To her surprise, there was nothing. Nothing came up at all. Angrily, she tried every single one - with no success. Now she knew definitely that there was a cover-up: it had to be. All that information was available a few hours ago, yet now... Well, she would have to start again. She got her notes out and started to read them, typing all sorts of references into the computer in the hope of finding another seam of information like the one she had discovered before.

Two hours later, she had still found nothing. But what she had stumbled across already only made her more determined. This must be big: it reeked of a government cover-up. And she was going to get to the bottom of it.

Doug arrived back home in the gathering daylight, his car sliding to halt outside his house, a building as scruffy as he was. He opened the front door and went straight upstairs to his back room, in which there was a computer. He decided it might be best to close the curtains, just in case... He put the light on as the computer rumbled into life and, when it was ready, inserted the memory stick and printed out a hard copy. He then put the machine off and secreted one memory stick in a plastic bag under the carpet, another in a hole behind his bathroom wash-basin, and the disc in the loft: the printed copy he took into his bedroom to read. There were a hundred and forty-seven pages of notes: it was going to be a long morning. He would call in sick later on - if they did not call him first. He put two pillows behind him and leaned against them on the bed.

Reading the notes, he realised that Mick had been a far better scientist than he had thought: his notes were impeccably written up and his sense of focus was exemplary. In fact, he made Doug look like an amateur. His experiments with the dogs was a cover for his nerve serum research and the last had been written up - judging by the spelling errors, hastily - probably only last night. There were many areas that Mick had been researching, but what caught Doug's eye was one where Mick had been officially involved in a similar area to his, but had got much further. The only difference was that Mick's brief - laid out 'unofficially' by the Secretary of State and the Home Office - was to create a serum that could be quickly administered and had the almost instant effect of stimulating the brain into unhindered loquacity, so allowing the military to interrogate enemy battlefield casualties or prisoners and so betray intelligence quickly. That was the parlazine part: but Mick's creation had the added advantage of rendering them inert at the same time, so avoiding any risk of retaliatory action. He read the usual bit at the bottom which stated that it was almost certainly fatal at the dose level indicated, but that was par for the course. So were many of his own projects; but Doug wondered why he had not heard anything about it: true, everything was supposedly secret from everyone else at Shepherd Scar, but usually the others had an inkling of what was going on, even if it was only general. But Doug had heard nothing. His own research was directed at helping stroke sufferers regain the ability to speak - as well as the rider, the unofficial reason, to develop a drug to stimulate the language-learning abilities of translators to help the military. That was where the money came from. After that similarity, their research aims had diverged. Concluding that Mick's seemed to be even more sinister than his own, he felt a slight sense of pique that Mick had divulged nothing to him: then he contented himself with the thought that he had not told Mick much about his research either, even at their meeting. They had been as tight as each other. Still, he had an opportunity now to continue Mick's research, which he could possibly claim as his own. After all, if he became famous as a result, Mick would be none the wiser...

He put the documents down for a moment and looked at the ceiling. He tried to work out where their research had crossed, and racked his brains to try and remember what Mick had said when they had had their conversation in the labs regarding their respective animals. Then he got to think about their conversation in the pub after that. Yes, the animals had probably all ingested parlazine one way or another, but Mick's inclusion of a compound called phenol hydresium - one that Doug knew of but had never used - had been apparently minimal; but the exact quantities had not been noted down either, as far as he could see. He was pleased that such a consummate chemist as Mick was sometimes as sloppy as he had been...

Doug pondered the fact that no government would have admitted to any of this research even if it had been shouted from the rooftops, especially with the animal rights lobby so voluble: so it would not have been difficult for Mick to pretend that he was doing something else 'unofficially unofficial', so to speak. He looked back at the notes, and saw that there was one compound he had not heard of: chromitic paradiosymine. Was it a real substance or one thrown in by Mick to confuse the authorities? He looked at the chemical equations and concluded that they looked odd. The amount of parlazine, if mixed with the other drugs, the phenol hydresium and, above all, the anthicin he mentioned, would have had a devastating effect on the brain. Perhaps that was the point. Then again... He looked at some of the other experiments that Mick had written up but could find no sign of chromitic paradiosymine anywhere else. Knowing Mick reasonably well, he wondered if this was, in fact, then, a chemicular red herring. For the first time in many years, he suddenly relished the idea of going into work again to get to the bottom of things, despite Mick's death and all the attention that would attract. Except, of course, now the body and evidence had gone, he was the only one who knew. Or was he?

It was at that moment that he heard a noise outside. Instinctively, he put the document into a huge file at the back of his wardrobe, marked 'Tax, 2018-2019' and closed the wardrobe door. He went into the back room. He nudged the curtain slowly aside, permitting the most minimal chink possible.

He was completely unprepared for what he saw.

By now, Jessie was angry. She had been going through the downloaded notes line by line, making cross-references in books, articles and on the internet wherever she felt she might have had some luck. But all her research and endeavour had come to nothing. The monikers 'SS' and 'MD' had thrown up nothing: even when she had tried to find 'unofficial government establishments' she had found little of relevance. No, the Freedom of Information Act had been well and truly hidden behind government bars. But that would not stop her: it made her even more sure that there was something being covered up - something big. Whole swathes of sensitive information did not just appear on the internet one day and disappear without trace the next.

She opened a local news website. She knew most of them and they seldom had anything of interest; yet occasionally they opened just enough of a chink of light to illuminate a whole world of information and stories.

She spent an hour browsing through these papers, occasionally typing in words to cross-reference like manganese tripuride and chromitic paradiosymine. 'I must be mad', she thought, as she suddenly wished she had not been wasting so much time on this. Perhaps she would forget it and have a good boozy lunch with one of her male friends, followed by.... But somehow the urge to follow the story persisted. Yes, the men could wait for another day. After all, she was still young: and her reputation and fortune had to be made before her biological and emotional needs needed to be addressed...

Idly, she found herself looking at the Liverpool Courier website news. The usual stories were there, burnished by tales of unfaithfulness in Speke and anger over a new roundabout in Toxteth. She scrolled through, glancing at a story from their reporter in the western dales, who had sent in a story about some sheep turning on a sheepdog and killing it. She laughed involuntarily - it all seemed so unlikely. Then the words 'research establishment' presented themselves to her... and she was suddenly alert and away again.

Apparently, a hill-farmer in the western dales had seen his sheepdog mauled to death by sheep which seemed to be acting as one. But the government establishment which the journalist had mentioned - and which had caught her eye - was, apparently, near to the farmer yet hidden away on the moors. This farmer did not know what it was, of course, but had always kept away as it seemed so hostile, unwelcoming and remote - and he had heard barking sometimes when the wind was light and coming from the right direction. He definitely thought that this event must be something to do with that. She smiled, but found herself searching in vain for an idea where the spot was that he was referring to. She was unaware of any research establishment on the moors but anything was possible. She looked at her watch: it was still early, so the staff reporter who had written the piece was unlikely to be in until a little later on in the morning: she would have to wait.

Yet waiting was frustrating. So she copied the article and its location, then went in search of the same story in another paper. Pulling out a map, she looked closely at the western dales and looked for any towns big enough to support a local paper, which she then referenced on the computer. It transpired that two other papers had carried the story, but sketchily: the latter though, she found, had contained the hill-farmer's name - Jason Brigthwaite - and also the name of the place near which the event had supposedly happened.

It was called Shepherd Scar. She began to think she had found something: the day ahead suddenly seemed full of promise, if not of the romantic kind...

Outside Doug's window in the gathering light was an array of creation. The animals were not big, but there were hundreds of them. Individually, he might not have seen them, but together they were a moving mass of life that were all over his garden. He knew that they were not friendly: not just because they were ranged outside his window and looking up at him - it was more ominous than that. Their movements were not rushed or random, but objective, collected and, above all, calm. Instinctively, he seemed to know that they were waiting for him, and had acquired the restraint of human intellect to wait for the right moment. Although he could not tell why, he perceived that they were aware that he was perpetrating hideous experiments on their cousins, and they did not like it. Nor did Doug. He had the innate perception that they were there to get him - a re-run of the mice biting him but on a far larger scale. He recoiled and let the curtains fall back across the window. As soon as he did so, there was a noise of screeching and squeaking that came from outside and, almost immediately, a sharp crack against the window that he had just looked out of followed by a receding flapping of wings. Then another. They knew he was there. He cursed himself for leaving the light on when he looked through the curtains: how long would it be before they found a couple of holes in his 1930s semi and invaded his space? With that number attacking him, he would not last for long: he had to get out. His car was outside the front of the house. He quickly started planning what he needed to take with him: but suddenly the true perception of what they wanted became clear. He had this feeling - an instinct - that they wanted to communicate with him: but although this instinct was understood, how could he do so? Talk? He found himself resisting this idea, which was nonetheless prevalent in his mind: how could he talk to them? And yet, perhaps there was no need: when he had been in the laboratory, he had felt that he knew what they were trying to communicate to him. True, he had probably ingested some parlazine - even other compounds that he had been working on - but he was still no wiser as to the volumes involved or why the effects had not worn off yet. Indeed, he felt that he understood their mood even better than before: so perhaps the effects were permanent and did not need to be replenished? Did they just mutate the genes or tissue of the host enough to create a physical and a chemical change for good? Had it really affected their - and his - DNA? Surely it would run out of potency after a while? Or, again, had he created something hitherto thought to be scientifically impossible - the undiminishing biological perpetuation of a diminishing chemical trace? All these thoughts crowded in on him as he looked around him for inspiration to relieve him of his predicament. Further - glancing at himself in the mirror as he wrenched a soft case out of the wardrobe and started packing - he felt that he looked younger. Or was it just that he had lost some weight? The stress of the last day would have justified that, but, stopping for a moment of vanity in his flight to escape, he really did feel that he looked less flabby, more toned and, yes, his hair looked fuller. Had he discovered the secret of eternal youth? That would really make him rich...

Again, a crack on the window reminded him of the presence outside and brought him starkly out of his reverie. Being rich - however he managed to re-run the experiments on an increasingly unwilling bunch of subjects - would have to wait. Survival came first.

He took the memory sticks and discs from out of their hiding-places again and put them in his shirt pocket: if he lost his suitcase, at least he would have his notes and references. As he packed some essentials, he again wondered why the creatures had not actually entered his home - he was sure they could. Were they just intimidating him? Playing with him? Making a point? Perhaps they did not mean to harm him? But then, why amass themselves here just to do that? Surely the law of the wild was to kill any threat wherever possible? And he knew that they knew he was a threat. But then it began to dawn that perhaps they saw him as a saviour: a sort of human catalyst who could reverse the domination of *homo sapiens* and return the rest of creation to supremacy. They had come to praise him, perhaps - not to bury him. Where that would leave him, of course, was anyone's guess.

He threw some more essentials into the bag and pulled on his anorak, into which he zipped his wallet and his mobile phone. He was unsure whether he was going to go back to work or make a break for it: it was only where he might go that eluded him for the latter option.

He stumbled down the stairs with his bag and stopped behind the front door. Outside, it all seemed quiet. He listened for a good ten seconds, then got out his car keys and looked through the letter-box. There was nothing there. This surprised him because, although he had only seen the creatures at the back, he had expected them to be all around the house, which now did not appear to be the case. He took a deep breath, quietly opened the door, and then ran for the car. Fortunately, he had not stopped to lock it for, as he crashed across the front seats, slamming the door behind him, a hawk noisily tried to dive-bomb him, so alerting all the creatures on the other side of the house of his escape route. Almost instantly, there was the sound of a tide of feet running around to the front, like one huge collective shuffle, and an indignant sound of squeaking and squawking. He started the engine, but by then they were all around him. What should he do? Just drive over them and make matters worse? By then, four or five birds of different species were cracking their beaks against the windows: some rodents had managed to get onto the bonnet and were staring at him through the windscreen. A sound like thunderous rain was coming from above him as the creatures ran onto the roof. He screamed in panic at the top of his voice: "Go away! Get away! For God's sake, go-o-o-o!"

The noise stopped. He found that they were still; just observing him again as the engine burbled. A calm after the storm. Except the storm was still all around him. Suddenly, though, he felt another wave of instinctive understanding affecting him: they were still angry and hostile, but perhaps more reasonable, as if they appreciated his fear and respected it. He stared at them: they stared back. Almost involuntarily, he shouted:

"I'm sorry. I wish I could help you... I'm sorry. Please..." This had turned into a sob by the end: and then he realised that they had started a quiet hubbub amongst themselves. Yes, they were conversing with one another, different species to different species. Then it stopped again, and they all looked back at him. He was sure they were going to savage him, and yet...

"Look, I know I do all these terrible things to you, your, your... relations," he admitted, although he felt utterly stupid talking to them like this. Yet somehow, he felt he knew that they understood. What was happening? "I do it for a living... It's the government's fault," he continued. Again, he felt ludicrous, as if he was bargaining with them, as if they were human. In the silence that followed, though, he realised that he must be making sense to them, at least in some primeval way, for they slowly started to descend from his car. "I might be able to help you," he added, more in increased hope than expectation. With that, there was more conversing; then they started slowly receding, leaving a clear path in front of his car, still watching him but now quiet yet intent. Without waiting, he put the car into gear and drove slowly out of the driveway, into the open countryside; on an impulse he decided to head south to city conurbations where there were fewer of nature's creatures and where he would be able to lose himself in their mass of humanity. As he drove, he wondered whether he was cheating the spirit of Charles Darwin or had just unwittingly made a Faustian pact with the animal world. Of course he could not help them... but would they ensure that he kept his side of the bargain as they perceived it?

When he got to the motorway, he put his foot down, for he knew that he could never return to Shepherd Scar: he would not get out alive again. Especially if the animals decided he was not helping them after all.

Above, two pairs of birds - two hawks and two kestrels - were following him...

Chapter 8

Sir Digby Crichton pondered as his assistant pottered around him, offering coffee, help with ministers' questions, and what to buy his wife for her birthday. But it all went over his head, as he had received another anonymous e-mail. At first, he was certain it was from the same source as the day before, but when he saw that it had been sent earlier that morning he was unsure: that problem had been dealt with. Or should have been. This time, the e-mail was telling him that there was concern that the state of the Shepherd Scar Research Centre was so dilapidated that there was the risk of environmental pollution, the effects of which would be uncertain but possibly catastrophic. As if to prove this theory, a local newspaper report had been added from the day before which concerned a hill-farmer who had been unfortunate enough to witness the savaging of his dog by a flock of sheep. At first, the news had provoked a slight smile, nature turned on its head, so to speak: but as he went further into the e-mail, the significance - and the authority with which it was again written - grew graver. The farmer had mentioned that he had lost his dog near 'some government research station', and Crichton felt that he did not need to check its location: he was sure that it was Shepherd Scar. Ironic that it was a shepherd, he thought...

The problem was that he knew very well that, being a government secret, a whole lot of clandestine research obviously went on there, which could quite possibly have caused the attack on the man's dog: nerve serums, truth drugs, mind-altering compounds, speech-inducers... a whole litany of creative destruction was being developed there. It was not all bad, of course: there was some good research going on into the helping of stroke sufferers - but it had grown out of work into just the opposite. And this farmer's sheep, due to their proximity, could just have been the unwitting catalyst of a whole lot of trouble. What made it worse was that he knew it was in a bad state of repair and a leak or an escape by one of the laboratory animals was a distinct possibility. Although how it might have got to a whole flock of sheep was somewhat bewildering.

He checked the location of the farmer's story to find only that it was in the proximity of Shepherd Scar, as he had thought. He called his assistant who, his not having responded to any requests before, had gone off in a sulk.

"Yes,?" she replied on the intercom, tetchily.

"Sandra, get me Dennis Fouracres on the line, will you? He's the principal of Shepherd Scar Research Centre."

"I don't think I know that one."

"It's under 'Unofficial Projects'."

"Oh. All right."

"Try him at home: I doubt he'll be at work yet."

A few moments later, his phone rang.

"Hello, Sir Digby", said the voice, not without a little concern. "What's up?"

"I was hoping you could tell me," came the reply, as argumentative siblings and the chinking of crockery in the background confirmed that Fouracres was, indeed, still at home.

There was a pause. "Not this sheepdog thing, is it?" he enquired.

"Mm."

"Ah. Well, there's no proof."

"Of course not". That was obvious: it was unofficial, so there was never supposed to be any proof. "But what about the chance of an escape of some sort."

"Ah, well, I suppose it's possible... We've been agitating for more funds to tighten the place up for -"

"Yes, I know all that," Crichton interrupted. "But there are stories in the papers already, and if it gets out of hand... What are the possibilities?"

"Well, it depends what got out, if anything. As far as I can see, not one animal has escaped."

"What about chemicals escaping, then?"

"Erm, well, I suppose it's possible. But there are several monitoring checks. I don't think it would be a problem. And they would be such small doses, even if they did leak out."

"So you're saying that nothing could have got out into the environment. Not much, anyway."

"As far as I can see, that's correct."

"And it's nothing to do with us."

"I don't see how it can be. The sheepdog thing's just a strange quirk of nature, I should think."

There was a pause, as Sir Digby composed his thoughts. Then: "So what about Mick Deakin?"

"What about Mick Deakin?" Then: "How do you know Deakin?"

"He's been doing some work for us. Unofficial."

"Oh. So why have I not been told?"

"Classified information."

"I see. Well, I was under the impression that he's working on a project for -"

"Not over the phone, please, Fouracres," Crichton interrupted. "But yes, that was part of it. So let me know when he shows up, will you? I'd like to talk to him."

"Er, yes; of course."

"I'll be on the mobile - I'm on my way up."

"Ah... right," Dennis replied, discomfited.

Sir Digby put down the receiver and folded his arms across his lap. Then he took a deep breath and made another call. When the respondent answered he dropped his voice.

"Everything done?" he enquired quietly. The response relaxed him somewhat. "Good." He said goodbye, replaced the receiver and stood up. "Sandra? Get Simpkin to do the minister's questions, will you? I might be away for a few days. Don't let anyone know where I am."

"So where will you be?" his assistant enquired as she entered the room. "Exactly," he said, as he left.

Chapter 9

Jessie put the phone down. She had been talking to the editor of one of the local papers, the Hickley & District News, who had confirmed that a Jason Brigthwaite had seen his sheep savage his sheepdog. And yes, it was close to Shepherd Scar, and, yes, there was a clandestine government research station there, although it was only rumour as to what they did in it. All this she knew, even if the location was now more precise. But she had not heard the other story he told her: that two ramblers had witnessed a number of foxes attacking some horses that had been used for hunting; they had only dispersed when the owner shot one and wounded another. Then, that night - last night - they had returned in even greater numbers and surrounded his house, howling until the dawn, despite the terrified wife and her husband shooting another seven. When he went out in the morning, he found his two horses dead in their stables, savaged beyond recognition. The editor had told her this in an off-hand manner, but Jessie was sure that a pattern was beginning to emerge. This sort of thing just did not happen in the natural world unless something was causing it. And she was beginning to think that Shepherd Scar Research Centre was a factor.

She decided that it was time to go up there for a

night or two and see what she could see. She packed a few things in a light bag, including some walking shoes, a thick jersey and a waterproof jacket. Then she added her laptop, some make-up and a nice dress. She put her phone on divert to her mobile, locked up and left.

Little did she realise that her absence from home would be far longer than expected.

A few hours later, Sir Digby Crichton stepped off the train at Manchester station and into a waiting car. Just behind him as he passed through the barrier was an attractive girl with a light bag and a laptop. He drove off, while she queued for a hire car. An hour later, she was on her way across the moors to Hickley, and from there a meeting with the paper's editor, who could take her to Shepherd Scar.

It would be a long day.

As ever, the breeze off the moors was as keen as ever. But it was not often felt so sharply inside, several of the windows having been broken, the glass lying in sparkling, random patterns both inside and outside. The principal of Shepherd Scar Research Centre, Dennis Fouracres, had intended to arrive at work to solve his first concern, which was assessing whether any supposed leak of chemicals had had any bearing on the behaviour of the sheep. But after he had put the phone down to Sir Digby Crichton, he had almost immediately received another call from his security staff to say that something far worse had happened: both his main labs had been wrecked - and all the research animals had escaped.

So there he stood, surveying the wreckage in Mick Deakin's lab; then he went into Doug's, where the scene was identical. The two police officers with him were completely subdued.

"I've never seen anything like it", said the police sergeant after a long silence.

"No, nor have I," admitted Dennis.

The animals had not just gone: they had destroyed the place. Everything was tipped over, broken, chewed through... All the chemicals had been pushed off their shelves and lay smashed in great pools and, sometimes, sulphurous, smoking puddles on the concrete floor. How they had annihilated so many windows, though, was beyond those assembled there.

"Animal rights protesters, d'you think?" enquired Dennis. The sergeant shook his head. "No. It's too clinical; and they usually leave their sledge-hammers lying around. And anyway, nobody heard anything. Your security guys seem to be quite sensible. Unless it's a grudge - and an inside job."

"They said that a Doug Sprake came in early this morning," the officer added.

"Doug wouldn't have done this," said Dennis. "And why? He made good money here. And they'd have heard him."

"They didn't hear who*ever* it happened to be," observed the officer. This stumped Dennis.

"Is he in yet?" he enquired.

"Sprake?"

Dennis nodded. “No, not yet,” replied the second policeman.

“Late, for him,” observed Dennis, looking at his watch. “I hope he makes an appearance.”

They walked out, sounding like a marching army as their shoes crushed various remnants of the lab, and complemented by the wind sending tinkling shards of glass around the floor. Apart from that, the place had an eerie silence. All the other staff were waiting for them in the entrance block, along with the two security men. Dennis took the latter into his office, with the police.

“So what time did Doug come in?” he enquired.

“About six o’clock. He seemed a bit worried - rushed in and out.”

“He was only here for a half-hour”, the other added.

“Not enough time to do all that damage,” said the sergeant. Then: “When did you do your last security check?”

“Around seven. Just after he’d gone. Everything was normal then.”

“I still don’t understand how you didn’t hear anything,” said Dennis.

“Well, it did happen on the far side of the far block” explained one of them. “And it was windy.”

“It’s always windy here,” observed Dennis sarcastically.

“Don’t you have any alarms?” enquired the policeman. “Or video security?”

Dennis paused. “We’ve wanted them for years,

ever since the animal rights thing took off. All we've got is those rusty gates down the road. But what with it being ultra-secret, and government cuts... they didn't want anyone to know we were here, really."

"Mm. I hardly knew it existed, I have to say," said the sergeant. "Well, we'll get CID in to have a look. But how you take fingerprints of hundreds of animals I don't know."

"You don't think the animals did it, do you?" asked Dennis contemptuously. "It's far too... pre-meditated."

"All the animals have gone, yet the only two labs destroyed had animals that were being experimented on in grotesque ways - unlike the others. Perhaps they're trying to get their own back."

'Stupid policeman', thought Dennis.

As Crichton and Jessie had been arriving in Manchester, Doug was heading into Stoke-on-Trent. He had no particular reason to go there, but he was hungry and so decided to try and lose himself there. He found himself in one of the seedier areas of the city and located a bed and breakfast down a dingy street full of graffiti and litter. Having asked the landlady not to disturb him, he had a bath, changed his clothes and sat on the bed to reflect upon the actions of the early morning.

That he had been let off, he was sure: it was a calculated, collective response from hundreds, if not thousands, of animals. They had suddenly decided to let him go when he showed fear and pleaded with them. He had understood their mood; he knew they had taken that decision together and that he should leave quickly. As a sceptical scientist, he never believed anything unless it hit him in the face: this was definitely hitting him in the face.

He decided to go for a walk, having hidden the discs and notes behind the chest of drawers. He made straight for an internet café and logged on to the Shepherd Scar Research Centre intranet, using his encryption encoder which he had fortunately remembered to include in his rush to escape. The first e-mail was from Dennis Fouracres asking him to get in touch. He knew why: it could wait. He had to have time to frame his response, although he could not wait for too long. The second e-mail intrigued him. It was from an unknown address, and all it said was "Stay low: I'll be in touch". He deleted it - must be an error, he thought: spam. Then he regretted it: why should anyone know he should stay low? He cursed himself, then found a news page and started looking through it.

A few stories down, he saw a headline that sent a shudder through his body. He clicked on it, and read the contents. It originated from a Liverpool paper and gave an account of a fishing-boat returning from its fishing-grounds being hit by a huge school of fish. The impact had been less big than persistent; but one lad who had slipped when the boat half-capsized had gone overboard and been submerged by the weight of thousands of fish. He had drowned and they had not found his body.

That story in itself was bad enough: what had made him alert was the fact that it was Liverpool: Scar Brook went into Bracken Mere; then to the Hildaburna, and then into the Mersey. Instinctively, he knew there was a connection. And just as instantly, he realised why the animals had let him go: they thought they could use him. The hubbub around him annoyed his senses so he closed his computer link and left, finding quiet in a park. So, if the animals could use him, what did they want? An antidote? Hardly. More likely, further amounts of the same to make a takeover of the planet easier and swifter. He could hardly blame them: the human race was a cancer on the planet, wrecking wildlife and habitats and polluting the sea and the air. Now they had a chance to get their own back. Well, it must be thwarted: with a deep sigh he decided that, despite his earlier resolution and the danger involved, he would have to go back to Shepherd Scar and somehow create an antidote by pooling his and Mick's research. If only Mick was not dead... The thought crossed his mind that the future of the world was on his shoulders. When he realised it might be true, he grimaced. He had to do something soon, and sat back to look at the clear blue sky. High above him, two pairs of birds were circling. He found it strange that there were birds of prey in a city, then realised with a chill that they must be his guardians.

He was going nowhere, doing nothing, without the natural world knowing about it. He went back to his accommodation and slammed the door.

Jessie arrived outside the Hickley & District News office and parked her car in a visitor's space. It was a Victorian building with attractive mullioned windows, built of the local stone which gave it a red tinge. Over a hundred years of wind, rain and grime had given it a seasoned look, and black rivulets of dried dust transported by the elements had created interesting patterns under the windows. These were caked with soot and looked as though they had not been opened since the building was constructed. The crenellations along the top of the four storeys made it look even older than it was. Extending from over the main entrance, a hideous, dilapidated dirty white canopy with tacky aluminium edgings that had partly bent away in some places - or completely come off in others - was supported by what looked like scaffolding posts. The legend 'Hickley & Distric News' in blue plastic letters hung precariously over the end. The 't' was missing. What a pity they had not kept the original lettering in view which had been beautifully engraved in the stone over the door but which was now mostly hidden by this ghastly encumbrance. 'Sixties', she noted to herself with disdain.

After spending some time in reception, Jessie was shown into the modern extension at the back which had been tacked on at the same time as the entrance canopy, she thought. The lady, Enid, was the editor's assistant and made no secret of the fact that she did not like her editor having his time wasted by passing young female journalists. Eventually, Jessie was escorted through a large opening and back into the old building, into the editor's office, where the high ceilings were dimly illuminated by low-hanging fluourescent lights. Enid left and, after the initial formalities, she asked Frank Wheatley - a young man in a sports jacket who looked too callow to know anything - what he knew of Shepherd Scar. "Virtually nothing," was the answer. His voice and bearing were more authoritative than his looks, she decided. "It was built to be hidden and clandestine, and it's worked. Nobody goes up there except sheep and a few lost walkers - the government marked it as a 'restricted area' on the ordnance survey maps. Still, I'll take you up there. Can't wait to see it myself, now, actually. Things are always more interesting when they're restricted, aren't they?"

She agreed. Then: "Anything in the news of importance today? I've been on the train and haven't seen anything for a few hours. Sorry, journalistic impatience - can't help it!"

"You and me both," he returned with a slight tone of admonishment. "I am an editor."

"Sorry," she admitted.

"Actually, there's only this, really," he said as he handed her a bit of copy off the news feed. "A boat's been attacked outside Liverpool."

She took it from him and read it. "Hmm," she said. "I wonder if they're connected."

"What?"

"The sheep killing the dog, the foxes killing the horses... and now the fish attacking the boat."

"Hardly," he replied, "they're nearly two hundred miles apart." She raised her eyebrows at him with a wry smile and then looked back at the news feed. He felt she was keeping quiet about something.

"Why the quizzical look?" he enquired after a moment.

"I think they're related. The sheep drank from Scar Brook, according to your report."

"That's right..."

"And that passes the research centre."

"Ye-es..."

"Streams flow into rivers. Rivers flow into the sea. Animals drink. Things get passed on."

"I see. Well, we'd better get up there fast and take a look, hadn't we..."

They both left the office at a far quicker pace than either had entered it.

Sir Digby Crichton passed through the crags as he approached Shepherd Scar Research Centre and was immediately faced with a flimsy police road block. As the blue plastic ribbons fluttered, he told the policeman there who he was and asked him why he was being impeded. The policeman's reply made him extremely anxious and not a little angry. Why had Fouracres not rung him? He then firmly asked the constable to move the road block further up the road - to the crags, if possible. He could then actually close the only gates; otherwise, all manner of people would know where the place was and they did not want that, did they? The policeman said he would do so and

Crichton progressed to the central block where he was met by a flustered Dennis Fouracres.

"Any sign of Deakin, yet?" Crichton asked without even exchanging pleasantries.

"No. Nor Doug Sprake."

"Bloody idiot."

"Who - me?" asked Dennis tetchily.

"That's not what I meant, although..." He let the words trail off as Dennis looked more perplexed.

"Erm, I have some bad news," Dennis blurted out.

"I've heard it already. You should have rung me."

"Sorry - but phones and internet aren't working today for some reason. Only mobiles. I should have called you on that I suppose, but it all happened so quickly. And my secretary's off today. Typical. And you were on your way up anyway."

Crichton was not listening to his excuses so Dennis decided not to say any more and kept quiet. He guided Crichton towards the devastated labs, both seemingly impelled by an unknown force. When they arrived, Crichton walked around with the air of a contemplative general, poking and lifting bits of debris disdainfully with a silver propelling pencil, looking at them, then replacing them.

"Well," he said at length. "An inside job. And that means the animals."

Dennis looked annoyed at this observation. "Really? So you don't think - "

"No. I don't. I think it was the research animals in here." The policeman threw Dennis a smug glance. "And it certainly wasn't Doug Sprake, wherever he may be now. He's too stupid." Then, after a pause and preceded by a deep exhalation of breath he added: "Might have been someone else, though."

"Who?" asked Dennis. "Not Mick Deakin, surely?"

"We'll need to have a private chat in your office. If it's still intact."

"Yes, it is," he laughed - then realised that it was the wrong sentiment.

"Without anyone else present."

"Fine," Dennis replied. And they both turned and made for its comparative calm.

"Cup of tea would be nice," said Crichton, as they walked off.

The sturdy four-wheel-drive car purred nonchalantly as they climbed fast up through the dales. It was becoming quite windy and the twisting ribbon of road glistened in an uncertain light. Jessie and Frank wound around its long, desolate contours, unsure of the expectation they were craving; he was a quick driver, but very safe, his expertise honed by having driven on these roads long before he'd succumbed to the formality of passing his driving test. You could get away with so many things up here, Jessie thought. That's why the government had put Shepherd Scar Research Centre here. Jessie found Frank warm and entertaining, if still somewhat callow for a regional paper's editor. But he certainly knew his local stuff, and that was what she was here for. He had suggested that, rather then drive straight up to the

Shepherd Scar Research Centre, it would be better to park some way off up a lane he knew well, get out and ascend the last few yards on foot. At the top, there was a good vantage point from which to view the Centre without being seen. He had been sure to throw some strong binoculars into the back of the car for that purpose, too.

Suddenly, he put his mobile phone off and asked her to put hers off, too.

"Why?", she enquired.

"Instinct. And it's good for people not to be able to get a fix on you. And ..."

"And if it rings at the wrong moment, it could be awkward," she smiled.

"Exactly." He smiled back.

Coming up over a rise which displayed a breathtaking view below, Jessie suddenly saw some animals moving in the middle distance. At first, she thought they were cows, but then realised that they were moving much too fast. And they were nearer than she had originally thought, which meant that they were smaller than cows as well. She pointed at them. "What are they?" she enquired of Frank. Frank screwed up his nose, squinting in the weak sunlight, as he looked in the direction she was pointing.

"Dogs," he said after a moment. Then, looking again, he added, "Strange; I've never seen dogs like that in a pack all together."

"They're beagles, aren't they?" Jessie enquired.

"Yes."

"Then someone's out beagling."

"I doubt it," replied Frank. Wrong time of day, wrong season... and I can't see anyone around in charge of them."

"So where have they come from, then?"

"Shepherd Scar Research Centre, I should imagine."

"Ah." The revelation sent a surge of excitement up her spine. "D'you think they've escaped?" she asked.

"Undoubtedly."

As they drew closer, the dogs made a point of running away from them, turning almost as one, rather like a school of fish or a flock of migrating birds. Rather than straggling and running in many directions as dogs normally did, they seemed purposeful and as one entity, instinctively understanding one another. Frank pulled over and they both quickly got out. A curlew screamed above as Frank took the binoculars out of the car and focussed them on the receding dogs.

"I don't believe it," he uttered after a few moments.

"What have you seen?" enquired Jessie, shouting above the wind.

"You can't see very well without these..." he handed the binoculars to her, "...but can you see a whole load of animals in front of them? Small ones, I mean... Like mice, or something?"

"Oh, yes," she confirmed. "There are hundreds of them. Difficult to see in the long grass, but... Yes. Mostly white."

"Research mice," Frank asserted. "And some rabbits."

"I wonder where they're all going," Jessie remarked.

"That's what we need to find out."

"Does this mean we're near the research centre?"

Frank nodded. "And we'll be able to see them better if we get to where we were already going to, fast," he said, jumping back into the car and starting the engine so quickly that Jessie thought he would be away before she had got back in.

Now she was even more pleased he was a good driver as he took hairpin bends with the expertise of a rally-driver. They drove to where a set of crags stretched imperiously leftwards for about half a mile, jutting into the sky and seemingly interfering with the course of the scudding clouds. Suddenly, he veered off to the left down a track that was not only unmade but full of holes, boulders and troughs and which immediately started to climb up towards the centre of the crags. Sheep scurried away, except for one flock just away from the road which looked ominously at them as they bumped past. Jessie looked back at them.

"Why didn't that flock of sheep run away like all the others?" asked Jessie uncomfortably.

"I hate to think," came the knowing reply.

A few minutes later, Frank pulled to a halt between two rocks that looked like twisted spires, wrenched sharply up on the handbrake as he switched off the engine and jumped out. Jessie followed, falling back as she got out as the car was on a steep incline. She pulled on her jacket: it was cold up here.

"Welcome to Shepherd Scar", Frank shouted, "it's

just over the edge there." Then he ran back a few yards and peered down to where they had just come through his binoculars, trying to find the escaping dogs in the wilderness.

"Ah, there they are," he cried. He followed their progress for a few moments, then gave the binoculars to Jessie, who had come up behind him. "Definitely mice and rabbits in front," he added.

"Where do you think they're going?" she asked. "They look very purposeful... They seem to be making for that little lake over there."

Frank went to the car and took out an ordnance survey map, which he held on to with difficulty as it contorted itself in the stuttering wind. "It's called Bracken Mere," he said. "Look". He pointed to it. What Jessie saw, though, were the words in red near it, which declared 'Restricted Area' in red. "Is that Shepherd Scar Research Centre?" Frank nodded. "It's over here," he shouted, and turned round, tossing the map back inside the car as he passed it. Then, falling onto his stomach, he crawled forward for twenty yards between two outcrops of rock that formed a small chasm about fifteen feet wide and looked through his binoculars over what was a sudden edge. Jessie did likewise. When she was alongside him, she looked too.

"Shepherd Scar Research Centre," he howled against the wind, pointing downwards.

So there it was. Jessie looked at the four low, grey buildings below, all joined together in the middle by corridors leading to the central entrance block. She noted the letters on each roof, and observed what looked like six square pools at the end of one of them. They looked very full. Overflowing, even.To the left of these there was a small stream. Frank had noticed other things, though.

"The police are there," he observed. "And several windows are broken. In fact, it looks almost as if there's been an explosion. Glass everywhere. And... that's interesting. A large black, official-looking car. There must be a government person there. Looks important."

"Why is there no perimeter fence?" enquired Jessie.

Frank shrugged. "I suppose they thought there was no need here," he said, indicating the height of the sheer, rugged cliffs. "They were wrong, though, weren't they?" he smiled. "The dogs got out - and the mice." Jessie laughed, too. She was enjoying herself. And she quite liked Frank, too, even if he was still a bit young. Her realisation of a feeling of warmth for him was still overwhelmed by her feeling of excitement at what she was witnessing, though, because suddenly all her instincts about what she had found on the internet only a short while before seemed to be bearing fruit. She could just feel it. There was a government cover-up: and she was in the right place to find out what it was, she was sure.

Then, for no apparent reason, she looked behind her. She started, because what she saw frightened her: between the car and their position at the edge of Shepherd Scar was what she assumed to be the flock of sheep that had eyed them so piercingly on the way up. The noise of the wind had cloaked their arrival and they were ranged behind them in an arc, condensed between the two outcrops of rock on either side, regarding them threateningly. She realised immediately that there was no obvious escape route and tapped Frank, who took no notice at first, his attention taken with events below him. When she prodded him more violently, he turned and instantly saw what she had seen. He said nothing; he just looked at the intruders that had spoiled his observations.

"I wonder if they're the sheep that killed the sheepdog," he shouted into her ear after he had taken the situation in. That made Jessie even more afraid: she had not thought of this until that moment.

Crichton and Dennis sat opposite each other at Dennis' desk, although the former had requisitioned the latter's chair. From his borrowed seat of power, he looked down at Dennis, leaned forward, put his fingertips together in front of him, looked at them and then, with a deep breath, spoke fast and without a break.

"Now, Dennis. Don't take this too personally but basically you don't know much about what's going on here." Dennis went to protest but a hand went up and Crichton continued. "We - the government - have been using this god-awful place to research one or two dirty little tricks that you know nothing about. Oh, you know the main things, of course - serums and so on to make various things happen under various different circumstances, particularly in the medical field. Well, officially, that is." His countenance became darker. "We've been researching into the possibilities surrounding battlefield casualties and making them speak, spill the beans, that is, about their missions. You know the first bit of that - but not the second. The second is..." and he took another deep breath... "The second is for them to then change personality to such an extent that, if they live, they become so aggressive they go back to their units and kill their comrades. I need hardly add that this also gives us a chance to know where the buggers are and wipe the rest of them out if necessary. It's a nasty little virus which then turns their brains to jelly. It's based on another compound we're researching here that you also don't know about, called chromitic paradiosymine. It brings on a very fast form of rampant senile dementia. And I mean, *very* fast. Minutes. Of course, they never recover. Well, that's if they're not dead already," he added with a slight smile. Then he looked serious again. "The problem, though, is that all that research - and a few more besides which I won't bore you with... yet - was in Mick Deakin's lab. It existed nowhere else - too sensitive. And now, of course, it's all gone. And so has Mick Deakin, it would appear. Unless he's turned up since I arrived."

"Well, no - they'd have told me," Dennis croaked.

"Mm. Well, let me tell you now - and this goes no further than this room for the moment - he won't ever turn up again. Deakin is dead."

Dennis slumped back in his chair. "Who...?" he

murmured. Crichton continued: "We don't know. But before all this happened, a lot of his research notes started to appear on the internet. We managed to shut it down quite quickly, but God knows who saw it. Trouble is, we don't know where his discs and research notes are now. They've all disappeared. Unless *you* know where he kept them?"

Dennis shook his head. "Secret," he said pointedly, "why would I know?"

The stand-off endured for a second when it was interrupted by a knock on the door and two turgid-looking cups of tea were brought in. After the canteen lady had left, Crichton looked at his cup of liquid. "Looks like some of the stuff you concoct here," he commented, with obviously no intention of drinking it. Dennis took a sip of his. "Yes, he was found dead this morning coming into work. Well, he was found at the bottom of the road leading up to here... At much the same time as Doug Sprake was seen here. Whether he's aware of Mick's death or not, I don't know. But as he hasn't turned up again today I suspect he knows all too well. Probably thinks we think he's going to get the blame. Stupid idiot."

"But if you know he's dead, you must have the body."

For the first time, Crichton looked uneasy and shifted in his chair. "No, we don't. It, um, was found by one of our operatives, coming up to question him. He was going to be waiting for Deakin early, outside security. To put him on the spot, find out if it was him putting his research notes on the net - or someone else. And - if that was the case - whom. But he found Deakin's body on the way up here... Strange thing is, I got an e-mail apparently sent after the operative found him dead... So..." He trailed off, grappling with the apparent inconsistencies of the story he was trying to relay.

"From Sprake, possibly?" Fouracres volunteered.

Crichton shook his head dismissively then continued: "Impossible. He knew nothing. Anyway, the operative went into Oldham to get the police and an ambulance, but when they arrived back there was nothing there. Even his car had gone. No trace."

"So do you really know he's dead, then?"

"Mm. I saw the photograph the operative took. But one thing was strange - he looked terrible. And much older than when I saw him only a few weeks ago; he'd aged, well... twenty years or more. Must have taken in some traces of chromitic paradiosymine, somehow."

"Who told you all this?"

"I said: one of our operatives. He tried to find Deakin's research notes before he left for Oldham. But they weren't in his car."

"So he didn't immediately come here to Shepherd Scar first to try and find them?"

"No - no point. Security wouldn't have let him in alone without a grade one pass."

"You could have called me. I'd have let him in on your authority."

"I daresay. But we didn't want to arouse undue attention. You know, other staff here... And especially you." He flashed a fake smile at the abject Fouracres, then continued: "After all, as I've implied, you don't know everything that goes on here."

Dennis suppressed the desire to get angry. Instead, he just carried on listening to Crichton. "So, as I say, the operative went into Oldham: then if he'd arrived as planned later on at the research centre with the police and an ambulance - and the dead body - everything could have been neatly swept under the carpet." There was a pause, then he added distantly: "Seemed tidier at the time. But now..."

"Why did no-one stay with the body?"

Crichton shrugged. "It was just the one man. And we couldn't risk one of our guys being seen with a dead body, especially Deakin's - too sensitive. Especially with his stuff having been splurged all over the net. Could get us into all sorts of trouble. All right if someone else had found him, though - especially as there were no research notes with him."

"Unless they were taken before your operative arrived."

"Mm. I hadn't thought of that." Then he added as an afterthought: "Bit of a mess-up really, isn't it?"

Chapter 10

Doug was back in the bedroom of his bed and breakfast accommodation, poring over Mick's notes. Outside, the occasional bird-cry above, mingling with the noise of a subdued radio, kept him assured that he was not alone. As he tried to see where Mick's research had crossed over with his, he was aware that he could not stay here for long, and he wondered if he would ever be able to get away from his aerial guards. He pondered the chance of a night-time escape, but then thought that if they found him again - as he was sure they would - they would probably be less forgiving the next time.

As he studied the contents, various things gnawed at him: why did Mick look so old when he himself had started to appear younger? And why had his superior at the Shepherd Scar Research Centre, Dennis Fouracres, not told him what Mick was working on? Did they not, should they not, work as one team? He was sure Mick knew much about his own findings and experiments - except the ones he was doing clandestinely, of course. Perhaps, then, despite Mick's admission that he had been working on unofficially official experiments, this was a double bluff. Perhaps, too, he thought with a start, that even Dennis Fouracres did not know what Mick was working on, either.

He kept coming across references to the compound in Mick's research notes that he had initially felt was a distraction, but now he could see it was mentioned more and more frequently: chromitic paradiosymine. It appeared to him that although many of the compounds they had been using were common between them, this one was used in Mick's experiments only. As he read more, he realised that this was no red herring and it was here where their research diverged: Mick was working on a serum that would completely change a person's personality. Allied with his compounds and research into inducing speech, Mick had been following a course which would make people change personality. The more he read, the more chilling it became: it was for use by the military and, although Doug had worked on the part to make wounded personnel more loquacious, his research had stopped there. He had been doing research to make compounds of use to stroke sufferers as well as battlefield casualties: Mick's was for military purposes only and the ensuing character-changing drug would reverse the loyalty of a soldier and make him violent towards those he had once been with. It also had the effect of ageing the brain prematurely - enough to ensure that the person who had taken it would not live for long afterwards.

He mulled this over: had Mick somehow ingested more than a trace element of chromitic paradiosymine, which was making him look so old? And what was it that he had or had not taken that was making him look younger? He delved into the notes with a renewed vigour...

An hour later, he felt he might know the answer; but he needed to get back to Shepherd Scar Research Centre to complete his findings. If he could. Would the animals let him back? Would Dennis Fouracres? And how would he justify his lack of attendance there after Mick's death? They must know about that now. He then wondered if they might think he had done it - professional jealousy or to gain access to his research for profit. He shuddered as he suddenly realised that his government department might be after him as well as the animals - for different reasons. Either way, he was cornered. Yet he still found something tugging at his senses that might make all Mick's research seem more obvious to him. He made himself look harder at Mick's notes, and then it came to him: was it the fact that he, but not Mick, had used manganese tripuride? There was scant reference to it in Mick's notes. And it did have properties that could suppress the ageing process: but without dedicated research he did not know whether it was stronger than chromitic paradiosymine or what would happen if they were put together. That was roughly where he was when all this had blown up. But had he, Doug Sprake, ostensibly found the secret of eternal youth? That would be something indeed. But why, then, had the animals reacted as one? They did not act or appear younger, just more aggressive - a trait of youth, perhaps? He wondered whether they might have more energy as a result, hence their new-found youthful aggression, but it seemed tenuous... But then, why should a form of teenage rebellion be confined just to the human world? It would happen sooner in animals because of their generally shorter lifespans, but it was a point nonetheless - and caused by a compound created by humans. Or just one human - himself.

This last thought hit him hard: in a spirit of naked greed, he had unwittingly started a chain of events that could jeopardise the whole human race - just for the good life on his terms. He felt ashamed at what he had tried to do and immediately made a vow to do all he could to reverse the effects of what he had started.

Back at Shepherd Scar Research Centre, Sir Digby Crichton and Dennis Fouracres were finishing their meeting.

"I'll have to shut this place down for a while," said Crichton: "Well, officially, anyway. You can carry on but you've got to be even more secretive than before."

"If that's possible," rejoined Dennis.

"Hm. There'll probably be people nosing about - the press, the BBC, and so on. Keep them out and don't tell them anything. Not just what we do or don't do here but also regarding any chemical leaks. And keep the animals' escape secret for as long as you can. It's all classified under the Official Secrets Act. The Freedom of Information Act doesn't cover this. Or, if it does, pretend that it doesn't until all this blows over." Dennis said he would do all he could. "And if Sprake comes back, let me know." Dennis agreed, and the two men parted, after Crichton had promised him extra money to cover a clean-up, restocking of the essential chemicals for their work - and added security. Even though the animals had escaped, violent visits from the animal rights lobby would almost certainly now be imminent.

Dennis returned to his office and sat back in his own chair, which made him feel slightly more important again. He mulled over what they had talked about and decided to take a walk around the outside of the centre to check the alleged leaks, which was something he had never done before. He stood up and walked out past the wrecked labs, through the linking corridor to the reception area, and the two security men. The whole place seemed eerily quiet. He stepped outside, just in time to see Sir Digby Crichton's car disappearing over the lip of the plain between the two rocks. 'Good riddance,' he thought to himself.

The day was beginning to fade and shafts of golden sunlight cast long shards of luminance across the eastern end of the enclosed plain, the tall spires of rock creating long gloomy shadows in contrast to the brilliant colour. Small patches of lichens clung to wet protruding boulders, glistening where the sun gave them some temporary warmth. If only this had not happened, Dennis thought, revelling in the majestic grandeur and beauty of the surroundings. He walked briskly around the outside of the buildings, having the odd word through windows - open or broken, sometimes both - with his colleagues. He looked in vain for any trace of the animals that had fled, but there was none. When he got to the holding-pools, he noticed that the concern over chemicals leaking into the environment was not an idle alert. For the last one, D3, was not only full but seeping over the edge; although this was normal procedure, the fact that it was thick, viscous and dark was not. The sludge, which should have been disposed of a long time ago had not been. The pool was nearly all composed of this - and that *was* a breach of regulations. It was so annoying, he thought: if this damn place was less secret it would be easier to get money to address things like this. As it was, any request for extra funds either took forever or got lost completely. Still, he would use some of the cash just promised by Crichton to rectify the leak, he immediately pledged to himself. He continued his tour; once, he thought he heard a shout from high above, but seeing nothing, he continued his circuit. Having made mental notes about many of the things he should do, he returned to his office, just as two men in rubber suits passed him to shut the pools off.

Just back in his office, his mobile phone rang. It was his secretary. He was about to ask why she was phoning on her day off, but she seemed very agitated and started talking before he could ask.

"Mr. Fouracres; I've just been watching the news. Have you heard what's been happening?" Dennis confessed that he had and that all was generally under control, despite appearances. "Well, I fear there's loads of people on the way to the centre - it's suddenly become a huge story. Especially as nobody really knew it existed before. And what with the animals escaping..."

"Who told the media that? I didn't."

"Well, they know. I've managed to get hold of security to alert them for a busy night. And the phones are all off there - I suppose you didn't know that?"

"Yes, I did. It would have been nice and quiet - except we had a visit from Crichton."

"Ah, he's been there, has he? Well, I'm not surprised. Anyway, as it's nearly five I think you should get out fast. "

"So why are there no phones, d'you think?"

"I expect the government did it to keep the hordes out for as long as possible. They might have told you, though." Privately, Dennis cursed Crichton for not availing him of that information - and much more besides.

"So what's the news, then?" he snapped.

"Well, you know about all these strange goings-on with the animals?"

"Yes."

"Well, have you heard about the trawler outside Liverpool? A man died when it was hit by a shoal of fish. Repeatedly."

"So what's that got to do with us?"

"The word is that it's leaking chemicals from Shepherd Scar that are to blame."

"Oh, how ridiculous," he retorted automatically, at the same time what he had just witnessed being paramount in his mind. "How on earth - "

"There is some evidence," she interrupted. "Apparently our holding-pools have not been maintained well and have been leaking substances into the environment. And some of them are very toxic, as you well know."

"Well, yes... But they are filtered..." he muttered flatly, wondering how this breach of regulation was already known about, before he had even known about it himself.

"I think you should get home," she said, "before all hell lets loose."

He put his phone off. Then he went to see his maintenance team and told them to keep the cocks to the holding-pools switched off indefinitely. When they asked what would happen to the liquids, which would now mount up inside rather than outside, he told them that there would be nothing mounting up for the foreseeable future and that they must more carefully store and mark any hazardous substances. Leaving them grumpily doing this, he then went round all the labs telling all the other staff to get out immediately but to ensure everything was locked up as well as could be, and that any contentious notes and discs were taken home with them. A glazing firm was already boarding up the devastated labs: he asked security how they had been asked for when all the phones were off. They did not know - they had just arrived, unannounced and unexpected. No-one had used their mobiles to call them. 'Must have been Crichton', he thought, and drove away from the research centre, stopping only to negotiate around the police road-block and the half-closed gates which the policeman had great difficulty in opening due to their previous lack of use. There was no-one there yet from the media, but there would be a scrum there in the morning, he was sure. He drove away as fast as he could.

Frank and Jessie looked the slowly advancing sheep in their eyes, which were malevolent and focussed. Unlike sheep normally, they did not look away from them even for an instant but kept staring - and were completely unimpressed by shouts and sudden movements, even when Frank picked up a large stick and brandished it. They could not get down the escarpment behind them - it was too sheer. And if they could have done, then so could the sheep. Jessie looked at the boulder next to her, which protruded over the edge. "If I can get over that, I think we can go round the back," she shouted above the wind into Frank's ear. "They won't be able to get over it for a while, and we can make for the car."

"I don't think they're that stupid," he shouted back into her ear; "but it's the only hope we've got. My side's no good. Go now - go on."

Jessie jumped up onto the rock and stood at the top for a moment, trying to get her balance in the blustering wind. Her foot slipped a little, but then she was over the top with Frank almost falling over her. They ran the twenty yards to the car behind the rocks and the sheep and opened the doors: the sheep, hearing the doors and then realising what was happening, tried to turn round quickly but due to their tight formation found it difficult to do so. This gave Frank and Jessie a few vital extra seconds: Frank thrust his hand into his pocket and pulled out his keys, which got caught on his trousers and fell with a jangling clatter to the floor of the car. He reached down, picked them up, and fumbled the key into the ignition as the first thud of a sheep's head rocked the side of the car - then another and another. Jessie found herself screaming as the butting continued and the car lifted off the ground for a moment. Then the engine fired and they were in reverse, a thump denoting that they had hit at least one sheep as they did so. Then the wheels were spinning and they were off down the track, mud, grass, lichen and water splattering everywhere, cascading down the escarpment with the sheep in full pursuit. As they got near the bottom they saw the dogs they had seen earlier running alongside, getting closer to them as they tried to head them off. And then, as the engine screamed, they suddenly saw a huge kite fly towards the windscreen, its extended claws scratching into the glass as it flew into them and then over. As they got to within a hundred yards of the road, the dogs jumped onto the car, barking and yapping, scratching and yelping; two got crushed under the wheels and great spurts of blood splashed the windscreen. Jessie had stopped screaming but was now white with fear: Frank had the look of a fighter pilot. As they hit the road with a bang and a huge jump into the air, another car was coming the other way, hooting and flashing its lights in an effort to avoid this idiot joining the road at that speed. Then they collided, sideways on, the sound of wrenching, tearing metal and squealing rubber mingling with the noise of dogs, sheep and birds. Jessie's door prised itself open in the impact: there was a gap of about an inch wide at the bottom. As the two cars came violently to a halt, the driver of the other car was flung through the windscreen, which shattered as his head crashed through it, blood everywhere, and his body thumped lifelessly onto the bonnet. Instantly, the dogs were on him, ripping the clothes and flesh from his body in a frenzy of primeval violence.

"Christ!", screamed Frank, as he revved on the accelerator to try and disentangle the two cars, "I think that's the boss of the research centre." It was then that Jessie saw the rodents through the gap under the door, which were suddenly there in their thousands, squeaking and shoving, using each others' bodies to try and get into the car. She screamed as the engine whined and the wheels spun on the tarmac - but the car would not budge. She started hitting out at the mice and voles and rats with the ordnance survey map. It went red immediately. Then she managed to wedge it into the hole and withdrew her hands as the car suddenly broke free from the other and veered off jumpily onto the road in a series of starts and not in a straight line. Frank put his foot to the floor as those dogs not still ripping the flesh off poor, Dennis Fouracres chased them; a few sheep stood in their path but by now the momentum of the car was enough to swat them out of the way with the crack of breaking bone and shattering headlights. Above, another kite and an eagle joined the first in attacking the car but by the time Frank and Jessie were a mile away and going at over seventy miles an hour, they gave up the immediate assault but kept watching for when they would inevitably have to stop.

Jessie and Frank did not speak for a long time. They were both white and terrified, hardly being able to believe what had just happened to them. And that they had escaped. At least, for now.

Chapter 11

After his resolve to rectify whatever he might have unleashed on humankind, Doug had left his lodgings in Stoke-on-Trent and driven north again, still followed by his aerial guards. He turned off the main road and, in a remote village, stopped his car and switched his phone on again: he knew he might now be traced but had to risk it for a moment. He called the Shepherd Scar Research Centre: it was just gone five o'clock and he had chosen the time specifically because he knew that Dennis Fouracres, after a lifetime in the civil service, would not be there and would have gone home. He wanted to tell security that he had had reasons for leaving the research centre and would not be back, but also wanted them to tell Fouracres that he would be in touch. His other motive was to find out what the official line on Mick's disappearance was, and whether the place had been shut down.

But the number rang as unavailable and he surmised that all communications had been cut. He pondered for a moment, then remembered that he had once been for a drink with one of the security guards… He found his mobile number and rang him. Success… it was ringing.

The news he received shocked him, and forced a

number of the carefully thought-out questions he had listed from his mind: Fouracres was dead, the victim, apparently, of a hit and run car just by Shepherd Scar; there were hordes of press and television cameras and hundreds of journalists trying to get into the place even though it had been officially shut down - although Brian, the security guard he spoke to, implied heavily without actually admitting it that the centre was still open. He also told him that his and Mick Deakins' labs were wrecked and that it seemed it was the incarcerated animals that had done it, all of whom had escaped. When Brian asked Doug when he was coming back, he thought better of making any answer and finished the call, quickly switching his phone off again. Even more reason not to be traced...

Things were moving so quickly that he could hardly think straight. So... if the labs were wrecked, there would be none of his compounds and chemicals there, unless the animals had not touched the storage rooms. Still trying to keep Fouracres' death out of his mind, he surmised that what he thought the animals wanted him to do was to try and create the compounds again. He realised that the small amount of money he had saved over the years would be inadequate to set up a lab, but knew that he had to do something: his sense of public duty suddenly became paramount. He would only be spared if he were seen to be solving the problems of Shepherd Scar - by either the government or the animals. Or both. He would clandestinely have to get Sir Digby Crichton to give some government money to continue with his research, whilst making the animals think that he was helping them. If Crichton was reluctant, he would blackmail him: he had enough on the man to do that. This had gone beyond honour or subservience to senior civil servants, even if he was a parliamentary under-secretary. In fact, it was that which would probably make his task easier.

A screeching cry from a huge bird on a telegraph pole a few feet away reminded him that he was trapped between two immutable objects: the government and nature. He was unsure which was the more sinister.

He looked at his pudgy hands and – although they appeared more svelte than they had been – took a deep breath and exhaled slowly through his teeth, making a soft whistling sound. Shepherd Scar was where he had to go after all, come what may. By the time he got there it would be dark, and he would try and get in without anyone knowing. He knew a couple of places where he could climb down the crags from above, although it was dangerous. But he could not go in via the official route. All he could do was hope for a full moon, the usual poor security - and understanding from the animals. For going back into the ecological cauldron that Shepherd Scar had become would mean that every aspect of his mission would be fraught, tense and perilous. As he drove off, what he would say in a phone call to Crichton was uppermost in his mind. On the telegraph pole, another bird joined the first, then both soared high to keep Doug's car in view.

Frank and Jessie parked up in a courtyard at the back of the editorial offices, which was full of cars and vans, the latter emblazoned with the legend 'Hickley & District News'. There was an opening there in what had once been the stables which was marked 'Editor', and they drove in. He threw a cover over the car and they went quickly round to the front and inside, the gravity of what they had just witnessed and its probable causes weighing heavily on their minds. After a long silence while they mulled over their thoughts, they had started to discuss the events as they neared Hickley and were aware of what they had to do.

"Where have you been?" asked a stressed sub-editor who harangued them as they came into the main reception area. "Your bloody phone's off. We thought we'd have to put the paper to bed without you."

"We've got the story of the week," shouted Frank as he powered past him, leaving him bewildered. "If it doesn't sound too clichéd, stop the presses."

"Actually, it could be the story of the century," Jessie added as she followed Frank. She sensed that the man they left in their wake resented such a young whippersnapper as Frank running the paper. As they went to Frank's office, several staff looked at them as if to imply that their being behindhand had actually stopped any news happening.

"Sorry, it might be a late evening for some of you," Frank tossed into the air as they entered his sanctum, ignoring his already discomfited secretary.

"Great story". The murmuring that this caused was shut off as he slammed the door closed. Almost immediately, it was opened again by a ruddy, sweaty man with a beer belly that came into the room a second or two before he followed it. "Not now, Arnold," Frank snapped at him.

"But the pageant - "

"Stuff the pageant for now, Arnold. This is more important. We have national - no, *inter*national - news happening here near Hickley. Please leave us and let us get it out. Thank you." This he was saying as he peered at the newsfeed on his computer. The door closed again.

"I was right," murmured Frank, casting a glance to ensure that the man actually had left the office. "It was the boss of the research centre we crashed into."

"And killed, too," Jessie added, not in an admonishing way but as a means of trying to make the fact sink in. "We'll have to tell the police what happened, Frank."

"Not yet," was the reply. "If ever. What's done is done and it wasn't strictly our fault. We have to use what we've seen to make sure something's done. We can't do that behind bars. Those sheep... I mean, they were savage. Primeval. And if it is whatever garbage is leaking out of Shepherd Scar that's causing them - and God knows what else - to act like that, then, as journalists, we have to make sure that everyone knows about it."

"In which case, they'll know it was us who killed Fouracres anyway."

"Ah. Yes. I hadn't thought of that." He looked worried again.

"Unless 'someone else' was up there and witnessed it. We could report it as such," Jessie ventured.

"Good idea. What, like a, a... walker or something."

"Yes, I suppose so."

"Good idea. And then they came to us, and they want to stay anonymous for obvious reasons." He seemed happier with that idea.

"But you'll have to get that car of yours repaired by someone who knows how to remove all traces of cars that have crashed into it," Jessie added. Then, with a twinkle: "And blood and bone. Fast. Otherwise, we're done for."

"Mm. I think I can sort that. A friend of mine who runs a garage. Used to be a mechanic and panel-beater."

"Useful."

"I'll go and do that while you write up the story."

"I thought you'd want to do that."

"You're freelance - you'll get a better angle and more excitement into it than I will. I've read your stuff before. You're good. And better than I am, even if I am a bloody good editor. Circulation's up lots since I took over." He smiled at her as he picked up the phone. Jessie was impressed with his altruism and his sense of priority, as well as the compliment he had paid her. In that instant, she saw a maturity in him that he must have always had but which she had missed; he was not the naive person she thought he had been when she first met him. She really was beginning to like him a lot.

A few minutes later, he was buzzing around her as she wrote up the account, adding bits of description and suggesting background information.

There was a knock on the door and Enid entered. "Did you know that Dennis Fouracres has been killed?" she enquired.

"Yes."

"The man who runs Shepherd Scar Research Centre."

"Yes, Enid, I know. Thank you."

"Oh. A hit and run; looks like they were trying to avoid some poor animals."

"Poor animals..." said Frank under his breath.

"And what happened to your car?"

Frank turned to look at her. "Enid, I had an accident. It happens."

"But there's blood all over it." Frank ignored her, suggesting a comma where Jessie had left one out.

"It wasn't you, was it?" she asked in a thin voice.

"No, Enid, it wasn't. Now please let us finish this story. It's important."

"I wish I could afford to ruin my car and not care about it," she muttered as she left the room, closing the door more forcefully than was necessary.

"Is she trouble?" asked Jessie. He nodded.

"Resents my being her boss. Thinks it should be her husband."

"Oh," said Jessie, knowingly. "Why doesn't she retire, then?"

"Still hoping I'll fall under the proverbial bus, I daresay." Jessie laughed, then realised it was the first time since their ordeal, which at least made her feel better.

"Why did you take her on?" she enquired after a few moments.

"I didn't, really. She was, shall we say, forced upon me by the proprietors. And they won't let me find someone else." Jessie instinctively felt uneasy at this. If the Hickley & District News had been a state enterprise she would have suspected something abnormal, but not a privately-run one. Then she became engrossed in her report and it went out of her mind.

When the story was written, Frank called a meeting of his editors. He introduced Jessie and explained how she had realised what was possibly going on at the Shepherd Scar Research Centre and had alerted him to it. Then he explained all that had happened, except for changing the fact that it was them that had experienced it: as far as the news team was concerned, Jessie had a contact who lived near Shepherd Scar, to whom the events had happened and who had told them the story. They had not heard of Dennis Fouracres' death until they had arrived back at the offices and someone told them. And his phone had been off because the person wanted to remain anonymous and they did not want a fix on their location. Finally, they had had an altercation on the way back with a wall while trying to avoid a sheep, but had subsequently hit both, hence the damage and the blood on the car. They all seemed to accept the story, except Enid.

Jessie did not like Enid.

Doug had not used his mobile phone since using its camera to photograph Mick Deakin's dead body. He felt lost, out of contact, without it, but knew he could not put it on or the government would know where he was immediately. Just like the birds; but he did not like being followed by anyone - and he needed to work alone. Then he had an idea: he would stop at the next car dealer's and swap his car for a second-hand one in the showroom. That way he would hopefully outwit the birds, who would stick with his old car. Before leaving the showroom, though, he would put his phone on, make a call to Sir Digby Crichton and tell him what was going on in no uncertain terms and what he needed - or else. Then, he would leave the phone in a car in the showroom. That way, the authorities would go on a wild goose chase when that car moved and they tried to track him. He smiled at his ingenuity but then frowned when he realised that it probably wouldn't work. It did in the movies, but this was real. Still, he had to give it a go in order to give himself as much time as possible to get into the Shepherd Scar Research Centre, undetected by man or beast.

A few minutes later, he found exactly what he wanted and drove onto the forecourt which was even more suitable for his subterfuge as it had a huge canopy covering all the cars. He got out, took his case and briefcase out of the boot, locked the car and went in.

A fat, pasty man, squeezed into a blazer with stains on both it and the mismatching tie, greeted him. "I want to do a swap with that car there for one of your lesser second-hand models," he said, coming straight to the point. "And I need it fast."

"Trying to get away from something, then?" the fat man asked in a thick Lancashire accent with a smile that revealed teeth desperately in need of a dentist.

"Not exactly," said Doug, lying with a new-found ease that surprised him. "Just want something different. That one will do," he said, observing an ageing two-seater in the corner.

"Ah, well that's a lot less then yours is worth."

"Great. We've got a deal, then?"

"Well, I'll need some details..."

"I can furnish you with everything," said Doug, who always carried his documents around in his car. "All I ask is that you sort out all the insurance, the registration book and whatever else after I've gone. In a few minutes," he added, as the man looked at him strangely. "Look, I've done nothing wrong, you can have my address, everything. But you can make far more for my car than I will on that one. That's the deal. It's yours. Just do it, please."

The man acquiesced. After a half hour, having looked at Doug's car while Doug waited inside, the deal was done, the fat man looking considerably pleased with this unexpected end-of-day business and a potential profit that would match his size.

"Send it all to my home address," he finished. Then: "What sort of car do you drive?"

"That one over there," said the man proudly, pointing to a vulgar-looking family saloon with discarded tissues and sweet-wrappings strewn across the inside. "Perfect," thought Doug.

"I just need to use the gents'," he said, and disappeared into a side door. When there, he took out his phone, put it on and called Crichton. He got him immediately. It was a short conversation, but Crichton was left in no doubt as to why Doug felt he and his government was responsible for what had happened and its gravity. He wanted immunity and help, or he felt that an environmental disaster was imminent. He knew that Crichton would not help him there and then and would stall until he realised he had no choice. He was not disappointed with that prediction. 'You can call me on the mobile', he had said when he signed off. Then he put his phone on silent. After that, he went back into the showroom and asked to see the man's car.

"Very nice," he said, as he surreptitiously but carefully hid the phone in the passenger-side door pocket under an avalanche of chocolate-bar wrappings.

Then, taking care to cover his head with his jacket on the way out to his new, substitute car, he drove off as fast as he could in the direction of Shepherd Scar. He kept looking, but he felt sure that the birds were still waiting for him at the garage. Despite night falling, his spirits rose.

Chapter 12

Crichton had been outside the House of Commons Whips' office when his mobile rang. Now, he was back at his own desk, somewhat perturbed at his conversation with Doug. He had been blackmailed before, but this carried far more concerns than previously. He knew he would be blamed for the leak at Shepherd Scar, but could not give Doug either cash or immunity without the say-so from a higher source - probably the Prime Minister himself. He could possibly divert funds for a clean-up without too much trouble, but money to continue the research on Doug's terms was distinctly dicey. And potentially very expensive. He would have to impress upon the Prime Minister its importance. In the meantime, if he could silence Doug, he would. He looked at the last incoming number on his mobile and wrote it down. 'Silly bugger,' he thought to himself, 'leaving his number available. We'll catch him in no time.' He then asked his assistant to get the police to trace the number, and find out where it was.

A few minutes later, a call from a police official confirmed that it belonged to a Doug Sprake, who lived in the village of Alterby. The phone itself was currently emitting a signal from north of Stafford. 'He's heading south,' thought Crichton. 'Good.' He hung up after asking the police not to do anything yet but to let him know where it ended up. Then he went to the Commons bar for a stiff drink. He soon realised how much he needed it, as there were reports beginning to circulate of a Japanese whaler north of the Irish Sea being attacked by a number of whales after one of them had been harpooned. He reflected on the fact that it was geographically not that far from Liverpool, where the pollution from the Shepherd Scar Research Centre would flow into the sea. What with the sheep, the foxes and the trawler - not to mention the devastation at Shepherd Scar Research Centre caused by the escaping research animals - this was a worrying additional event. Very worrying indeed.

Jessie and Frank were in the printroom as the paper started to come off the presses. She had never been in one before and she found the thunderous noise and speed of it all very exciting. Although it was a small room and printrun by national standards, the shaking of the old building lent a reality to her feeling that this was news that would make the earth tremble: she felt very much that these revelations would open people's eyes to the significance of the cover-up. Frank pulled one of the copies off the belt and held it up for her to read. The headline said: 'Secret Government Research Centre To Blame For Savage Animal Attacks'. Her name appeared underneath: 'By our special reporter, Jessie Scott'. She read the rest of the article, smiling quietly to herself amongst the noise at what she had written. Then Frank was tapping her shoulder and speaking into her ear, telling her that he had already downloaded the story onto the web, specifically to the Press Association. That meant she could expect to be rung at any moment.

He was not wrong: within the hour they were both giving interviews for local and national television, radio, and over the phone to other news editors across the nation, as well as one from France, two from Ireland and one from Japan, who wanted their views on the significance of the whaler which they now knew had been overturned by the whales. A television satellite link was set up in the office by a camera crew which had spent the day camped outside the Shepherd Scar Research Centre but had not been allowed an interview or a look round: this interview would be live on the Ten O'Clock News, and possibly Newsnight after that, when the Under-Secretary for Home Affairs, Sir Digby Crichton, was rumoured to have agreed to participate.

"Do you think your paper's proprietors will mind all this attention?" Jessie asked during a lull between interviews.

"They'll love the publicity," Frank answered, "At least - they will until something goes wrong."

The newspaper staff, unused to such attention, were agog with amazement, and Frank noted that it was the first time he could remember that many staff had not headed straight home at the earliest opportunity.

At that same moment, Doug, who had decided to

drive on motorways with his replacement car to ensure greater speed, was approaching a service-station. Believing that the birds were not following him, he had decided to pull in for a meal, and to kill some time before what would be a nocturnal visit to Shepherd Scar, now under forty miles away. He parked as close to the entrance as he could, then put his jacket over his head again and ran into the foyer. He received some strange looks from passers-by because it was not raining, but once inside he assumed a normal posture and made for one of the outlets that pass for restaurants. As he made his way, he became aware of some title music that he knew and realised that although the sound was low he had discerned the music for the news, coming from above him on a giant television screen. Immediately, he stopped to watch but was horrified at what he saw. Straining to hear above the hubbub, he made out that a Japanese whaling-ship had been overturned in the Irish Sea by whales being hunted for their meat - or, supposedly, for 'research', though no-one really believed that, least of all the Japanese. The way that this item was referred to made him realise that this must be relatively old news but a new story seemed to underline the crisis he had helped to unleash on the planet. Around him, people were taking little notice, and those that did had that disaffected air the public shows when it feels it nothing to do with them. The report told of a breakout at an ostrich farm near Chester, where hundreds of these birds had attacked their handlers and killed one of them. They had then gone on the rampage and were attcking anyone they could find. When a farmer shot one, the rest cornered and attacked him before he escaped: when the police and an ambulance arrived, they, too, had been attacked. The man was seriously injured in hospital. Then the news anchor turned to a screen where an attractive girl named Jessie Scott was giving her views 'live from Hickley' on why she felt these events were happening. His blood ran cold when he just managed to hear her mention the Shepherd Scar Research Centre and some alleged chemical leaks from it that were in breach of just about every safeguard on the globe. He suddenly found he could hear better because the hall was much quieter - people had started to listen. When he saw a picture of Dennis Fouracres - the reason was obliterated by a loud guffaw from a person near him who was not watching - he realised that the chance that they would say they were looking for a Doug Sprake was almost inevitable. He quickly got up and went to the door as fast as he could without looking suspicious; hungrier than he had realised by the expectation of eating food that had been thwarted, he just got to the doors when his picture appeared, along with that of Mick Deakin. He just remembered to pull his jacket over his head again and got back in the car, locking it instantly.

He thought back at what he had seen. Hickley. Where was that? He found a map in the car and looked it up. It was not too far from where he was: he would go and find this girl, Jessie, if he could. She might be able to help him - and he, her. He could tell her where to look and also show her Mick's notes and more, in return for cover and help in putting this catastrophe right. He was sure to find her: she would be well known by now as he could see that the town was not very big, and the building in the background of her television interview looked as if it must be somewhere in the centre. He turned the ignition and headed off, hungrier than ever, into the night.

What Doug had not seen in his haste to leave was a picture that appeared just after his: it was of a fat car salesman with a dirty mismatching blazer and tie who had been killed by a flock of birds and a swarm of wasps and bees as he got out of his car at his home. A few dogs had contributed, too. The animal world had taken its vengeance on the one who had replaced him. But it also meant that they had lost Doug - at least, for the moment.

The first interviews over, Jessie asked Frank if she could check her e-mail before they went back to the cameras to face Sir Digby Crichton and one of the usual acerbic presenters on 'Newsnight'. When she opened her mailbox, she found an anonymous message. All it said was: 'You're doing a great job. I can help you further if you keep this communication a complete secret and wear a red scarf on your interview on Newsnight. Then I'll give you more information. Hope you see this in time.' That was it. She thought deeply as Frank put a cup of coffee in front of her. She shut down the e-mail. There seemed no point in trying to reply - she was sure it would go nowhere. Whoever it was probably knew how to cover their tracks.

"Got a red scarf?" she enquired of Frank.

"Not my colour," he replied. "What d'you want one for, anyway? It's not that cold."

"Never mind."

Frank was slightly taken by surprise at this change of tone. She had always been so communicative up until now.

"I think Enid might have one," he offered. "She's always cold. I'll go and have a look."

She thanked him and went back to her e-mail as he retreated into the empty newsroom. No-one else of importance had been in touch.

Sir Digby Crichton sat in the back of the car as it sped towards the BBC's London news studios. He did not want to be here but had received a personal call from the Prime Minister, on holiday in Italy, who had told him to appear. He felt even more indignant as this PM had the worst record in history for not appearing in public or parliament if a tricky event could not be given a positive spin. Now Sir Digby was being forced to go in front of the cameras to prove that the government had nothing to hide - which they did. But if this got out of control then it could possibly bring down this very same government. He had seen the news and wondered how Jessie Scott had got her information in the first place. It could not have been from Doug Sprake: he did not know some of the things that had been alluded to. Mick Deakin... well, he was dead before all this blew up. And the notes that had appeared on the internet had been shut down almost immediately. He was hoping that that security breach was as yet unknown. He shifted uneasily in his seat as the car arrived. To say he was nervous was an understatement.

Doug was ravenous. He peered into the night, his stomach churning, as the car rattled towards its destination. Every so often he felt that he saw an animal or a bird monitoring his progress, but thought that he was probably imagining it: he was fairly certain that whatever pollution had escaped from Shepherd Scar Research Centre was still mostly concentrated on the immediate area around it. What exercised his mind more, though, was the virulence of the compound, despite its being diluted as it coursed down the brook and then out to sea: it was as if it resembled a digital computer copy, able to replicate at the same strength without any diminution of effect, millions of times. As he drove, his mind exercised itself again over that point: had Mick been working on some genetic compound that had the ability to maintain its strength without being over-strong at the initial point of contact? If he had been doing some research in that area it was not apparent from his notes. Not the ones he had read so far, at any rate. Although there was that one compound he had come across that he did not know much about: phenol hydresium. Was that the catalyst that set off a biological chain, and yet also stimulated the animals' brains into maintaining its efficacy? He wondered as the miles rolled by: then he started wondering about whether it was having an effect on humans: would there be a sudden rise in domestic violence, for example, as the compound got into the drinking-water supply? He hoped that modern filtration systems would alleviate the impact: after all, who drank water straight from streams now? Only animals. Confident that humans were probably safe from the immediate effects of his actions, he sped on through the night.

The topography started to change again and soon he was in amongst hills, getting taller and steeper all the time. Then he saw the signs: Hickley. Seventeen miles. His foot slammed down onto the accelerator.

A few miles further on, he saw a petrol station and felt he had to eat something, even if it meant risking his identity with the animals. It had a canopy as well, which he hoped would cover him again from any birds looking out for him: he pulled in as close to the kiosk as possible and entered, then bought some pies, chocolate bars, crisps and fizzy drinks, as well as some sweets. A good diet had always been alien to him. He put his jacket over his head again and ran for the car. He looked up to check for wildlife: it still seemed clear.

Jessie and Frank were standing outside the newspaper building, as before, surrounded by a camera crew and a forest of lights. As the night was unusually dry and time was tight, they had decided to stay outside rather than move into the building, which gave Jessie an added reason to wear the crocheted mauve-pink scarf of Enid's that Frank had pilfered from her draw. He hoped she would not see the interview: Enid could be quite forceful when she wanted to be. And she had taken a dislike to Jessie for some reason, which would only compound the anger. They were wired up with microphones and earpieces so that they could hear and contribute to the discussion from London: according to the PA, the interview was only a few minutes away.

It was at that moment that Doug found himself entering Hickley: it was a typical hill town, which probably had had mining and cotton manufacturing by the middle of the industrial revolution but was now not really sure why it existed. But it was there, and Doug made for the centre. He was unsure how much Jessie knew or whether she was a charlatan, like so many people in the television medium, who knew very little but puffed themselves out to be experts. Still, he felt that she had a good style and was honest: if she could help him, then he would do all he could to help her if she was willing. Which he felt she would be. It was then that he wondered why he felt so sure: perhaps it was another effect of the compounds he might unwittingly have ingested. Well, all this could be discussed with Jessie, he thought.

He turned a corner and saw some bright lights a couple of hundred yards away: that must be the television interview - there were no other bright lights at all in Hickley.

He got as near as he could and parked the car. Yes,

there she was, the girl he had seen an hour or so before, standing beside the editor of the local newspaper. He got out and stood close to the interview area, where there was also a monitor on which he could see the live programme from London. A small crowd had gathered, and a floor assistant was trying to silence a disaffected drunk who noisily wanted to know what was going on. Just next to Doug was a large four-wheel drive car with 'BBC' written on it and a tall pole with a microwave link pointing heavenwards on the top: inside he could see a stack of tightly-packed monitors and a stressed-looking man with an even more stressed production assistant. That must be the director, he thought. Although why he looked so stressed with only two cameras was beyond him.

Then the interview started. It was difficult in the chill night to hear much as they were just too far away, but he could get the gist. Then a chill ran down his spine as he recognised Sir Digby Crichton on the monitor. This must be big, he thought: Sir Digby was only rolled out when things got tough for the government on environmental matters. And Doug knew that Sir Digby knew everything. As he could not hear well, he tried to lip-read what the man was saying, but all he could ascertain was that he looked rattled. 'Good', he thought. Then it was all over, the lights went out and the night enveloped the huddle of people again; the meagre warmth and luminance vanished in an instant, as if death had suddenly swept away a vibrant and living organism.

Jessie and Frank stood there, suddenly looking like normal people again rather than the artificially highlighted entities in a crucible of light only a few moments before. "That's a wrap for tonight", said an authoritative yet bored voice. Then a sound assistant was taking off their microphones and slunked off.

Jessie and Frank went to move away, back in to the building behind them.

"Excuse me," Doug found himself saying to the receding couple, in an unnaturally high pitch: "I think I might be able to help you."

Jessie turned. Her reaction was written all over her face: 'Who is this overweight anorak and how can he help *me*?'

"Sorry," said Doug, pressing forward. "But I saw your earlier interview and I think we can help each other." Then he dropped his voice and said quietly, so only she could hear: "I'm Doug Sprake and I've been doing some of the research at Shepherd Scar."

Jessie's face registered interest immediately. "Come inside," she said, and guided him through the wires and spectators and past the front entrance security.

She realised who he was, of course: she had seen his face flash up on the screen, someone the police and the research centre wanted to interview. Doug realised at once that he had done the right thing in trying to contact her when, closeted in the editor's office, she unhesitatingly told him all that had happened to her and Frank at Shepherd Scar. In one sense, she had to: Doug was one of the last people to see the research centre functioning normally, and he knew more than she, Frank or anyone else. The three of them discussed every detail of their respective experiences: none thought of giving a sanitised version such as the one that Jessie and Frank had given the media. Doug, for his part, told of finding Mick's body, taking and copying his research notes, the disappearance of the car, and his episode with the animals.

At this, Jessie gave a slight smile. Suddenly, she realised who the 'MD' was and it confirmed without doubt that 'SS' was Shepherd Scar. But for the moment she said nothing: she wanted to know why Doug had come to her rather than any one else.

"I've got to go back and see if I can replicate the experiment without animals," Doug continued. "That's why I need your help. I have to have someone to share this with in case I meet the same fate as Mick."

"You don't think he was murdered, do you?" asked Frank, slightly disbelievingly.

"Well, I didn't do it... and nobody else has come forward. I doubt Fouracres knew anything, and even if he did, it's too late to talk to him now."

"Sorry," whispered Jessie. "But we couldn't help it."

"I'm sure..." Doug trailed off.

"I bet Crichton knows something," Jessie observed. "What a nasty, slippery man. I'm glad we weren't in the studio next to him. Typical of this government. All cronies and placemen. Ugh. I hate them."

"Mm. Me, too," agreed Doug. "But if this is as serious as I think it is - what with the leaks at

Shepherd Scar, the attacks and the way these are beginning to happen further and further afield... then we're all in trouble - and the government will get it in the neck."

"I intend to make sure of that whatever happens," Jessie proclaimed. Then: "By the way, Doug... presumably my wearing the red scarf was my confirmation that you wanted to talk to me."

Doug looked confused. "Sorry?"

"Well, I wore the scarf. Now you've contacted me. That was why I did it, wasn't it?"

She could tell from his countenance that he had no idea what she was talking about. "It was you who sent me the e-mail, wasn't it?"

"Er, no. What e-mail?"

She looked hard at him for a few moments, then said, "Did you post the research notes on the internet?"

"No. What research notes?"

Suddenly more serious, and after a look to Frank, she added: "Have you got the notes you mentioned - Mick Deakin's, I think you said - with you?" Doug nodded and took out a memory stick from his pocket. "They're all on here," he said.

A few moments later they were all crowded round a computer. "That's them," she said after scrolling through only a couple of pages. The ones I saw had notes and comments inserted into them, though. Otherwise, they're identical."

"So you're saying that Mick Deakin put these on the internet?" Doug asked incredulously.

"It can't be anyone else," she replied curtly. "They're his notes. Now he's dead." Then, after a pause, "It was so unlike me not to copy the notes there and then, but there were so many of them. All I did was take the web addresses. Then the next moment I looked, they and all the references and links I'd saved had vanished completely. I was furious with myself."

"But that's when you knew it was a cover-up," Frank suggested.

"Absolutely. They all follow the same patterns."

"I still can't understand why Mick put them on the internet," said Doug.

"He wanted the Freedom of Information Act to be just that," Jessie observed. "He must have known someone was trying to suppress something so he wanted to expose what you're doing at Shepherd Scar Research Centre before anything happened."

"And then it did," Frank added trenchantly.

"But I still don't see why," said Doug. "It was drawing attention to something that everyone - Mick included - would have wanted to keep quiet."

"Then there must have been another reason," Jessie stated firmly. "Money? Another person who wanted the information for their own country? Or a military dictatorship? There are plenty of people who'd like the details of the wicked things you're doing in that place. Now the lid's off, God knows what'll happen. I think it stinks."

Doug and Frank both nodded, deep in contemplation.

"So who sent the e-mail to me?" she tossed in

brightly. "It can't be Mick Deakin. He's dead. Killed after his notes hit the internet, it would appear."

"I think it's Crichton," Frank said.

"Me, too," Jessie confirmed.

Doug looked up at them. "I suppose there's no-one else. But *why* did he send you the e-mail, Jessie?"

"Simple. He wants to know what I know. Confirms it's me on the programme by wearing a red scarf and hey, presto, he concludes that I saw Mick's notes on the net. How else would I know so much? I suppose I'm next to be found dead in a car somewhere."

"No, I think I have that privilege," said Doug with a chill in his voice. "Which means we have to get in to Shepherd Scar tonight. Before the animals find me again."

Sir Digby Crichton left the BBC hospitality suite after two very strong drinks and asked to be driven home. He felt that he had managed to keep the lid on things for now and had given public assurance that the cause of all these strange animal goings-on were nothing to do with Shepherd Scar Research Centre. And that there were no leaks of such significance that so many untoward things could happen at all - they were pure speculation. And the research done there was benign, too, even though some research animals had been used occasionally but not in a cruel way, of course. Because the BBC was 'friendly'towards the government, he had not had too hard a ride; their disdain and ridicule they had reserved for Jessie Scott and Frank Wheatley. Yet on the way back, the assured, smiling face of Jessie Scott was nonetheless foremost in his mind and it troubled him. She knew too much and had argued her points well. Too well; it was clear she knew the truth. He was going to find it difficult to keep her quiet, not least because a pretty girl like that would attract much media attention. In fact, she was so pretty that he could not help feeling that he had seen her before somewhere. Recently. He suspected that she must have seen Mick Deakin's leaked notes before they were shut down and he worried how many more might have done the same. Or had she been in league with Deakin all along? Had Deakin been about to go completely public? Were the notes just the first part of more disclosures about what was going on at Shepherd Scar, and was this Jessie Scott going to be the mouthpiece? He shuddered at the thought of the notes appearing again but felt that MI6 and GCHQ would find them even more swiftly next time. He wondered if he should rein Jessie in, talk to her, frighten her; then he concluded that this would probably make matters worse - she was a spirited individual. He would have to try the subtle approach. And he knew how to get in touch with her...

BOOK TWO

The Nightmare Begins...

Chapter 14

The fallout from the chemical leaks at Shepherd Scar Research Centre were beginning to have a much wider effect. Contrary to hopes that the immediate blight was contained to a radius around the area, the virility of the compounds entering Scar Brook and washing down to Bracken Mere and then the Hildaburna to the River Mersey were beginning to create a huge shift in the ecology of the planet. The attacks on the sheepdog, the horses, the trawler, and then the Japanese whaling ship had each been seen as isolated incidents confined to an area of Northern England and the Irish Sea; but as more events began to be reported, the scale and profundity of the catastrophe began to magnify. Most recently, a whole battery chicken farm had seen its young inmates suddenly fly at the door of their incarceration when a hapless attendant opened it: he had been savagely pecked as they escaped past him into the light, a swathe of fluffy yellow contrasting with the grey concrete, mud and grime outside the sheds. The British government, inevitably, tried to play down the warning signs, but when attacks started in other countries, they had to start making excuses on several different fronts.

In Scotland, grouse and pheasant being beaten from the heather to be shot, were in a couple of cases seen to form a tight flock and assail the shooters after a few had been fired at. One man had been seriously injured when, having loosed a barrel at a bird and missed, it had instantly acquired support from surrounding birds and they had flown straight at him, blinding him in one eye and causing him to despatch the second barrel which had hit a beater. In France, migrating birds had been shot at as they flew over Brittany, the Massif Centrale and the Camargue: in each area there were reports of birds turning on their attackers and leaving them in no doubt that nature was turning from a passive state to an active one: the revolution had begun. And where birds were shot, the gun dogs and other carrion beasts had ingested traces of the compounds and acquired the ability to instinctively understand their species and others. In Italy, the same was happening: trigger-happy hunters were suddenly in shock when huge flocks of birds attacked them when fired upon. And so the poison spread further and wider...

An incident in Belgium even managed to stir the

European Union: a debate on further integration was uncharacteristically postponed. Cows, having ingested the compound in their fishmeal additives, had refused to be loaded onto lorries when being taken for slaughter: they instinctively knew their fate from other rodents, insects, reptiles and birds that had witnessed the carnage of abattoirs, and innately, suddenly instinctively, passed on their knowledge. Then they had run amok and caused injury to the farmers and the buildings: when one was shot by a farmer, he was butted to death by the others, who had instantly turned on the farmer as a response. In India, elephants had started to attack villages in reaction to being kept off land by electric fences and villagers beating them back with sticks and stones. In Africa, poachers killing elephants for their ivory had been trampled to death by a huge herd which, hearing the cries of pain of a trapped elephant, had charged and crushed the poachers who were about to cut off its tusks with chainsaws. And in America, deer hunters were attacked by angry bucks when a doe was shot; one man had been severely injured as they tried to tie the dead beast across the bonnet.

Because France was closer to the epicentre of the pollution, it had suffered disproportionately - along with Britain and Ireland - and more stories were becoming heard about: in one instance, protesting French farmers had burnt a lorryload of Welsh sheep in retaliation, as they saw it, of cheaper prices. But when they had returned to their farms, they were set upon by their own sheep who had been innately and instinctively appraised of the act; two men had died and one was seriously ill in hospital. In a research establishment on the Rhone, research mice and guinea-pigs had escaped by chewing through their cages: when their teeth had been broken on the wire, another had then taken over until severed. Then they had released the others and wrecked the laboratory - as they had done at Shepherd Scar: before escaping, they had also chewed through electricity and computer cables, causing hardware and software crashes, data loss and complete chaos. And where data was shared with parent companies farther afield, such as America and Germany, the subsequent effects were even more extreme.

A beekeeper in Luxembourg had been stung to death by his swarm when he had tried to cull a hive by killing the queen. His protective clothing was useless against the cloud of insects that enveloped him...

It was beginning to be realised that the animals were acting very selectively and only responded when they were abused, exploited or threatened by humans. In some cases, even animals who were predators would help their usual prey against humans, and would then revert to the normality of nature, red in tooth and claw, after the threat had receded or been killed off. Indeed, a herd of antelope in South Africa - the compound having been transported by housemartins and others after their eight thousand mile migration from Britain - had lost four of their number to hunters with rifles; immediately, the human intruders were attacked by a pride of lions. Three men and two women had been savaged to death and the others had run for their lives. The lions had then disappeared back into the veldt after having killed an antelope for themselves.

It was as if the natural world was starting to protect what was rightfully its own against the ravages of man: survival in place of sport.

As for humans, it was not yet understood why they were not affected; why had they, too, not acquired a higher sense of instinctive understanding with the animal world? For the moment, the line was that nearly all food was cooked at some stage and this sterilised the compound. But for Doug, who had ingested the compound at first hand, he was aware that he felt much better than before - and he looked it, too. And he seemed to know what the animals were thinking. But the results would be different when the compound hit the oyster beds around the Irish and French coasts...

Although Doug was astute enough to understand the implications of what he and the government had unleashed onto the world, the events were still relatively isolated and, in many cases, unknown outside the countries where they happened. Indeed, had he known more of what was happening, he might have changed his mind about the night's adventure that he was about to embark upon: he had been grateful for Frank and Jessie's insistence that they come with him on his mission to Shepherd Scar

Research Centre because he could do with help in removing vital pieces of kit and compounds. And after hearing what had happened to their car, he was glad that the one he had was not his own; if that was found near the research centre after a mishap, then that was the end of his being able to do anything about it. After all, he would be hounded by the government and the media, then probably prosecuted under some ancient act, when the best thing he could be doing was getting an antidote out into the natural world before humankind's continuation was severely threatened. A show trial would be a useless waste of time: what was needed was action.

After he had adopted a semblance of a disguise - a beany-cap and a bulky jersey - he rubbed in some insect repellent: it was also to change his smell in case the animals recognised him, which he was sure they would, but it might buy them a bit of time. While he did all this, Jessie had gone down to a Chinese takeaway and they had gorged themselves on it in the office to give them energy and keep out the encroaching damp cold. Jessie replaced Enid's red scarf but borrowed another neutrally-coloured one, and Frank applied insect repellent as well as spraying himself with an odious-smelling after-shave. He changed into another jacket and pair of trousers, while Jessie also applied the cream and changed into the clothes she had taken in her small bag. Prior to donning her thick jersey, she then sprayed herself with a cheap moisturiser. It was all they could think of to try and cover the animals' best chance of reidentifying them. Frank was poring over the ordnance survey map when the others announced they were ready to leave.

"I think I've found a track on the other side of the plateau," he said. "It means a longer walk but perhaps the animals on that side won't recognise us so readily."

"I wouldn't bet on it," replied Jessie.

A few minutes later, they were on the way to the scene of their earlier nemesis. Doug went ahead in his appropriated car and Frank and Jessie followed in her hire car: they had not thought it advisable to return in the other one, which, anyway, was still being repaired and having its earlier evidence removed. They were fortunate in that it was a clear night and the moon was nearly full, obviating the need for torches which would have attracted attention and nearly every insect in the vicinity.

As they climbed, they were quiet, but Doug's head was in a supercharged state. Perhaps it was a mix of the drugs he had ingested and the excitement, or the thrill of being the one man on the planet who could reverse this increasingly terrifying experience; or perhaps it was just that it was him against nature. Although he had been doing this all his life, now it was more personal. The natural world had given him a chance to survive - but he was still unsure whether the reason was to help them to conquer the planet or to help things revert to how they had been before. Judging by the reports he had heard - and his heightened instincts - he felt it was the former.

When they got to the turn-off to the Shepherd Scar Research Centre where Doug had found Mick's car and body, they went straight on. They had put their headlights off completely after passing through the final village on the way up and were content to risk meeting something coming the other way. At that time of night, and under the threatening circumstances which were now becoming so well-known, it was unlikely. They had switched off their engines at the top of the rise and coasted down the incline; then they used their momentum to turn off through an open gate in a wall and the two cars bumped to a standstill on the lumpy turf.

Doug looked about him before opening the door. All seemed quiet. Frank and Jessie waited: the proximity of their experience earlier that day had made them very nervous, their tension mounting with the climb. But now they had to get out.

"I think that's the way there," whispered Doug as they did so, pointing to a small crack in the rocks a hundred yards away. They moved off quickly and quietly, Doug nursing a crowbar and wire-cutters under his jacket. Ostensibly, the former tool was to get in to the research centre: in reality, it was also to protect himself. They had each armed themselves with a similar piece of equipment, and Frank was wearing his cricket box under his trousers. They each carried an empty rucksack on their backs which would be filled with the compounds if they got in; all had decided to take protective goggles in case of aerial attack, which they wore on the tops of their heads like sunglasses: birds always went for the eyes first.

They had memorised the unknown route as far as it was possible to do so: the night was calm and quiet, with only an occasional hint of a breeze. It was almost too quiet, thought Doug. There seemed to be nothing making any noise whatsoever. In fact, apart from their breathing and footsteps, there was no sound at all, like a film where the soundtrack had been erased to make normally heavy-footed people seem silent. He found it unnatural, and held up a hand to make them stop.

"Can you hear anything?" he whispered.

"Like what?" Jessie whispered back.

"No; I mean, there's nothing. Not a sound. It's so unnatural. I don't like it."

Now he had pointed it out, Jessie did not like it either. Still, they could not turn back and after twenty minutes Jessie and Frank found themselves looking over the Shepherd Scar Research Centre for the second time that day, but from a different direction. It was spread out below them, but not from such a high vantage point as earlier, and the holding-pools on the far side were almost completely hidden behind the bulk of D block. Doug, puffing somewhat due to his poor diet and lack of exercise, looked at his previous place of employment. Apart from a small pool of light throwing diffuse shadows on the ground outside the reception area where the security men were, it was all dark. Far away to the left at the end of the vague line of asphalt there was a pinpoint of light, partially hidden by outcrops of rock.

'The police road block,' thought Jessie, who had

seen it on the news.

It all seemed too unassuming, too easy. No hostile animals, no added security, no reporters, minimal police presence and no apparent barrier to entry. It was one thing to keep the place secret when it was so, but now it was in the news they were all troubled by the lack of activity.

"Is there another way of getting this stuff?" Frank enquired, reflecting the unease they were all experiencing. Doug shook his head. "The only place I know it exists is in there," he croaked.

So they had to go in. That was it. Doug lowered his frame over some rocks and let himself down a little: the others followed. Again, the silence stifled them, like the lull before the storm. Then, sooner than they had expected, they were on the flat plateau and only a hundred yards from the side of block B: they would have to pass the reception block where security was located, but being in the middle of all four blocks, it was a good deal further away. They slowly went to the right, hugging the base of the cliffs, and then, when the security block light was hidden by the shape of block A, they moved closer to the end of it. They had to pass around the back of this, then check that security had their backs to them as they crossed the open patch to arrive at what had been Mick Deakin's lab in block D. Having done this without much effort, or arousing the attention of security, they skirted the end of the block in order to go between it and the holding-pools. After that, they would be outside Doug's old lab.

And then they realised why it had all been so quiet: as Doug carefully looked around the end of the block, he saw something moving by the last holding-pool about forty yards away. Then he could just make out more movement, as if there was more than one. Then he realised it was very many more than one. He swung his arm round to push Frank and Jessie back, pointing with his finger at the place he had seen.

"Animals," he whispered, his voice trembling. "I think there must be dozens of them; I think they're drinking the stuff." The chill that went down Jessie and Frank's spines was like touching an iceberg in the Caribbean. The animals were actually lapping the polluting compounds up as they dripped over the edge, and seemed to have the knowledge and foresight to know what they were doing and why. They had attained reason, and their collective understanding was becoming wider; with every sip, too, it was more capable of being spread further. Doug then saw in the dim light a large number of birds of prey on the edges of the pool and they, too, were drinking. It frightened Doug to see the totality and commonness of their purpose, to the exclusion of anything else: it had become a fanatical requisite. He surmised that they were all coming from the other side of the block and the holding-pools because that was where Scar Brook ran away into its soggy pool before disappearing underground. He feared in that moment that there were literally thousands of animals there, quietly and singularly drinking for the annihilation of humankind. They would surely kill them if they were alerted to their presence: yet now the three of them were in view of the back of the reception area, and the outlines of the security men were visible. They were in the middle of a deadly situation. They pulled back behind the end of the block, out of view of the animals but in full view of the security guards had they decided to turn around at that moment.

"We'll have to get in here," whispered Doug, touching the boards that covered the broken windows. Then: "Or go in the front after all. I don't fancy bumping into that lot," as he waved his hand in the direction of the natural world, which was becoming less so by the second.

Jessie thought for a moment. "Why don't you go into the front and explain to them what you're doing - they know you, after all. Just tell them what's going on and, well, if they try to arrest you, they'll be aiding the takeover of the planet. Surely you can reason with them?"

"I think there's more reason in that lot than them," Doug replied, intimating first the animals, then the security guards.

"It's all we can do," emphasised Frank. "I don't want a repeat of this morning."

"Mm." Doug thought for a moment. "No; better that you go in, Jessie."

"Me?"

"Yes. They'll have seen you on TV. You can talk to them - distract them - while Frank and I get in up there" - he pointed to where the corridor to the building they were against joined the reception centre

- "there's a window and it'll be easier and quieter to get into than here. I had left one in my lab just open, but that won't be any use now - all boarded up like this, I'm sure. And I'm not going round there past that lot to find out."

Jessie was not happy with the idea but realised that it was the only way of possibly getting in. Their whispered parlance over, she began to think of her nice warm bed and why she was not in it. Then, she took a deep breath and, keeping close to the side of the block, she approached the small patch of window behind the security guards. The others followed until they got to the corridor then hid in the corner where it met the security block as Jessie tapped very lightly on the security men's window.

One of the men looked furtively around, and his eyes bulged when he saw Jessie's face against the window, looking even stranger with the goggles parked on the top of her head. She immediately put her finger up to her mouth to imply silence. By now, the second security man was looking at her, too. Both looked astonished and unsure what to do next: how had she got in past the police roadblock? She implied a pleading posture and intimated that they open the window. After a moment, one of them came forward and shouted through the window: "Who are you? How did you get in here?" She implied silence again and the terror that was behind her. The men turned to each other and she could hear their muffled voices, although she thought she heard the word 'police'. She tapped again and shook her head: the man's hand was on the phone. She shook her head more violently and mouthed the word 'help'. She was never one for the damsel in distress routine but this time she would just have to do it. The man took his hand off the phone and came over. They talked again, then one cautiously opened the window a little.

"What are you doing here?" he said in a loud voice. Jessie instantly and emphatically put her finger to her mouth again. "Sshh!" she allowed to leave her lips, "The animals..." Then, forgetting decorum, she pulled the window open, much to the astonishment of the two men, who recoiled a little, got in and quietly shut the window.

"I'm sorry," she said, still in a quiet voice. "But there are thousands of animals out there who are drinking the compound in the holding-pools. They know what they're doing. Did you see the news tonight?"

A flicker of recognition went over the two men's faces. "Yeah," said one of them: "You're that reporter." She nodded. One to her, she thought. "Then you know what's going on," she added.

"The pools have been shut down," said the other. "The place is closed."

"The fact is that I wanted to talk to you because you might know what's happening," she found herself lying. "Yes, I'm a reporter and I couldn't get past the roadblock so I came the hard way - over the top." They looked incredulous. "This is the biggest story ever to hit our putrid little planet," she continued: "If you can help me get to the truth we can all avert a global catastrophe." They did not look convinced. "Look, if those animals know I'm here then we'll all be dead", she went on. "Whatever's in those bloody pools is about to cause the destruction of the human race. I need to make sure that you know that and so do your superiors. Do you understand?"

"Our boss was killed yesterday afternoon."

"I don't mean that boss - I know about him. I mean Sir Digby Crichton, the government. At this moment thousands of animals are drinking that stuff and becoming more capable of killing us all. Now, I don't want you to do anything except very, very quietly show me the labs that were devastated. But quietly, or they'll do the same thing to you."

"I'm not going in there," said one.

"Nor am I," said the other.

"Then give *me* the keys: look, I'm on your side, not the government's. If they don't do something about this we're all dead, but they don't seem to realise the importance of it all. They need to be pushed, and as the reporter who was on TV earlier, you know I'm the best person to do that. Please."

"You can go on your own. There's nothing to see, though. Just a mess."

"Great." This was what she had wanted. To be allowed to go there alone. "Just give me some time to look around and I'll soon be gone. You never need admit you've seen me. But whatever you do, stay in here and don't make a sound or the animals might come and get you. Look what they did to the lab."

The bigger of the two men went to the wall and

took a bunch of keys out of a metal key-box. She imagined Frank and Doug just on the other side of the wall, less than a foot away from him.

"Here you are," he said. "Turn right. It's at the end of the corridor. But close the doors behind you. If any of those animals gets in we don't want them in here."

"No worries," she said, and left them quivering. She went into the corridor and let the doors swing closed. Then she went to the window and opened it. Doug and Frank were still hiding in the corner. As Doug gave her a thumbs-up, she intimated to them to wait for a moment and went through the second set of doors; then she paused for breath. Her heart was pounding in the claustrophobic stillness, not just with the subterfuge but also due to the lies, the danger, the importance of what they were doing, and what they yet had to achieve. Then there was the small matter of getting out again, probably laden with bottles of lethal substances. Her bed had never seemed more welcoming, nor so far away.

Chapter 15

Sir Digby Crichton was having a sleepless night. He had hardly spoken to his wife when he returned from the BBC studios, being deep in thought. Subsequently, she had taken a sleeping-pill and was now snoring noisily beside him. But it was not that which was keeping him awake. He was thinking of all the ends he had to tie up to keep this story from harming the government, which had compromised the Civil Service and put placemen into every part of its administration to protect against events like this; but even with these safeguards, there were still people who would spill the beans for enough money. Or out of pique. Or lapsed loyalty. Still, it was this government that had wrecked the notion of loyalty, as well as a sense of country, so it could not blame anyone else but itself on that score. So, if the government was harmed, how could he get out of it with his nose clean and a large sum to retire on?

He turned onto his side and thought about the unfortunate death of Dennis Fouracres. This man's demise could complicate matters if anyone decided to construe that the government had done it, but as in this instance that was not the case, this would be easy to bat away. He really did not know much anyway. He had just been a political appointment, a figurehead.

As for the events surrounding the leaks at Shepherd Scar, though, they were not so easy to dismiss. He had already had a meeting with the editors of all the national papers and told them emphatically that there was no cover-up and no cause for alarm - nor any proof. He was hoping that that would be enough. But again, he was not too sure. Deep inside, he knew the facts were compelling but could not allow himself to believe them. The compounds allegedly leaking from the Shepherd Scar Research Centre did seem to be having some of the effects on animals that they were supposed to have on humans, if the reports were to be believed: but there were also vital differences. For example, why did the afflicted animals not die off quickly after ingesting the compounds? That was one of the effects they had been working on; revive, repeat, relapse was the brief, yet, rather than dying, the animals seemed to be increasing their lifespans, not suddenly dropping dead all over the place as they were supposed to.

He slipped out of bed, his silk pyjamas swishing against the Egyptian cotton sheets. Ah, Egypt. He had not been there for a while; perhaps it was time to go again. He donned his dressing-gown and slipped noiselessly out of the bedroom and into his study.

When he was there, he opened up his laptop and sent an e-mail.

The security men sat at their desk, flinching at every noise they heard, inside or out. Jessie's tirade had got through: they were terrified, and just where she wanted them - out of the way.

She, Doug and Frank had entered the chemical store with little difficulty, thanks to the help of the crowbar. Mercifully, the animals had not realised its importance and left it alone – as had the authorities. The crack that the door made as it opened, though, had worried them somewhat lest the animals heard and decided to investigate. The security men were not worth bothering about...

Doug was selecting phials, bottles and cylinders with the dexterity of a harpist: he went round picking things out and handing them to Jessie and Frank, who carefully put them into their rucksacks. He had mentally noted not to put some compounds with others; those that might react harmfully together if broken he put into separate rucksacks to his own. But he was sure to put at least one of each of his main compounds, where possible, into each rucksack for safety. He also needed some sharps, glass test-tubes and dishes, although he could improvise with those later if necessary.

Jessie was looking around, too, amongst the rows of chemicals on the sliding racks, when suddenly she saw a name she recognised: chromitic paradiosymine. She picked it up off the shelf and went over to Doug.

"We'll need this, won't we?" she whispered. Doug took one look at it and walked off, saying, "No. I wasn't using that at the time all this started."

"Well, I think Mick was," she retorted, "It was in his notes."

Suddenly, Doug was next to her again. "Of course.

You're right. I wonder..."

"It might be the missing link," she smiled nervously.

"Yes, yes."

"And what about phenol hydresium?"

Doug looked astonished. "You're amazing," he said, "It should be over here." He went to the last row of racks and pulled it quietly out, then picked out a large bottle of mulberry-coloured liquid. Then he took two more out and gave one to her and one to Frank. "Just one more to get," he said, and disappeared behind the racks at the other end of the store.

It was then that they heard the noise they had been dreading. Like a thunderclap, they heard what sounded like a multiple battering-ram outside the boarded up lab outside the store, and a sound like sporadic hail on the roof. The animals had heard them - or been notified by some insect or rodent.

"Time to get out," Doug barked quietly, and they left the room, the weight of the compounds in their rucksacks dragging them down as they retraced their steps back to the reception area.

As they burst into sight of the security men, one shouted "What's that?" in a terrified voice as he referred to the noise; the other took one look at Doug and said: "Doug Sprake. What are you doing here? I'm supposed to - "

"Don't bother, if you value your life - get out now. Have you got a car?" The man nodded. "Good, get into it now - and we're all coming with you. Run."

They ran out of the door, the guard aiming

towards a clapped-out family car.

"Shit," thought Doug.

"Mine's better," said the other, and they found themselves getting into a small jeep-like vehicle. Then the birds saw them and started to dive-bomb the vehicle, just as Jessie got the last door shut, but catching the wing of what looked like a kite, which screeched loudly and incessantly as the engine revved into action. 'I don't think I can bear this again,' Jessie was thinking as, suddenly in front of them on the strip of road, she saw dogs running at them. Further ahead, she could see the bright lights of sheeps' eyes as the car's full beams went on.

"Just keep going," she and Frank shouted. The man needed no encouraging and put the car into second gear and four-wheel drive with extraordinary dexterity. The first two dogs were brushed away with yelps and cracking noises, but the sheep put up more resistance and even stopped the car for a second; then the rodents were there again, jumping up at the windows, being squashed under the wheels and crawling all over the roof, as the birds started their onslaught as well. The driver was crying and swearing both out of fear and what this was doing to his new car but he kept going relentlessly. When they got to the roadblock by the gates they saw that the policeman was little more than a bloody red mess - death had visited him already. Fortunately for them, he had obviously tried to escape in his panda car but had been attacked whilst opening the gates, which were just wide enough for them to scrape through - literally.

Immediately outside the gates were four animal rights protestors - or what remained of them: the car bumped straight over them but they were a gory mess already, their placards broken about them and their balaclavas soaked in blood.

'The animals aren't selective, then,' thought Doug as the car sped down the slope.

"Shall we try to get to our cars?" screamed Jessie.

"You must be joking," shouted Doug. "Just keep driving."

They turned off the lane at the bottom and onto the main road, passing the point at which they had unwittingly killed Dennis Fouracres only a few hours before, and where some traces of the previous carnage were still evident. Then there were cows in front of them, obstinately moving slowly towards them. The driver managed to swerve to hit one sideways; the car bounced off its flank and into the side of another, which crumpled as they hit the horns of a third, these breaking off with a sharp double crack as they embedded into the car's side. The bird with its wing trapped in the door was still flapping and screeching but no-one dared open it lest it flew in and attacked them, or, worse, let in the teeming rodents.

Then it all subsided, and the driver put his foot down. It was all so déjà vu, Frank and Jessie were thinking. The second security man was in the back with them, and Doug looked pale but resolute in the front, his arms surrounding his rucksack on his lap with absolute intent. With the exception of the bird flapping in the door and the screaming engine, all was quiet. Frank leaned across Jessie and opened the door for a split second, releasing the bird, then slammed the door shut again. It fell in a heap on the road, then righted itself; as the car receded, Jessie could see its wing was broken, sticking jaggedly upwards at an awkward angle. That bird would not be following them, she thought.

When they got back to the Hickley and District News office, they looked around them and fled inside as one - they were aware that, by the law of nature, stragglers would be attacked first. They got inside and shut the doors. Then they went upstairs.

"You can stay here to work, if you want," Frank offered to Doug. "There's a room over there with no windows so nothing should be able to get in and no-one will be able to see what you're doing. It's actually the editorial room, but if the law comes, we'll just say it's a store-room."

Doug was grateful for this: Frank had obviously been thinking about it on the way back. "I'd better start right away," he added after thanking him. "If you can give me some glasses from the canteen, saucers, bowls, that sort of thing, that'll help. And Jessie, can you print off those notes of Mick's for me? And then you all try and get some sleep. I'll still be here in the morning."

They each deposited their bottles of compounds into the 'store-room', as it would now be called, and Doug arranged the tables into rows, redistributing the chairs to the periphery. Frank brought him a collection of crockery and a pair of scales from the kitchens, which he put on a table in the centre of the room. He then put all the compounds that were the same together and, when Jessie brought him the notes a few minutes later, he took them and sat down to study them again. He knew he was going to be very restricted as he had no means of measuring accurately, no scientific equipment and, above all, nothing to test his research on. Despite this, he was optimistic, as most humans are when there is no alternative.

"Where are your printed notes?" enquired Jessie as she was leaving. "I burned them before we left for Shepherd Scar," he replied. "I've got all the discs in my pocket - they never leave me. And I e-mailed you a copy, in case..."

She nodded and left. She needed some sleep. She went back into Frank's office, where the two security men from Shepherd Scar also sat, looking awkward and out of place, waiting for they knew not what; Frank was dozing in his editor's chair but sat up as she entered.

"I don't dare go home," he said immediately. "There's a hotel next door if you want to get a room. It's not much cop but it's a bed. That's where I'm going. And our friends here."

"What about our 'natural' friends?" she said, gesturing skywards.

"We'll run. It's very close." She nodded. Any bed would do right now. And while Doug was trying to resurrect his research, there was little she could do to help.

"What are you two going to do now?" she enquired.

"Sorry, we seem to have wrecked your lives."

"S'alright," said one. "I hate the job anyway. Boring." The other assented quietly.

"The police will want to see you, I suspect," said Jessie. "What are you going to tell them?"

"Dunno. But I might take John here back up there at daylight to get his car."

"I wouldn't," she retorted. "Unless your car is more important than your life. Just go and tell the police that some people broke in to the Shepherd Scar Research Centre - don't say it was us, obviously - and the animals attacked you as you tried to get away from them. You can tell the police that their man didn't make it."

"They'll soon know it was us when they find our cars," Frank stated flatly.

"Mm. Although one's hired, the other exchanged; might take a while."

"Mm. But I don't know if our animal friends will let the authorities get to them" mumbled Frank.

"So there might be some good in them after all."

Frank nodded, with a nervous smile.

One of the two security men stood up: the other followed. "Can we take you up on that taxi?" he asked. "We live quite close to each other."

"Certainly," Frank replied. "But don't wait outside and, when you get home, run like hell and shut all doors and windows. You saw what they did to the policeman - and what they would have done to us."

"When will I get my car back?"

"I'll see to it in the morning," Frank replied. "Gus

is going to wonder what's happening: two bloody cars in one night - if you see what I mean. It'll look like new when he's finished with it. But not a word to anyone, please. What we're doing is very important and if the government gets to know where we are and what we're doing then the whole urgency of this will be compromised."

They nodded. "Go and wait for the taxi downstairs," he continued, taking a large number of coins out of his pocket. "Here's some money. There's a coffee machine there and some sandwiches. They're not usually more than a couple of days old."

The two men thanked him and left, still uneasy and still wondering what on earth they had got themselves into.

Jessie found herself looking back at Frank after they had disappeared, and asking, "Are you married?" Frank did not seem surprised by the question: but then, after what had happened that day, everything was unsurprising, even a private enquiry by a pretty young girl.

"I was. My wife left me when I got this job. I was seldom at home and she went off with someone who could give her more attention." The last part of the sentence was said with a trace of bitterness. Best left alone, she thought.

"You're not, are you?" he asked.

She shook her head. "Too young for all that."

"Mm. Me, too."

"I'd just like to check my e-mails if I may," she stated, changing the subject.

"Of course. I'll ring the hotel."

"At four in the morning?"

"They're used to it."

He went out to Enid's desk and called the hotel while Jessie logged on. There were two e-mails. One was from an old flame in America trying to get back in touch. The other was far more interesting.

It was an anonymous e-mail again - but attached to it was what she had first seen that day on the web: Mick Deakin's notes with all the mis-spelt additions and comments. She cried out with delight. This time, she saved them immediately, then printed them off and ran in to see Doug, who was hunched over the table reading the other ones. She put them in front of him.

"Look what someone's sent me. Mick Deakin's notes with all the additions - just like I told you."

Doug looked surprised and startled. "Who sent them?" She shrugged her shoulders. "Who cares?" she answered.

"I do," said Doug. "I want to know who else knows about all this. If it's not Mick - well, it can't be - then who is it?"

Jessie's delight was somewhat short-lived. But it would still be a huge help, she thought.

Back in London, Sir Digby Crichton closed his laptop with a smug smile. "That'll cause a few hiccups," he said quietly to himself. Then he went back to bed and slept soundly, despite the increased volume of his wife's snoring.

Chapter 16

There was a knock on the door. Jessie woke, the sun streaming through the chinks in the shutters she had closed when she had gone to bed.

"Your breakfast's here," said Frank's voice from outside. "Shall I bring it in?"

"Oh, yes," she replied. "Come in."

Frank did so. He was dressed in jeans and a T-shirt, which made him look completely different to before. 'Quite a nice physique', she found herself observing. She sat up in bed, making sure that she was not displaying anything that she should not be. Not yet, anyway. Frank observed that she must be a truly attractive girl as she looked better without make-up than with it, especially in the tousled state he found her in now. He put down her breakfast tray on the bed and sat next to her.

"Any news?" she asked with a yawn.

"Yep." She could tell by the tone of his voice that it was not good.

"Well?"

"The Home Office has been in touch. The Minister wants to talk to us."

"That's good, isn't it?"

"In theory, yes; in practice, it means that they might get in our way, slow us up, try to suppress us...

Shut us up, even. And once they know who the cars we left up there belong to, I suppose we could be done for criminal trespass too, if they so wanted. And I suspect that they would - to add pressure on us. Also, I think we should be around to help Doug: ignore them. We wouldn't be there to protect and help him if we're busy helping the government..."

"... to cover things up," Jessie completed the sentence.

"Mm. I wonder if we ought to disappear. I haven't spoken to anyone; there's just a message left with Enid."

"Ah. Enid. So she'll be on their side, then."

"Anyone's but ours." He paused. Then: "She's probably telling them now when I'm free and can see them."

"So why don't you stop her?"

"I think it better that I let her do her worst but then I just find excuses not to co-operate."

"That won't work," Jessie said curtly. "Once you're enmeshed in the system they'll make sure you never get out. Trust me."

After a moment, Frank concurred. "I know you're right," he said. "So I'd better go and appeal to Enid's sense of loyalty."

"Huh! That won't work either. If she thinks she can get one over on you and replace you with her husband..."

Frank looked dejected. "So what shall I do?" he enquired at length.

"I think you should tell her that it's in her interests

- and that of your paper - to do what you tell her with regard to the government. Then she'll know that if she screws you up the paper will go pear-shaped as well. They have ways, this government, of putting nasty stories about against people who speak out against them. Like, you're unbalanced or have psychiatric problems. They did it with a business organisation. And, guess what? They put a placeman in there instead."

"And a local paper would be easier to silence than a business organisation."

"Exactly."

"Jessie, you're wonderful," he sighed.

"You're not so bad yourself, Frank."

He looked at her. The respect and attraction between them was palpable, but somehow the gravity of the events overshadowing them made them implicitly aware that developing a personal relationship now was not the right thing to do. He took her hand and kissed it. She held it and leaned forward, giving him a kiss on the cheek. Despite what they both felt, their emotions would have to go on hold for the moment.

"Does Enid know about Doug?" she asked suddenly.

"I hope not. I think I'd better get back. And I also think we're going to have to move him to somewhere else. My house is a good place."

"Can you get Enid out of the office for a bit?"

"Unlikely. Anyway, she always seems to know what's going on even when she's not there. And there are too many other snoopers," he added. "We should have done it last night, I suppose, but it just seemed more important that he get on with it. If we have to move him , though... well, we'll just have to risk it."

She nodded. He got up, gave her a peck on the cheek and left. She felt alone without him. She quickly ate her breakfast, got up, showered and, having looked around her carefully, ran from the hotel across to the newspaper building.

Arriving in the newspaper's reception area, she found herself up against other reporters and a BBC television crew. She categorically refused to give another television interview and ran upstairs. Frank was talking to Enid in his office when she arrived. After the frigid pleasantries had taken place, Frank announced discreetly, "I've told Enid everything." But he had managed to get behind her when he said this to Jessie and gave a big wink and a shake of the head when he said it. Their innate sense of understanding made him sure that she would comprehend his meaning. "We've discussed the Home Office request for a meeting and Enid is going to stall them. She knows that it's not in the paper's interests, or the editor's - any editor's -" he said this in a loaded way, "to have the government interfering with this story and that it's in all our interests here to keep them away. I'm on holiday and uncontactable, and you've done your job and have, for all we know, moved on to something else." He smiled, then continued quickly lest Jessie asked a question that might compromise his subterfuge. "And as for that research scientist... what's his name..?"

"Doug Sprake," Jessie added helpfully.

"Yes, Sprake; we don't know where he is." This he added in a slightly over-emphasised, histrionic tone.

"But *do* we?" Jessie asked unsurely.

"Categorically not," he emphasised. Then he continued: "So, Enid, your very important job is to keep the Home Office away."

Enid stood up, inflated with her sudden feeling of self-importance, and left. Jessie was unsure whether Enid was aware of either the subterfuge or the reality.

"Bit of a risk, that, wasn't it?" she said after the door had closed behind Enid.

"Yes; but she knows so much already that I think it's better to keep her involved and on-side. She knows nothing about Doug being here."

"So why did you mention him?"

"I want her to feel part of this. She doesn't know that he's locked in there, though. All she knows is that we met up with him and escorted him to Shepherd Scar. After that, he went his own way. I've 'lost' my key to the editorial room and hidden hers. It's only today that we'll have to be careful. We'll move him tonight. If you want to talk to him he's on 376", as he pointed to the phone. "Don't let it ring too long, though: if someone in the office hears it they might try to get in to the editorial room and answer it. Which we do not want."

Doug was underlining various points on the printout that Jessie had given him the night before;

Frank had lent him a laptop and he had been surfing the net to find as many cross-references as possible as they were needed. He had found a lot of references barred, but put that down to Crichton. The phone rang and he answered it quietly. "I think I'm onto something," he whispered excitedly when he heard Jessie's tones. "And I think I know why I've started to look better than Mick did: he was experimenting a bit on himself - bloody fool - and was taking increasing doses of chromitic paradiosymine to see whether it made him feel or act differently. Apparently, it would seem that he didn't trust the results on his research animals. It was his way of speeding up his results."

"And it did just that - killed him."

"Exactly. So I'd better be careful."

"Why?"

"I think I must have ingested some trace elements of manganese tripuride at various stages and I think that's the difference between him and me: I hadn't told you this but I've started to look younger and he... well, he just looked awful - he'd aged suddenly, terribly, when I found his body. So I don't want to overdo it in the other direction."

Jessie laughed. "No, you don't! I don't want to have to change your nappies!" She thought it was funny; however, Doug remained silent on the other end of the phone so she decided to ask a serious question: "What about the compound that you were *both* working with?"

"Which one? Parlazine? Anthicin? Phenol hydresium? Chromitic paradiosymine? They're all pretty volatile so it's going to be difficult to isolate them from all the other possibilities. And it's all theoretical, of course - no proper kit." She heard him sigh heavily: a man with the world on his shoulders - almost literally. "When the bottles got broken in the labs, the compounds just went down into the drains and into the holding-pools - supposed to be a safety measure to cleanse the toxic waste. But what I don't know is the amounts that went in, when, and with what. But despite that, I still need to find an antidote, then get the governments of the world to manufacture it in industrial quantities and then ..."

"Then?"

"I'm not sure. Get it out into the wild, I suppose. Starting with Shepherd Scar Research Centre." Then he put his phone down.

As this conversation was progressing, an army of police was on its way to that very place to secure it. They had initially been ordered by the government to keep reporters and the media out of the research centre, but the events of the night before were now beginning to be known. This was mostly because Jessie and Frank's supposed 'secret witnesses' accounts - emblazoned across that morning's Hickley & District News - had been syndicated on to the national press and television news; all this was suddenly diverting attention back to it. This was underlined by the two security men deciding to go to the police to tell of their experiences after all, for they could not just disappear: they needed their jobs. At first, they had only said that they had been attacked by animals and fled, but when it became evident that their car's location was currently unknown to them, the full story slowly started to come out. According to them, three people had got in to Shepherd Scar Research Centre, each carrying a rucksack. And one of them the security men identified as the man police were looking for: Doug Sprake. They had said, too, that a policeman at the roadblock was dead, which was dramatised specifically by the police to throw suspicion onto Jessie, Frank and Doug.

It was for these reasons that a separate representation of the law was also on its way to the Hickley & District News office. Frank had given a breakfast television interview again that morning inside the newspaper's reception area after he left Jessie, all of which was making the government even more nervous. To compound it, news was coming in that a horde of turtles on a Greek beach had started to attack holidaymakers who were too close to their buried eggs. It had provoked little interest other than local at first, but now it was beginning to be seen in a wider context. The worry was that it was even further away from the supposed source of the catastrophe than before. Which only meant that eyes were starting to bear down on the British government ever more heavily, and something had to be seen to be done...

At that moment, Jessie looked out of the window to the front of the building and noticed a number of dogs - all of them beagles - looking at it with a quizzical eye. They were not in a huddle, but dispersed about the small front car park and so did not attract much attention. But she felt that they must have followed their scent all night and traced them here: it was time to get Doug out - if not themselves. She went in to Frank and told him what she could see: when Frank looked, he, too, was concerned. "I'm sure it's them," he confirmed. "One or two, maybe not; but, what...? A dozen? They've found us. We must get Doug out before there are any more."

He rang Doug's number, telling Jessie to somehow get rid of Enid if she could while Doug made a break for it through the back. Jessie went out and asked Enid if she could show her where some stationery was, which she begrudgingly acquiesced to, and led her away. Then Frank went in and helped Doug to pack as much as he could: "Leave anything you can't take now," he said, "we'll bring it to you later." With Enid not there, nobody noticed the figure of Doug leave the office with Frank down the back stairs. He opened the fire escape door, yanking up the bar with a hollow, metallic ring that echoed up the concrete staircase. "There's a news van there," he said; "Get in it and cover yourself up. I'll be down as soon as I can." He gave him the keys and disappeared: Doug looked around then ran the few yards to the van and did as he had been told. A few minutes later, Jessie and Frank - with Doug under a blanket in the back - drove out of the rear of the building under the courtyard arch, watched by the glaring eye of Enid through a fourth-floor window. She was angry: she did not like not knowing what was going on. She turned away and went to her desk to find her keys.

As the police arrived at the front of the building, watched by inquisitive townspeople, a film crew and a number of dogs, Jessie, Frank and Doug were passing the kebab shops and light industry sheds that formed the depressing hinterland of Hickley. They were soon out on the moors again.

Chapter 17

Two police helicopters hovered over Shepherd Scar as an array of cars filed up the narrow lane to the research centre road-block. An ambulance was with them - too late to do anything but there to take away the policeman's body - and ENG news crews from the BBC, ITV and Sky, as well as other reporters. Many had already gone in, realising that the place was now empty and unguarded; but most stood uneasily at the front of the reception and security block, slightly jittery at the oppressive surroundings, the decrepit and partly ravaged buildings and because of what they heard had happened there not once but twice before.

No-one had gone around the back near the holding-pools; it was as well that they had not for, as the police helicopters arrived, clattering overhead, the pilots could see that a huge host of creation was still lapping up the polluted liquid. Hearing the sudden noise, a flock of birds flew up and, sensing the danger, flew straight at one of the helicopters; there was a sound of beating wings and thudding bodies as the flock hit the rotors top and back; then an increased whining and pitch of the engine as feathers and corpses were distributed in bloody chunks across the sky. Then the helicopter tilted and started to swing in the air before coming crashing down, spinning, to the right of the centre. It all happened so quickly that the news crews hardly had time to start filming; everyone was stunned into silence and disbelief as a roar comprising the noises of every type of animal rose in volume from behind the buildings, mixing with the mangling, crunching and clanging of the helicopter. Then, it was getting nearer, and some of the assembled people started to run for their vehicles; two news vans collided into each other as they tried to escape down the narrow, solitary road. Then the animals arrived around both ends of the buildings and started to assault, bite, peck, chew and sting any representative of the human race that they could. Screams and shouts augmented the noise of the carnage: one policeman in a red car who got out an automatic rifle was silenced almost immediately after he had despatched some dogs, sheep, birds and foxes, the vengeful throng leaving him a bloody mess like the one by the gate. It was chaos: crews and police fought each other to get into their cars but those too far from them did not make it. The second helicopter had veered away from the scene when the pilot saw what was happening to the first and he was screaming into the microphone to send in the army, almost incapable of describing the scene but shouting that they had to be destroyed. In the back, a cameraman was filming the scene: soon the pictures would be around the world with the message that the Shepherd Scar Research Centre had become the crucible of the animals' revenge on humankind.

Two cars made it out of Shepherd Scar - one ITV satellite van, shooting pictures as they went - and a police car. At the bottom, by the junction where Mick's car had been found only a few days before, these two stopped and shouted with each other: then, there was a crash of metal and bone and their cars both heaved and bounced forward as a herd of cows and sheep charged them as one from behind. Then the dogs were in front of them, the rodents and the insects underneath and within, and the panic and the screams started again as they fled the place in different directions.

The cameraman stopped filming when they were a mile or two away, then put another memory chip in the camera: his sound recordist was bleeding beside him but was still monitoring the sounds around them. The driver, a young camera assistant, was white with fear and red with cuts: he had managed to spray the car with some insect killer which had nullified many of the insects: those that were not dying he swatted with his call-sheet. He had been wearing thick gloves to carry cables and equipment but they had served a more useful purpose - they protected him when he had picked up a number of mice, rats and other rodents and either smashed them against the dashboard or thrown them out of the window as the men escaped.

The police car was less lucky: one policewoman had been bitten in the throat and was bleeding profusely. "They will not believe this at HQ," the driver was mumbling as he sped along back to

Oldham, the blue light flashing and the siren wailing. When any car came towards them they made it stop and turn back...

At that same moment, Jessie, Frank and Doug were in a pub, discussing what to do next. A television was on in the corner with the sound barely discernible, yet something suddenly made Jessie look up. There was a newsflash and some shaky aerial pictures of what looked very much like Shepherd Scar.

"Oh, my God," she exclaimed. Doug and Frank looked to where she was facing and their reaction was similar. They rose and went closer to the screen, trying to pick up the commentary. At that moment, there was a screech of brakes outside and three fearful men ran in, one holding a camera, the other a sound kit, and the last wearing thick gloves. All were bloody and their clothes ripped; their faces, forearms and legs were also puckered as if they had been stung many, many times. Jessie recognised the cameraman as the one who had filmed her interviews the night before: a rugged, burly but overweight man of forty-five with a genial disposition and a hatred of the government. He and Jessie had got on well. He was shouting for the landlord who contemptuously came out on hearing him then, when he saw them, asked if they were all right.

"No, we bloody well aren't," was the reply. "Give us three large scotches immediately, please." The landlord complied as Jessie went over to him.

"What's happened?" she asked him.

"Oh, hello," he said, recognising her. "Christ - I've never seen anything like it in my life."

"That?" she said, implying the screen. He looked up, nodded and then started sobbing uncontrollably as his drink was brought, which he downed in one.

"They attacked us all - helicopters, cars, press, police... Carnage. Unbelievable..."

"What's going on up here?" the sound recordist asked blankly. "I've never been up North before. Is it always like this?"

Jessie confirmed that it was not, and that this was an exceptional set of circumstances. But what they had all seen only made their job all the more important. She went over to Frank and Doug, who were in a subdued state watching the unedited pictures of the events that had happened only half an hour before. The sound was up now as the few people in the pub watched what had been happening only a few miles from where they were; a couple left quickly, and their car was soon heard disappearing rapidly into the distance. Then there was a face on the television that they knew: it was Sir Digby Crichton, saying that there was no need to panic and that the army would soon have everything under control.

"Now I feel a lot better," said Doug sarcastically.

What really angered the group further was that Crichton was saying there was still no proof that the events were caused by the alleged leak at Shepherd Scar, nor the research programmes that had been followed there. "What planet is that man on?" the sound recordist gawped.

"He's been told to say that by the PM," said the cameraman indignantly. Then his mobile phone rang; when he answered it, he was gruff to the point of rudeness: "I'm recovering from being assaulted by thousands of fucking animals," he stated ineloquently, "and if you don't believe me, watch the news. I'll be back shortly with more. Just give us a break, OK?" He listened for a few moments longer, uttered a brief swear-word, then switched it off and threw it down. Jessie was getting used to living without her mobile: they would be too traceable if hers was on, and Frank was now in hiding, so his was off, too. The cameraman looked at him.

"You're the editor of the Hickley & District News, aren't you?" Frank admitted as much. "You'd better get back, then; I've just heard that your offices have been attacked by a whole load of dogs. They've savaged some police and your staff. Some police marksmen killed them but two people are in hospital."

"Are you going there?" Frank asked.

"I'm supposed to be."

"Would you take me? I can't let these two go back."

"Yeah, OK. As long as you let us film what we like there."

Frank said that this would be no problem. He then turned to Jessie and Doug and pulled them away from the others. "Go to my house – you have the address. Just turn right out of here; then down the lane a mile away on the right, it's signposted to Little Micklethorpe. It's the first house you come to - huge.

Here are the keys: Doug, get stuck in as soon as you can. I think the loft's the best place. I'll see you later."

As he turned back, he noticed that the sound recordist had put his headphones on again and was listening intently to what he was picking up on his pole with the furry end, a very worried look on his face.

"I think we'd better be quick," he said. "I'm not sure what it is that I can hear but there's a lot of it and it's headed this way."

The landlord found that his pub had emptied faster than had ever happened at closing-time.

Jessie and Doug went in the car and Frank with the camera crew. As they disappeared, the landlord went out to his now empty car-park and saw what looked like a huge black cloud on the opposite horizon. It was vast, dark and filled his view. There was a deep buzz, augmented by a rumbling noise. And whatever it was, it was coming his way. He turned and ran in, shutting and locking the doors and windows. Then he got his gun out and went upstairs. Looking through the top window he saw a terrifying sight...

An hour later, Sir Digby Crichton was still fending off questions, live in the studio, when the news anchorwoman's eyes suddenly narrowed as she listened to the producer on her earpiece and she interrupted Sir Digby, saying, "We've got some new footage of the events at Shepherd Scar. I think we should take a look." With that, the cameraman's footage of events from the ground was shown, including the birds attacking the helicopter, the animals' assault, the escape and the activity within the news car. Every so often, they cut away to Sir Digby's face, which was a picture of horror, disbelief and panic.

When it was over, she asked him simply: "And do you still really believe there is nothing to be concerned about?"

Chapter 18

Back at the newspaper office, Frank had gone in and witnessed the after-effects of the invasion there. A thin, gangly police inspector was awaiting him in his office, and Enid was giving off an air of disdain at Frank's prior disappearance.

"Were you at the Shepherd Scar Research Centre last night, sir," the policeman enquired immediately.

"No."

"Were you there with anyone else?"

"No."

"And what about the witnesses whom you supposedly got the story from, then? Where are they?"

"I have promised them anonymity."

"And were they helping you to get in to the research centre?"

"No, officer."

The man looked disappointed. "Pity. I was hoping that you might be able to give us all an idea what to do about this, this... shambles. The government's in chaos, the army don't know whether to intervene, animals are attacking humans all over the world, and yet we understand you have first-hand experience of both the research centre and the whereabouts of Doug Sprake." Frank shot a barbed look at Enid.

"Which would help us all no end to sort this out."

"If I knew where he was, I'd tell you. Though I suspect he's better off without government intervention because he knows so much. He should just be allowed to get on with creating something to stop this - an antidote or whatever - rather than having the government silence him. Which they would."

"So how do you know all that if you don't know where he is, then?" the inspector smiled sweetly.

"He told me. He knows what happens to people the government doesn't like. Look, I've only spoken to him. I don't know where he is now."

The inspector nodded. "I see." Then: "So who do you think killed our policeman up at the research centre?"

"I'd have thought that the events of this morning here would give you the answer to that one, inspector. It was the animals." There was a pause while they contemplated one another. "Look, is this going anywhere?" Frank continued. "I have a story to write, an editorial meeting to go to and various jobs to finish."

"I can't find the key to the editorial room, Mr. Wheatley," said Enid pointedly.

"I'm sure we shall find it somewhere," he riposted firmly. There was another pause.

"Are you hiding someone in there?" the inspector enquired. "Like Doug Sprake, for example?"

"Why should I want to do that?"

"So... are you?"

"No, I'm not."

They looked at each other. Frank did not want him to go in there: even though Doug was not there he would see his rough experiments and know that he had been.

"Ah, there's the key," Enid piped up, having opened one of the draws in Frank's desk with a dexterity that surprised him. "We'll prove it for the officer, shall we?"

Frank was floored. "Ah, er, OK. Right." He got up and followed a sprightly Enid to the editorial room, which she unlocked. 'What am I going to say now?' he was thinking, as the door swung open. The inspector entered. Frank looked past him but was surprised to see that it looked tidy and as normal. There was no trace of Doug's experiments or that anyone had been there at all. He shot a look at Enid, who just forced a smile. "I always like to help the police," she added to her expression.

"Thank you," rejoined the inspector, with a note of dissatisfaction. As he passed, it was Enid's turn to shoot Frank a look that said 'I've got you out of that one haven't I?'

At the pub, the landlord watched as the black cloud of insects buzzed around his premises, taking away the light and imitating the flurries of a violent but dark-coloured snowstorm. The noise was deafening, and made worse by the bashing against the windows of insects who were trying to find out if their prey was inside. A few had managed to get in through various cracks in the floors and masonry, but hummed around him then went searching in other rooms. It was as if they knew exactly what or whom they were looking for. Then he heard other noises outside and, through the fog of insects, made out a number of different animals, all looking intently towards his pub. There were hundreds of them, and also rodents - even reptiles, although these were less abundant. He crossed the landing and looked out the back, and was terrified to see that they were all around the building. He prayed that they would move on soon and was relieved that his wife was away at market and their son was at school. Except that, if he got out of this alive, they would not believe what he told them unless they had seen it for themselves.

Then, like a cloud lifting, the noise subsided, the sun came out again and he heard the animals running away, all in the same direction, the only evidence being trampled grass, flattened flowers and a lot of faeces.

The police had not had the chance to reconnoitre the surroundings of Shepherd Scar: it was for that reason that the two cars that had been used to take Doug, Jessie and Frank to the research centre the night before had not been found. Instead, they were the subject of a very different investigation - by the animals around the research centre. A selection of dogs - the beagles' numbers had been augmented by other breeds now - were busy sniffing them inside and out: the windows had been smashed and the interior was a mass of furry animals and insects.

Outside, sheep, cows and even horses now looked on with a kind of detached intent, as if awaiting the next step in the revolution of the species. After each had finished their separate investigations, they loped off or flew away in different directions, each seemingly a disconnected being but each having acquired a heightened instinct... and the inherent ability not only to use this as individuals but to pass it on to others...

Doug had been propelled into action by the events of the morning and was being helped by Jessie to set up his experiments again, this time in Frank's loft. In the rush to get out of the newspaper buildings, he had left some of the compounds he had concocted behind, but was hoping that these would follow shortly. As for his research, he felt he had made some significant advances, as he had told Jessie earlier: but he was still no nearer to solving how he would create the correct balance of parlazine - which he was now sure was the fundamental ingredient - with the other compounds. How he would test their effects, too, would be time-consuming and difficult with the limited equipment at his disposal, and the march of global events was making the necessity of an antidote all the more pressing. Further, what complicated issues more was the fact that he did not know whether any other chemical had crept into the equation as it seeped down the drain at Shepherd Scar.

The loft was big, and had one window in the roof, under which was a large table and a couple of chairs; in this area it was light, although dingy elsewhere. It had obviously been converted recently, and a new, narrow staircase led up to it, in contrast to the age of the rest of the building. He wondered why Frank had not put more windows in, but would soon be grateful for that oversight. For, as he tried to set things up, he became aware of a distant but fast-approaching droning sound, and stopped to listen. Then Jessie was pounding up the stairs.

"Hide yourself!" she shrieked. "The animals are coming!" She, too, had heard the noise, but being less busy and not immersed in thoughts of chemical formulae, she had heard it before Doug and reacted with amazing speed, shutting and locking all doors and drawing the curtains: she had also emptied a bottle of bleach outside the front door in a frantic attempt to cover their scent which she knew the dogs would pick up - but it was a forlorn hope.

As she got half-way up the stairs, Doug had already thrown a blanket over himself and was cowering under it in the dingy corner; then the room went dark as the thick cloud of flying insects descended over the roof, the droning noise of millions of beating wings sounding like the call of doom. Jessie stopped and decided to go down one floor to cover herself, as Doug had done, but with a sofa throw. Then the beating at the windows began and she could hear the dogs sniffing, long and protracted, under the downstairs doors. Then there was yelping which she interpreted as excitement: she was sure that they knew they had found their quarry. She had her mobile phone in her pocket, and decided that this was the moment to put it on. It took what seemed like ages to log on: she started to dial Frank's number but was almost immediately interrupted by her voicemail ringing. She instantly switched it off and then tried to ring Frank again.

Frank had just got back to his office after seeing the police inspector off the premises and had closed the door, so containing himself and his assistant, Enid, with whom he was not a little angry.

"What the hell did you do that for?" he sputtered.

"I thought you needed some help."

"Like hell."

"Yes, I did," she said indignantly. "That's why I cleared away the evidence. I knew the police would be here sooner or later. It's all in the basement, locked away."

Frank relented a little. He had to keep her onside now, after all.

"So how did you know about Doug Sprake, then?"

"I didn't. But when I saw you leaving by the back door this morning with an unknown man and that woman -"

"Why don't you like her?" Enid ignored the question and continued. "When I saw you leaving, I knew something was up and realised that it was probably Sprake. What with all that's been going on around here and Shepherd Scar and all the media interest, it seemed likely and I had to protect you. That's my job."

Frank was not convinced, but had to go along with

it. He was sure she would use it against him - or Jessie - at a later date. But for now...

"OK. Thanks," he managed. "Did you get it out without anyone noticing?"

"I put it on the tea trolley and covered it with a tablecloth."

Frank almost found himself admiring her. But he still could not think that she was doing it to help him; there must be an ulterior motive.

"So was it you and the others at Shepherd Scar last night? And not a witness?"

"That's enough for now, Enid."

"So it was you that killed Dennis Fouracres - accidentally, of course - then?"

"I said that's enough, Enid." A little smile of triumph crossed her lips.

"Cup of tea?"

"That would be nice, thanks."

She left the office just as his mobile phone rang. He did not recognise the number, but he certainly did the voice. It was a panic-stricken Jessie.

"Oh my God," was all he could say after she had told him what was happening. "Keep quiet now but ring me if everything calms down again. I'm thinking of you, Jessie - I'll do something, I promise."

With that, Enid came back with his tea.

"Is she in trouble?" she asked coldly.

"Yes. Jessie's at my house, which is being invaded by insects and animals and humankind's future on this planet is possibly being threatened as a result."

"Ah. So Sprake is there as well, is he?"

"I didn't say that."

"No, but that's what you mean." Then, after a moment she added: "I don't think *she's* the future of the planet, somehow."

Frank bridled. "She - as you call her - is the reason all this has got out. If it wasn't for 'her' then the government would be covering all this evil stuff up. Now we have a chance to expose them and hopefully save what's left of the planet - at least, from a humankind point of view. So please either help me or stop being snide and bitter."

There was a pause, and she sniffed, as if clearing her disdain for the situation but taking another viewpoint. Then she looked at him.

"I do have a plan, actually" she confided. But it involves a government contact."

The cacophony was unbelievable. Doug, under the blanket in the loft, was terrified. He knew they knew he was there, he thought, and were probably very annoyed that he had given them the slip the first time. He expected that they had a very unpleasant death in store for him, and any entreaty he could communicate to them he was sure would be rejected. It had worked once, but forgiveness was not a natural phenomenon: it had evolved through sophistry within the human race alone... Downstairs, Jessie, under the sofa throw, was wishing for the first time that she had never seen Mick Deakin's notes. At first, the confrontation with the animals had been exciting before the fear set in: then it was very frightening; now it was terrifyingly tiring through being commonplace. Now the birds were flying at the windows in an attempt to smash them and so let nature's flood within: but she noticed that the windows were double-glazed and the shatterproof glass was standing up to the onslaught, even though it was becoming scratched and pock-marked with the attack.

Then, after a few more moments of blind terror, everything fell silent again, like the combined din of hell and chaos suddenly being relieved by enlightenment. Sunlight flooded back into the rooms and the incessant sniffing had ceased as well. Somehow, though, she felt that it was only a respite, and the attack would be longer, more savage the next time. And there would be more of them, too, she thought. She pulled the throw away from her eyes and peeked out. Nothing moved, save some leaves outside the window. She slowly and noiselessly crept on her hands and knees to the underside of the window and surreptitiously looked out. Apart from the garden looking as if it had seen army manoeuvres, everything seemed tranquil once more. Then she heard a bird twitter and instinctively dived under the window again. A moment later, she heard a noise behind her and, terrified, turned to see her expected attacker.

But it was Doug. "It's OK - they've gone," he said without expression.

"How d'you know?"

"I just do. Remember, I've had some of this gunk, too." She did not look convinced. "I think they just wanted me to know that they're watching me."

"Us."

"Us. And they want me to make some more. That came over very strongly. A whole load more birds are due to migrate soon and I think they want as many as possible to have ingested the stuff."

Jessie was aghast. "You're not serious, are you? Surely they can't be that calculating, that scheming?"

"I think they can. Remember, it was made for humans, *by* humans: it's just got onto the wrong side of the natural divide. And it affects their instincts, or genes, DNA, nervous system - whatever - in a way that we don't comprehend yet."

"You."

"Touché. *I* don't comprehend yet." With that, he turned resignedly and started to return to the loft. "I'd better keep going. I don't know how much time we've got. They want the stuff as soon as possible and one thing I don't know is how impatient they are. Or not." He was trudging up the narrow stairs by the time he had said this.

"You're not going to make it for them, are you?" she asked nervously.

"No, but until I know what it is, I can't make an antidote. That's the problem."

"Do you think they'll let us out?" she enquired.

" I doubt it."

"What about Frank? If he comes back, do you think they'll let him out again?"

"No. They wouldn't even let him in." He was in the loft, now. "We're prisoners," he added, the distance of his statement adding a resonance to the words.

Jessie sat back against the window and decided to ring Frank: he must not come to his house. And that upset her as much as she knew it would annoy him. She really wanted to be with him again, and hoped her feelings were reciprocated. She went to the phone, but it was dead: 'Chewed through,' she concluded. So she put her mobile on again and rang him.

Frank took her call with Enid sitting beside him. Jessie explained what had happened and that he could not come back to his house or he would be a prisoner, too. Or even worse. She felt that the house was surrounded and that the animals were only waiting for Doug to produce more of the liquid. How they expected him to make it there, though... But if Doug could convey that to the animals without betraying the impossibility of the task, perhaps that was their ticket to escape... When he could get it made - or if - then Doug felt that the animals would expect it to be taken to Shepherd Scar, which he believed had become the focus of animal pilgrimage, rather like Rome, Jerusalem or Mecca were for humans.

Frank listened intently. Then, quite abruptly, he said: "Enid has had a brilliant idea." The silence made him know that Jessie either did not believe him or it was code for her being next to him and that she should speak carefully. Either way, he had to lead the conversation from now on.

"Enid suggests we tell the government everything - Doug, the serums -"

"You've told her about Doug?" she shouted in a

whisper down the phone.

"Yes - and Mick's notes, our two escapes, the animals around Doug's house, what they've done to him and the fact he understands them... in return for their help and co-operation in getting the compounds made. She feels that Doug will be protected. What do you think?"

"No."

"Why?"

"Because they'll only take what they want, cover up the rest and compromise us. Doug will not be protected and when it's all over they'll probably force him into the open and blame him. You know what happens to scientists who fall foul of the government. And as for us..."

"Mm."

"Frank, don't listen to her: she's trying to compromise you - and me, and Doug."

"Mm." After a pause, he added: "But I don't know how we're going to get this stuff made and distributed in the vast quantities we need if we don't get government help."

"I hear what you're saying, but - Christ - I think there's more to it than that. If it's so bloody secret, so incredibly important, why did they not protect it better? OK, OK, so as not to attract attention. Rubbish. I've researched stories like this before and I think it's a cover for something - or someone - else. It means that unofficial things can be done, shipped in and out, without anyone knowing. Off the record. And that's what I think they were doing. Then all this blew up and exposed them. I think it's more sinister than it appears and we're stuck in the middle. As soon as they know where we are, we're done for. And someone - and I think we both know whom that might be - will be delighted. It'll make whatever he's doing invisible and get the government off the hook. But whatever he's doing that isn't right, they'll still help him because it'll make them smell of roses and will also go down as making it look as though something's being 'done'. God, Frank, I thought you realised all this. You've seen how they work. They're immoral bastards."

"Mm."

"Stop just saying 'Mm'. Talk to me."

"I can't. I'll call you in an hour. Put your phone off until then in case they're getting a trace on you. Speak soon." With that, he put the phone down.

He turned to Enid. "I think she's right," he said. Enid looked indignant. "But I think we might steer a course through the middle."

"What shall I tell the government, then? I'll have to reply."

"As I said before: tell them that I've left the country and can't be contacted, and that we know nothing other than what's been reported in our papers. We don't know where Doug is and Jessie's disappeared, as, again, we said before. The only difference - and you can tell them this - is that you believe that someone in government is covering something up that is bound up with this crisis." Then he looked at her more earnestly and added: "We feel it's unrelated to this crisis but is nonetheless compromising a solution to it."

"Is that a real conclusion or a bluff?"

"I'm not sure yet. But something's not right. I agree with Jessie."

"And you want *me* to tell them that?"

"Yes, you. You have the contact. But you haven't spoken to me: I'm out of the country."

"But the police know you're here - you spoke to them this morning."

"I've just gone."

Enid gave him a sullen look, turned and walked out of the office and back to her desk. Frank felt good: as long as she did not say that he really was there this would mean that her government contact would be her problem. And if anything came out, then it would be her responsibility, not his. And if she was trying to fix something for her own devices, the buck would now stop with her. Which is why he knew she was so angry inside: she felt she had compromised him but now he had turned the onus onto her. She was, at that moment, in an ugly mood.

Enid opened her e-mail and clicked on 'reply' to a message. Then she started typing: 'Dear Sir Digby. I do not think I can help you. My editor is now out ofthe country and we do not know the whereabouts of the other people you wish to contact. However, I am of the opinion that there is more to this than meets the eye, otherwise reactive events to counteract this crisis would have happened sooner. Sorry that I cannot help further. Yours, Enid Croft, Editor's

Assistant, Hickley & District News.' She looked at it for a moment then sighed and sent it.

Frank was watching her intently. As she sighed, he felt that there was something she knew that she was not telling him. Something was being tweaked in his subconscious but it would not reveal itself. He hoped it would soon, because Enid knew a lot. In fact, far too much.

Chapter 19

At that moment, all along the Brittany coast around Cancale, in northern France, the town was thriving on its usual trade of oysters, driven in on the backs of tractors to the port area. There, numerous restaurants fed the appetites for those flocking to the town for this specific local culinary delight. The breeze that blew off the emerald sea was cooling the town on this early autumn afternoon and foreign and French tourists alike were devouring the raw oysters with gusto, prising the shells open and swallowing the creatures whole as they had done for centuries.

On this day, though, as demand was exceptional, a new bed had been harvested just around the headland. The word was that this season's oysters were better than those of previous years and the town was recording record attendance as a result. But unbeknown to people, there was a difference, for the location of these particular beds - further out into the estuary than usual - had experienced a different current to the others. It was known that these beds bred larger, more succulent *crustaces*, but they were usually left until the very end of the season because they were more difficult to get at and it was also when most of the non-French tourists had disappeared; but this year was unusual, and they had to provide for their customers.

However, what was going onto the plates of the assembled gourmets would start to leave an unexpected impression - and not just on the people; for the many stray cats and plenty of pet dogs would also partake of these creatures, either as scavengers or due to being given the shells to lick after the main contents had been consumed.

Imperceptibly at first, several dogs and cats had started to congregate together on the road: in itself, this was unusual, cats and dogs normally being natural enemies, but they had started to sniff and smell one another. After extended proximity, they then seemed to know what the others were thinking. Some of the restaurateurs tried to disperse the animals but when they stood their ground these restaurateurs realised too, by some sort of innate instinct, that there was a hostile intent about their stubbornness. It became apparent to those eating the oysters there was a strange, all-pervasive feeling that they suddenly knew what the animals wanted: it was to chase all these *bons viveurs* away. It was silent, profound and menacing.

As the numbers of strays and pets grew - the latter often not responding to their owners' calls to come with them - a strange feeling fell over the previously happy scene: people started to feel uncomfortable and decided to leave, but they were not quite sure why they felt the way they did. Yet they knew it was a fear, a fear borne out of a primeval instinct that nobody had ever had before. A couple of dogs bit their owners as they tried to retrieve them, but for the most part it was a quiet and steady withdrawal. Within an hour, the town was virtually deserted of people, and, as night fell, the doors and windows were bolted, leaving the streets to the animals. Staring out from the insides of their closed businesses, the *petits commerçants* were baffled, yet seemed at the same time to completely understand, despite the fact that hardly anything was said. It was as if true instinct - acts and communication without apparent reason or discussion, so long buried in the human psyche - were being revealed once more.

Jessie was furious, yet felt completely helpless. The man she liked and respected was being influenced by a jealous harridan who wanted to depose him and obviously felt she now had the means to do it. At the same time, she, Jessie, was stuck in a house surrounded by hostile animals, birds and insects that would not let them out until they got what they wanted. Upstairs, a not very attractive man was trying to save the planet yet did not have the wherewithal to do it. She was not good when confined to a space, either, and she desperately needed to be doing something. To cap it all, she needed to keep her mobile off in case someone traced her whereabouts. It was all too stifling. She went downstairs to see if she could make a coffee. A huge, drawn-out sniff under the back door made her know that they were still there, even if they were only the guards. She put the kettle on and was glad when it started to boil: they had not got to the power supply yet. She made two coffees and went up to Doug, who was in the process of tasting a compound from one of two saucers in front of him, taking notes the while.

"Should you be doing that?" she enquired.

"Not really. But who else can I test it on?" He waved his hand vaguely to imply the animals outside who were there but who he could not touch. "Anyway, remember that it was made for humans but it's become something they've adapted to. I'm trying some experiments backwards, if you see what I mean - then I'll do them forwards again."

She looked at him. He looked younger than before, she thought. Then, perhaps it was just the light, as he was standing under the window. But he definitely looked thinner.

"You're not having too much of that, I hope," she joked. "You're losing weight."

"Am I? Are you sure?" he shot back at her. "I admit, I don't feel hungry..."

"Yeah. I think you look younger, too."

"Since when?"

"Since I first met you a couple of days ago, I suppose. You certainly look different to the picture I saw of you on TV the other night."

Doug was pleased about that. "Thanks," he said. Then, as if he had not comprehended the compliment, he added, "Look, do you want to help me?"

"Of course."

"It'll mean ingesting some of this... stuff."

"Oh, my God. Erm..."

"Look, the point is this. I'm trying to find the difference between two sets of research, where they divide: mine and Mick's. If I do it all myself I might compromise the other. They might even interfere with one another. If you take one, and I the other, then we have a faster chance of annotating the differences. When I've done that then I think I might know what to do next."

"I can hardly refuse, then, can I?" she said, not without an element of concern.

"Look at it this way," Doug continued enthusiastically. "The one I was taking when you came up is something that I think - *think* - is what I was doing when all this started. I took some an hour ago. Now you say I look younger and I have to say that I feel better - which is what was happening just before I spoke to Mick the last time. Now, this one -" he tapped the other saucer - "is what I think Mick was researching. It was joint research bar a few differences that impacted the end product. My research I think has had an effect on reversing the ageing affect of stem cells, which is why I'm looking and feeling younger. The difference between me and Mick was that he became - according to his notes - more talkative and could remember things better: classic parlazine effects. They affected me, too. But the compound that you picked up at Shepherd Scar - chromitic paradiosymine - was, I think, the different ingredient. So I need you to try that one - added to these - to see what happens."

"What do you *think* might happen?"

"If it works, you'll feel as if you want to talk but after you've told me everything then you won't feel so good." Jessie looked horrified. "It won't be for long - and it's a tiny dose. Mine was to make people talk after suffering from strokes - although there was a military aspect, too, of course... Mick's - as far as I can see - was to make people change personality, take on a vengeful streak, then talk and then become paralysed. And then die," he added with an almost boyish relish.

"Oh, thanks! Why can't I have the one you're on?"

"Because we'd be doing the same experiment twice. I need to do this separately. And you're the only person in the world who can help... to perhaps *save* the world."

It all sounded so ludicrously dramatic, yet it was true. But she had never had to make such a terrifying decision. "You promise me it's only a tiny dose?" she enquired.

"As far as I can see, yes. And I've upped the anthicin content so it'll be less painful and far less virulent. And your brain won't turn to jelly."

"Thanks," she said without any enthusiasm.

"You might even understand the animals, too," he added. "That would be very useful, so you and I can communicate without talking - an instinctive comprehension."

She raised her eyebrows momentarily. "I'll do it if you give me a tenth of the smallest dose you *were* going to give me," she said at length with a tremor in her voice. "I can always take more, but if I take too much then you've lost your guinea-pig."

"Right," said Doug. "Here." He took a teaspoon and dipped the tip into the second saucer, withdrew it and offered it to her. She took it, whilst feeling that he had acquired a slightly manic air and was possibly oblivious to her fate. But she felt compelled to do it nonetheless and, taking a deep breath, sucked it off the spoon, then swallowed it.

She sat down on one of the chairs and Doug did the same; he looked at his watch, noted the time and then looked at her with his pen poised over his notebook.

At first, she felt nothing. Then, after two minutes, there was an inkling of a tingling sensation in her cortex and a feeling of lightness. Then the inside of her head seemed to see multiple flashing coloured lights and yet her eyes seemed to be seeing what was actually in front of her with a purple frizzy glow around the edges. Yet both seemed detached from the other. Then a headache descended across the top of her head right across from her forehead to the base of her neck, and it went tense. She was feeling nauseous and convulsive and she thought she was speaking yet she could not be sure: she certainly did not know what she was saying and the pain became more intense. Then after what seemed only a few more seconds the pain went and she felt as if she was floating, yet her conscience seemed separate from her body, which was as if it was in a different room. Then she was feeling aggressive yet she did not know against whom or why - or even where they were to be aggressive against. Then it all went dark and she lost consciousness.

When she felt some senses returning and started to stir, Doug was there holding her head and begging her to wake up; it was darker than before, and she instantly remembered Frank's face but not his name - and that she had not phoned him. She realised she was lying down and a dull but intense pain covered the whole of her head but was still particularly acute in her cortex area. She felt cold and was trembling. Then Doug was putting bedclothes over her and making her sip water. She could hear his voice a thousand miles away amidst the throbbing of her pulse, which reverberated with every beat and simultaneously intensified the pain.

"Wake up, wake up, you're OK. Well done, well done." Doug's words began to take on more meaning and she suddenly had a craving for the water she had been sipping; she wrenched the glass from him, but he continued helping her as she gulped the water down, spilling as much as she drank.

"I'm so sorry," he could hear Doug saying. "Thank God you only took such a small amount." The relevance of what he said was lost on her but its meaning was clear.

Then she found herself wanting to vomit and Doug was with her in a cold room that reverberated as he pointed her head down a white opening. Her head seemed to drain of every fluid as she evicted whatever she seemed to have inside her and then she was lying on the floor again. Almost immediately after that, quite suddenly, it was as if the sun came out again and her pain virtually disappeared - just a dull, thudding headache. She struggled to get up then parked herself against the toilet bowl.

"Jessie, are you OK?" was all she could hear, but she was unclear who was saying it. Then she opened her eyes and the face looked familiar, even if she was unsure who he was.

"Jessie," he said again.

"Who are you?" she found this dislocated voice asking, but realised it must be hers.

"It's me; Doug. You've done it, Jessie - perfect symptoms. I think - I hope - I can create an antidote now. You're amazing. Sorry, I was under the influence of the research I was doing on myself when I asked you to do it. I only realised after you'd been under for a couple of hours that I could have killed you. I'm so sorry - thank God you're OK." And he was hugging her and clasping her to him. Then she passed out.

Frank had tried several times to reach Jessie on her mobile: the hour he stipulated had become four and the light was dimming outside. Enid was sullen and uncommunicative and had received a reply from Sir Digby which only confused matters further: he had requested a meeting with Frank as a matter of the gravest national urgency, and demanded that they give any help possible to the police to find Doug Sprake and Jessie Scott. The former person she was happy to keep quiet about, but the other she wished she could turn in; but she could not reveal one without revealing the other, so for the moment she would do nothing. Then her phone rang and it was reception telling her that the police were back and on their way up already. She hesitated, wondering whether to warn Frank or pretend she did not know; then she realised that she was implicated in the fabrication too and he must leave. And very quickly.

She purposefully rose and went in to tell him: he was on the phone trying to get through to Jessie again but she ripped it out of his hand and instructed him in an emphatic whisper to leave, and why. Now. He picked up his mobile and left by the back stairs again, but when he got to the second floor he heard what sounded like heavy boots coming up. He darted into the first floor and hid in the ladies' lavatory. After a few moments the steps receded and he carefully opened the door and was onto the staircase again and out in the courtyard for the second time in twenty-four hours, trying to look nonchalant as he headed for the archway. After that, he was unsure where he was going.

Back in Frank's office, the police were arriving - more this time. They went to Enid and asked to see the editor. In a loud voice that the whole office could hear she said that Frank had left immediately after their earlier conversation. The inspector glowered at her.

"Someone told us he was still here," he said angrily to Enid. "And I thought that that someone was you."

Enid blushed and tried to imply that she had thought he had come back for something but it had been someone else.

He turned to the office and asked in a loud voice: "Has anyone seen the editor recently?" There was a pause, then someone spoke up in a positive voice that nonetheless tremored as she spoke.

"I thought he was on holiday," it said. There was a general murmur of agreement. The inspector looked even more sceptical.

Enid was annoyed, too: she was sure that this girl, Harriet, was after Frank and resented it, even though the response was the right one.

"Well, where does he live, then? We'll need to search his house. That might throw up a few clues." Enid opened her contacts file and wrote down the address, handing it to the inspector, who then passed it to another officer. "Get down there," he snapped.

"You won't find anything there," Enid said faintly, aware of what Frank had told her happened earlier that morning. "I don't think you should go."

Misunderstanding her meaning, he looked at her harshly and said: "Don't worry - we have a warrant."

"That's not what I meant," Enid found herself saying under her breath.

Outside, Frank had crossed the enclosed courtyard, full as usual with its vans and cars; he was now under the arch - where he came face to face with a large number of dogs of many different breeds, sizes and parentage, who glared at him with a hungry expression. Looking up, he also noticed some large birds of prey, dark even in the dulling sky and framed by the arch: there were about ten of them, and he decided in an instant that they all knew exactly who he was. Whether they would attack or not, he was not sure, until he heard a low, frightening buzzing sound and in a split second knew what that meant: not only would they almost certainly attack but their newly-honed instincts made him sure that they knew he was connected with Doug. All the terror of the two escapes from Shepherd Scar came flooding back and blind panic took hold of him: he was suddenly running back to the relative safety of the building - police or no police. Except that the rear door had swung shut and there was no return that way. He ran to the right in the hope that he would find an open window, but an autumn chill had set in and none were unlatched. The buzzing was getting louder and suddenly the sky was black and all manner of insects were flying towards him, blotting out the light. The dogs, who could have caught him with ease, seemed content just to push him into a corner and stare, like Romans idly watching a gladiatorial spectacle but with the roles reversed. He ran back to the door and started wrenching the bar up and down in a manic, frantic manner; then the door came open and he realised it was Enid. He fell inside and she slammed the door shut, crushing a few insects as the door clanged closed, and trapping a few wasps and bees who instantly started to sting him; Enid was swinging her body and arms around trying to swat them with a rolled-up file, and then the others flew off, trying to get out again and banging on the insides of the windows as they tried to rejoin their swarm.

"Nice holiday?" said a man's voice halfway up the stairs.

Chapter 20

It was nearly eight o'clock when Jessie had woken up, and the evening had turned into a gloomy porridge of long shadows and uncertain shapes. She was lying on her side on a long sofa under a window. The house seemed quiet, although she could hear some noises upstairs; she could see the face of the man she knew it to be, but could not remember his name. In fact, she could not remember where she was, although she had a good recollection of the layout of the place. It seemed as if her consciousness was a panorama of unrelated thoughts and it made her feel detached and insecure. She tried to get up but half fell into the wall, whereupon she slumped back onto the sofa, rubbing her eyes and wondering why her brain felt like a gelatinous mass.

Then Doug was in the room. "Are you OK?" he asked. She looked at him.

"I know who you are but I can't remember your name," she said flatly.

"Oh, shit," came the reply. "Here, drink this. As much as you can."

"What is it?"

"It's water."

"Oh, I thought it was... I don't know... Something else."

"No - no more of that. Just drink it - now." She did as she was told, gulping it down. "I've made you a sandwich," he continued, "and I think you should eat it. Sorry, I can't cook, and the electricity's off now, anyway. Probably bitten through by the animals."

Again, she did as she was told. It was the best cheese sandwich she had ever tasted. At least, it seemed to be at that moment.

"Can you put the light on?" she asked eventually. He shook his head. "No. I said; the animals must have bitten through the cables."

"Did you?"

"Did I what?"

"Say that." He nodded again, and looked concerned. He was terrified that he might have wrecked her memory. Which, after all, was what the drug had been designed to do in its military incarnation.

"What's my name?" he asked her, a slight tremor in his voice. She looked at him and then slowly shook her head.

"I don't know." He looked down at the floor as she flopped against the back of the sofa. Then an idea came to him.

"Phenol hydresium," he said to himself. He ran upstairs and came back with one of the bottles rescued from Shepherd Scar. He opened it and poured a small amount into a teaspoon. Then he tipped it into the glass: he knew it was a rough and ready amount but felt that if he did nothing then she might never fully regain her memory.

He asked again if she could remember his name,

but once more she shook her head. He looked at the glass: would he really have to administer this? Then he asked if she could tell him the name of the newspaper editor she liked.

"Who's that?" she replied. That was it: he had to risk it. He picked up the glass, went to the tap in the bathroom and filled it. Then he came back.

"Frank?" he volunteered.

"Who's that?"

He took a deep breath. "OK; drink this. Now." He wrenched her up and forced the glass to her lips, which were a blue-ish colour. Now he was even more concerned. She drank it, complaining that it was a little bitter, but drained the glass nonetheless and then fell back again. Doug was sweating, his hands like damp sponges as he clasped them together. He watched her as the gloom became denser and wondered how much longer it would take him to come up with an antidote, working under these conditions. He also knew that, should the animals tire of waiting, they could be inside the building within minutes. At least, the insects and rodents could: there were enough cracks, air bricks and drains to get in for her and Doug to be overwhelmed in no time at all. No, they must be waiting, holding back to see when he would produce more of whatever he had created before. In the meantime, he and Jessie were at their mercy. But at least if this worked on Jessie it would give him a lead: he just wished that the stakes were not so high.

At that moment, he heard the sirens. Initially they were far away but he was sure they were coming here.

Frank had relented, he thought, for the love of Jessie, if for no other reason, of which there were plenty. He was then even more worried that she would not recognise Frank and found himself willing the phenol hydresium to have an effect. As the sirens became closer, he was aware of increased movement outside. He peered through a window and saw what looked like the ground heaving. Although it was now dark he could just see several different types of animal down there, increasingly restless as the wailing grew in intensity. He could not see the sky but was sure it was full of birds; and then it started - barking, screeching, mewing, baa-ing, chirping... a cacophony of sounds united in vengeful indignation at the approaching vehicles. He went round to the front of the house and peered through another window, and could then see the stabs of headlights slicing into the dark and the flashing beacons swirling a ghostly blue light around the hedgerows. Subtlety was not a salient feature within the police force, he thought.

He then hoped that Frank was not with them: he would not survive a third time, he was sure.

Frank was sitting between two officers in the back of the police car. He had been harangued by the inspector for withholding information and for the intention of evading police questioning, and was now under arrest, feeling forlorn and helpless. He had given the police his home address, the whole affair prompted and led by Enid, who he was sure would come out of all this smelling of roses. But not him, he felt: the editorship would soon rest with her husband, even though he was completely incompetent.

The car bumped down the hill and soon they arrived at their destination. He and his guards got out and they escorted him through the front door, first checking that there was no attacker from the animal world in the sky or on the ground. It all seemed quiet, though: the animals seemed to feel that they had made their point for the moment, and had not attacked Frank even when he was escorted away. They had been there all right, but around them here appeared lifeless, dark and unremarkable, the only light to sear the gloom being one over the entrance and some distant street lamps. This was where the police station had been built, over a century ago, when it had been in the centre of the town; but as Hickley had grown with its mining and cotton manufacturing, it had expanded westwards, leaving the original buildings in a land of limbo.

Frank had managed to get out of travelling to his home: he felt he knew what sort of reception there might be and only worried about Jessie and what could happen to her. And Doug, of course, but that was different. He had, though, kept these thoughts to himself as he believed the only way to make the authorities realise at first hand the gravity of the situation and the ferocity of the natural world was to let them witness it again at first hand. He hoped as well that the new confidence resulting from the animals' novel and innate mutual comprehension across all the different species would compel the authorities to do something useful at last. With that in mind, he was sure that he would soon hear some news from his house: he would not be disappointed.

Jessie groaned and clutched her head as the headlights hit the curtains: Doug rushed from the window and held her as the noise outside reached a crescendo, a mix of indignation and revenge, it seemed - although that might have been just his understanding of them due to his heightened perception. He heard a car door open and the noise got louder: then there were human screams outside and a long blast on a horn which he knew meant that someone had collapsed onto the steering-wheel. Then Jessie was shrieking and waving her head around next to him, adding to the din, and he wondered if he had arrived in hell. Then there were gunshots outside and he ran to the window: a policeman in a red patrol car was firing an automatic at anything he could see, which was everywhere around him, shooting indiscriminately as the hordes attacked him and his companions. A number of dogs were pulling policemen out of the cars and savagely biting them as the insects stung and the rodents ran over them, adding to the savagery and pain. Doug could not bear to watch: not only because he knew all about it from first-hand experience but because he felt somehow responsible. And Jessie was groaning again. He went back to her and asked her how she was feeling, but was surprised by the answer.

"I feel as though my head's on a string, somewhere

else... away from my body. Doug, I think I'm going mad." Doug: she had said his name! The drug must have had an effect. He was elated despite the carnage being perpetrated outside and then suddenly thought of Frank. Was he outside with the police in this mayhem? He rested her head against the sofa again and ran back to the window. There was blood everywhere and at least four bodies, birds already pecking at the carrion offered by the dead police officers. He peered out but could not see a trace of Frank and concluded that he would have not come here if he could possibly avoid it. Feeling relieved, he ran back to Jessie.

"I think Frank's OK," he affirmed breathlessly.

"Frank?" She seemed distant again and he wondered if she had relapsed and forgotten him after all, but then continued, her voice rising to a crescendo by the end of the sentence: "Frank? Is he there? No - tell me he's not there!"

"No, I don't think he is," Doug confirmed, relieved that she also seemed to have some comprehension about what was going on outside..

"Thank heavens for that." And then she was sobbing into his shirt as, quite unexpectedly, the noise outside stopped, just leaving Jessie's sobs to punctuate the sudden silence.

"What's that?" she suddenly exclaimed, becoming tense and alert.

"Nothing."

"That's what I mean. Do you think they're coming for us, now - as a sort of revenge?"

"I have to say I doubt it," he replied. "I think they want more of their new fix. Mind you, when I've provided it, perhaps they'll come for us then."

Before he had been killed, one of the police officers in the car had got a message back to headquarters describing what was happening to him. It became national news in an instant and Frank, still in the police station, heard an account from the desk sergeant, whose first words after telling him of the incident were: "Did you know that this might happen?"

Frank looked down then said, "I couldn't be sure. It's a tragedy, but perhaps the government will take things more seriously now. It happened at Shepherd Scar Research Centre so you must have realised the risks when you went to my home."

"Why should we have thought that your home would be as dangerous?"

"Because the animals are holding the man hostage there who can sort all this out."

He could tell from the look on the sergeant's face that he thought he was stark raving mad to have said this. Then he looked at his notes.

"You mean Sprake?" Frank nodded. "I thought you said that you didn't know where he was," he said flatly.

"I lied. I was trying to protect him. But now... I think now that it's all in the open more the government can't spin or deny anything and it's best to get him out so he can continue his research properly and in safety." He omitted to tell of Jessie's presence though, because although he was worried about her, he did not want them to know she was there as well. It might play into the government's hands too much. "Look, I'm sorry for the men you've lost but we have a huge and terrifying incident on our hands of national, no, global dimensions. The supremacy of humankind on this planet is in peril and we have to do something about it soon. I suggest that, rather than keep me here, you let me get back to my newspaper. After all, I do have some experience of all this myself." Then after a pause he added: "Even if most of it is second-hand. And I have contacts who can help sort this out as well; I think we should keep this in the public domain as much as possible, too, because the government doesn't like it. My newspaper can help that."

The sergeant looked at him and then told him to wait there as he left the room. A few moments later, he was back with the Superintendent.

"What do you think we should do, then?" the senior man asked.

"I need some privacy and to get back to my office. Then I need to speak to a contact."

"And who might that contact be?"

"I'm afraid I can't divulge that at this moment. But it's vital to what happens next." The two men looked at him. Then, with a sniff that implied he did not like the situation one little bit, the superintendent just got up and said, "OK. Hoppit. But we're watching you." Then he left. The sergeant cocked his head at the door as if to tell Frank to go but he did not want it to be heard on any recording, if, indeed, there was one.

When he got into the foyer, Frank asked if he could be run back in a panda car, as it could be dangerous for him.

"Not many left now," came the ominous reply, "but I'll see what we can do." A few moments later he was being driven back to the Hickley and District News. When he arrived, he went straight up to his office and was somewhat irked to find Enid sitting in his chair, despite the lateness of the hour. In fact, a number of people were still there, and all but Enid seemed pleased to see him back. 'Right, this is the moment,' he thought to himself, and closed the door on the rest of the office. Enid suddenly looked a little frightened.

"I wasn't expecting you back," she said meekly.

"So I see," Frank replied. "Now, Enid; what's going on? Why are you stitching me up like this? What's in all this for you, apart from the obvious with your husband?"

"I don't know what you mean," she said, her attitude changing from softness to aggression on an instant.

"Come on; you put me in an awkward position with the police, you seem to know everything that's going on whether I've told you or not; you tell the police about Sprake and God knows what else and you seem to be having a very close relationship with Sir Digby Crichton."

She stared at him. "Well, he is a relative," she said, after a slight hesitation.

"A relative?" Frank was incredulous.

"He's my father's younger brother." Frank could

feel the wind being taken out of his sails.

"Well why didn't you tell me?" he sputtered.

"None of your business," she said pointedly. "But he promised me a nice job - if I wanted it - at the Home Office. If I keep him abreast of things."

"I see. And how much have you 'kept him abreast of things', then?"

"Not as much as you think." This was said with feeling, and she almost spat it out. Then she seemed to soften a little and she continued, "Actually, although we're genetically close, I don't like him. Not at all. We couldn't be further apart as people. He's like my father; slippery. I think I'm on your side more than his. I don't think he's taking all this seriously enough and can't help feeling there's a reason. In fact, if he's anything like my father was, he's probably covering something up."

"It obviously runs in the family, then," Frank found himself saying, to his regret. She shot him a withering look. "At least I don't fall for any pretty face that comes into the room," she riposted curtly. So that was it, Frank thought. Jealousy: she was jealous of Jessie. Why? Enid was old enough to be his mother, almost.

"You've treated me differently since she came onto the scene," she replied when asked. "As your EA, I expect a close relationship. That has not been forthcoming. And you've kept me out of many of your decisions, as well as my not knowing where you are half the time or who I should be talking to, or telling what, or not. She knows everything, though. It's been very difficult."

"It hasn't been easy for me, either," Frank returned. "But, as I said to you before, it was 'she' who uncovered all this and got it into the open. We've almost been killed together, too - twice. That creates closeness. And without her the government would be denying everything; and this, probably the greatest potential disaster ever to have afflicted humankind, might have happened almost without our knowing about it until it was too late. Now we have a chance. And I think all this is more important than a petty jealousy about a girl I think I happen to be falling in love with."

There was a pause. Then she said, "Ah. Well, that's all right, then." With that, she got up and made for the door, then turned and said, "But I still think my husband would be a good editor."

"That's as maybe. But right now she's in danger at my house; as you know, there have been four more deaths - at my house - and I'm very concerned that Jessie might even be dead, too. And if Doug's dead... well, we probably all are. So let's see what we can do to find out what's going on and then help to come up with a solution to save us all."

Enid looked down. "Please let me help you, then," she said. "Trust me, please."

Frank paused, then let out a sigh and said, "OK. But I think you know everything now anyway."

Enid gave a strained smile. "Yes, probably. Look, I've just got to make a call, then I'll be back. You see, I know something about Sir Digby that you don't, and I think it might be important."

Chapter 21

Sir Digby Crichton was having a meeting with the Prime Minister at that very moment in 10, Downing Street. The latter was annoyed as he had had to cut his holiday short: pressure on him was growing, and it was all too much for his deputy. Basically, he just wanted to know what the hell was going on. Was it really Britain's fault that all these things were happening? And why had the carnage at the Shepherd Scar Research Centre not been hushed up? Wasn't the place remote enough and how had the news crews got in? And what was all this about four dead policemen at a house in Yorkshire? Sir Digby was trying to remain outwardly calm, but it was not easy when the world's media was hounding you twenty-four hours a day and you were trying to protect a Prime Minister who had done nothing to help in the first place and who was not interested in anything other than his good reputation or how he could benefit from the situation.

He took a deep breath and looked directly at the Prime Minister, despite his being flanked on the sofa by his press controller and the Home Secretary - his direct boss - as well as a large number of unelected 'advisers' who were standing around. This was going to be hard. However, he began.

"As you know, Prime Minister, the Shepherd Scar Research Centre has been a virtually clandestine operation for several years - "

"Which government sanctioned it?"

"One of ours." The disappointment was palpable: he would not be able to spin that one away, Sir Digby thought to himself, and continued: "We have been researching a number of top-secret projects there with the ideal of creating several compounds for the help of people with speech difficulties - stroke victims and that sort of thing."

"So why was it so secret, then?" the press aide fired off.

"Because it was being used in parallel by the military to produce, er, 'other things'.

"What sort of other things?"

"Nerve serums, character-changing drugs for, well, for example, to change a soldier's allegiance against his previous colleagues... er, speech enhancers to make him spill any confidences he had to us... that sort of thing."

"Why was the military involved in the first place?"

"Because we knew that we couldn't afford the research for the public good without help from other sources. And as the military could see advantages to them in our research we also wanted to keep it in-house, so to speak - in Britain. We had to defray costs, too, or the public accounts committee would have been all over us. With the military involved, we could keep everything secret - national security and all that. It was, as we would now say, a win-win situation."

"Why wasn't the private sector involved so that we could blame them and kick the shit out of them when it all went wrong?" asked a man at the back of the room, whom Sir Digby assumed to be there for the ideological rather than the practical point of view.

"Because it gave us a head start in new medical technology for the battlefield at a time when private firms were not being 'included' in a lot of government projects for ideological reasons." There was a pause, then he added, "I have to say, too, that, at the time all this type of thing started we were just coming out of the Cold War and *most* things of importance then were publicly-funded. Funds, of course, have been diminishing for years," he added pointedly.

"Should have been cut off years ago," said an overweight man to his right, whom he recognised as a junior treasury minister.

"It's - well, it *was* - a potential money-spinner," he riposted, "and we are still in competition with other state-funded drugs operations, notably France."

He knew this would silence the more extreme elements in the room, and then continued: "The cuts in funding haven't helped with our security, particularly at places like Shepherd Scar," he pronounced with more weight, "nor with precluding the reasons for the grave problems we now find ourselves facing." This he added with even more gravitas in order to stress the point, and looked around at the assembled bunch of governance. It was not an inspiring sight, he thought to himself.

"Do you really think it's our fault, then?" the

Prime Minister asked suddenly and indignantly but with a fear in his eyes.

"Yes, I do. I have been suggesting raised funds for security and environmental improvements for years. So, although it was freak incident - that whatever's got out of the lab, has - it could still have been avoided."

"That's not what you said on TV," said a young woman behind him in a smart suit. Digby smiled: "Just doing my job," he replied, without looking at her.

The rest of the meeting was taken up with what should be done next: they would have to swallow the fact that it had happened and, although they would try to limit the damage, they had to accept that it was 'at least a possibility' - which is how it was worded - that the Shepherd Scar Research Centre was to blame for some of the acute environmental problems which the world was now facing. Humility and regret was the tone to be set, tinged with an indignation masquerading as resolution.

Towards the end, when it had become more like a selection of focus groups all discussing minor points in order to give a broad government response which would abrogate any responsibility with the minimum of political damage, a note was handed to Sir Digby. It was something he would have to attend to immediately and it put him into a state of controlled panic. He asked to be excused a minute and left the room.

He went immediately to his office but eschewed the official car: the walk would do him good and he needed to clear his head. This was serious.

Enid was waiting for his call. It was strange how things came in bursts: one day, all was controlled; the next, everything seemed to be running away from him.

"What's happening?" he snapped, when he got through to her.

"I've had word from your sources that they're not happy," she replied. "What do you want me to tell them?"

"What are they not happy about?"

"That this is getting out of hand and sooner or later it'll all start to implode. The fallout, I need hardly add, would be devastating." There was a pause. He could sense the gravity but dared not discuss the detail over the phone.

"What are they worried about?"

"That your ability to deliver your product - whatever it is - is being compromised by your proximity to the government," she replied. "They don't think that you'll be able to fulfil your side of the deal."

"If I wasn't close to the government we'd never have got this far at all," he replied. He knew it was a truism, but he had to say it nonetheless. "Are they fretting about the exposure of Shepherd Scar?"

"That's about the nub of it, yes."

"Tell them I'll meet them. I can explain everything and that they have nothing to worry about." Enid knew he was trying to convince himself of this rather than the other party, but decided to say nothing. He continued: "Tell them I can get out to them in a day or two. Just organise it. But keep me posted."

"I shall." And the phone went dead. He walked to the window and looked out. It was one of those early October evenings when London was unsure whether it was enjoying a belated summer or getting ready for another austere winter. Above, the last swallows still circled over St. James's Park, emitting their high, falling cadences over the hum of the traffic before they migrated from the capital. Although it was dark, there was a balmy feel to the air, and the timelessness of this great city weighed upon him. He loved it: what a pity that he would soon have to migrate from it as well.

Enid walked back into Frank's office and sat down. He looked up, told her he was just finishing a piece and would be with her in a moment. She smiled and looked down at her crossed knees, as if they would give her focus to what she wanted to say. Then Frank had hit the 'save' button and it was on its way to composition for insertion into the next edition. "Well?" he enquired, stretching his arms above his head, "What is it you want to tell me about Crichton?"

Enid looked at him, then took a deep breath, exhaled as if unsure where to start, then took a breath again and started. "As I told you earlier, Sir Digby Crichton is my uncle - my father's brother. I never met him until I was sixteen when I went to see him in Egypt during the school holidays. He was in charge of a government diplomatic mission there, or something. Anyway, sadly, I found him to be just like my father, who I'd been keen to get away from. It was like getting out of the frying-pan and into the fire. They're both the same - distant, arrogant, hard, unscrupulous, but utterly charming when necessary. He took me around some factories in the area that was under his control and introduced me to loads of local businessmen, most of whom I've forgotten. One, though, stood out. His name was Abu Bhakraim and my uncle said he ran an import-export business. I never knew what, of course: at that age I wasn't really interested. All I know is that I didn't like him, or the fact that my uncle kept getting gifts and money from him, which struck me as odd in the diplomatic service. Then I came home and never saw him again."

Frank was wondering when she would come to the point, although, as a journalist, he was enjoying the story.

"I left home as soon as I could, met my husband, had kids... and never saw my dad again. When he died, I wasn't too bothered, and he left me quite a bit of money, although most of it went to a woman I'd never heard of, let alone met. My mother got nothing and died soon after. By that time, I was living up here. Then, one day a couple of years ago, I got a call from Digby, right out of the blue. He said that he knew I was in a difficult financial situation and would I like a better-paid job. I was astonished - I hadn't heard from him for years; I just saw him on TV every so often and knew that he was doing well as the Under-Secretary for Home Affairs. But I never wanted to get in touch with him."

"What about this call?" Frank probed, aware that there was more to do than listen to some ramblings from his assistant.

"I'm coming to that," she replied with a slight hint of annoyance. "As you know, my husband works here but we always needed more money, so when Digby said he could get me a job here - working as your assistant - I grasped it with both hands." Frank was suddenly more alert: perhaps something was about to be explained that had bothered him from the start. "What I didn't know was why he was so keen to have me here."

"Well?" Frank probed.

"I know you didn't want me - I suppose that's why I'm a bit grumpy sometimes. But your bosses - the proprietors - I now know were told to take me on by government insistence."

"The government in this case being your uncle, Sir Digby?" Frank asked.

"Exactly. But I didn't know that. Until recently. When it all began to come clear." She took a deep breath again, then continued. "I think that he has - or had - some clandestine business arrangements going on at the Shepherd Scar Research Centre. The fact that it's remote and virtually unknown was great because I think he was doing so-called government research for himself. Fouracres was nominally the head but Digby was in charge. And I think he's doing something for middle-eastern clients. Now that all this has blown up, I've got a good idea what it might be."

"Nerve serums, character-changing drugs - that sort of thing," Frank volunteered. She nodded. "So you think he's running his own lethal businesses under government auspices and cover?" She nodded again. "Jesus Christ."

"Mm. But when all this happened - the leaks and everything, the animal attacks - suddenly there was a huge interest in the place. But I think he thought it would blow over. Instead, of course, it's got worse."

"What alerted you to this - I mean, about Fouracres not really running the place?"

"His wife called me just after he was killed. She suspected it was Crichton's work instantly, in case he knew too much. Actually, I don't think he knew anything, very much."

"What? She thought that Crichton had him 'rubbed out'?" Enid nodded again. "No, on this occasion, you're wrong, Enid. Crichton did not kill Fouracres. We did."

"I knew it," she said with a twist of a smile.

"It was an accident," Frank confirmed hastily. "We were escaping from a violent animal attack and we hit his car."

"The one I saw?" It was Frank's turn to nod. "The one I talked to you about?" Frank nodded again. "I *thought* you were lying," she said, with a deadpan expression.

"I don't think either of us have been precisely in concert with the truth," Frank observed. "Anyway, is what I'm discerning from all this that your uncle Digby is doing illegal drugs business for middle-eastern groups?"

"I believe so."

"Terrorists?"

"Probably."

"Abu Bhakraim?"

"Almost certainly. I don't know what he does, but I'm sure it's not good. And I saw him up here once. He didn't recognise me but obviously he must know I'm working in this office."

"You still haven't explained why your uncle wanted you in this job."

"No... Well, I think it must be that, because I'm working with an editor at a newspaper which is the closest there is up here to Shepherd Scar, I'd pick up on any currents or titbits and pass them on to him if he enquired. A sort of early warning system."

"But different events started to happen for other reasons and by then it was too late," Frank concluded. Enid nodded. "And so now he's trying to keep us - the media, you - off his back as well as the government."

"That's it in a nutshell."

"And why have you told me all this?"

"Loads of reasons."

"Well?"

"He's been in touch with me a lot over the past couple of days. What with that and what you've been 'involved' with, I've suddenly started to put two and two together. And I've just put the phone down to him. I now seem to be a sort of middle-man. He's just asked me to organise a flight to Egypt for him. He gave me a number last week and told me to keep it secret. I think it's someone in Bhakraim's organisation, but I'm only allowed to know him as a contact - no names. And I'm certainly not supposed to have any idea what 'the product' which he keeps talking about is - although I think it must be something that was being cooked up at Shepherd Scar. Perhaps your colleague Doug knows something about it?"

Frank shrugged. "Perhaps. Although I suspect it was the other one - Mick. Or even someone else. There were quite a few working there before all this happened."

"Well," Enid continued, " he must be getting desperate because he's suddenly asking me to do all these things rather than his Parliamentary secretary. So it must be all getting too close to the government and his comfort."

"Phew," Frank reflected. "Anything else?"

Enid sighed again. He had never known her do this even once before, now she was doing it all the time. "When that girl came into the office - Jessie - I just sensed that she was going to be closer to you than I am. And so I knew that it was going to be difficult as your EA. Especially as I was foisted upon you and you're obviously now having a relationship with her."

"We're not yet, actually," Frank interjected, suspecting that there was a personal something she was about to add that he did not want to hear anyway. "And I don't even know if she's still alive."

"Why don't you call her?"

"My home phone's dead, her mobile's switched off so no-one knows where she is, and they've been surrounded by hostile representatives of the animal world."

"I hope she'll be OK," Enid said, "I really do. For your sake. And, even, hers. Now I must go and organise my dear uncle's trip." She got up and walked to the door. Frank then found himself feeling as if a huge load had been shifted from his shoulders and he said, "Thanks, Enid. I suddenly feel a lot better about you: this is going to work, now."

"I think so, too," she replied.

"So keep me informed about what's going on with him. It's great for our paper and we might even get a change of government out of it. Mind you, if we're all going to be taken over or annihilated by the animals - or even some middle-eastern plot - then it might not make much difference anyway."

Enid laughed, and left his office. For the first time, Frank realised that actually she must have been very pretty once. A nice smile, too. Then his phone rang. In an instant, he was ecstatic and relieved. It was Jessie.

"Thank God you're OK," he sighed down the phone, tears of relief coming involuntarily, suddenly and in volume. "Why didn't you put your phone on after an hour like I said?"

"I can hardly begin to tell you," she replied. "Look, Frank, I've got to save this battery because it's all I've got and your home phone doesn't work: the animals are all around us still but not attacking. We've got four dead police outside who were killed when they tried to get into the house -"

"Yes, I know - I was nearly with them."

"Well, you wouldn't be alive now if you had been,"

she said without expression. Then a wrenching feeling gripped her throat as the emotions and strain of the past hours began to affect her; "I wish I'd never started this now, Frank," she said as the saliva welled up, complementing the tears that were now cascading down her cheeks.

"Yes, you do," Frank interjected softly, but Jessie was now literally in full flood and she continued: "I think Doug has made some progress, but only because he tested it on me - God! - he'd gone a bit odd by taking another combination of stuff and didn't want to mix it up. Nearly killed me and I was out for a long time - it was awful - the pain... that's why I didn't call."

"Christ. It's so good to hear your voice."

"Yours, too."

"Is Doug all right, then?"

"I think so; I think he's recovered. Look, you've got to get us out of here. God knows how, but please think of a way: I'll have to go now but I'll put the phone on again in a couple of hours and say goodnight. I don't want my phone to be traced. Look after yourself, you lovely man."

"Not half as lovely as you are," he responded sweetly - only to be met by the buzz of the line going dead. He ran in to tell Enid the news but she was on the phone and put her finger up to her mouth to imply silence.

"Yes, uncle Digby... yes. OK...", she said pointedly.

"He's got to help us," whispered Frank to her, pointing at the phone as if Sir Digby was actually in the receiver. Enid gave an understanding look to him but continued talking to her uncle as she scribbled a note to Frank which read, 'Not a good moment. I'll call him again later when we've talked.' Frank nodded and went to the fridge for a beer.

Somehow, it had never tasted so good.

Chapter 22

Outside in the wild, the unintended consequences of the leaking poisons from the Shepherd Scar Research Centre were spreading in a sporadic and patchy fashion. Where there was an intensity of wildlife, the interaction between the species ensured a great deal of contamination and cross-infection, but where the human influences were greater - or there were vast open spaces between the affected concentrations of wildlife - the process was slower, yet no less profound.

In some places, too, the effects of the chemicals missed the natural world altogether: in others, it was swift, violent and unpleasant. In Scotland, for example, a salmon farm had been infected by spawn and faeces dropped by birds from an affected area far away: the resulting amphibians that were born had then been eaten by other birds and animals in its vicinity. Due to these hunted animals and insects being ingested - rife with traces of the serum - some salmon had leapt out of the loch cages in unison, several at a time, to knock a young fish-feeder into the water. Then he was not allowed to surface, being held down by an aquatic ceiling of swerving, aggressive salmon, their morphic field being re-attuned to their new sense of purpose until the young man had drowned. Then many had escaped, the lure of freedom passed to them by wild salmon outside the cages, jumping over the heightened nets into the open waters outside. There, they passed the condition further afield, which would happen even faster when the salmon had spawned upstream. This instance was the first where wildlife had taken a human life for sport, rather than revenge...

Globally, the threat was moving slowly but inexorably to the point where animals' shared natural instincts would enable quick and devastating reactions to any situation, whereas humankind's myriad of languages, once its greatest glory and advantage, would suddenly seem hopelessly inefficient and out-of-date...

Doug looked at Jessie, his sallow face earnestly trying to elicit an answer. They had moved downstairs to the middle of the house for the conversation so as to be as far from the roof - upon which hundreds of birds and rodents were assembled - as possible. She, for her part, was wrestling with the question, while at the same time trying to put out of her mind the fact that, despite his pallid colour, Doug looked healthier and thinner than before.

"OK," she said at length, "let's do it."

Doug stood up as she switched on her mobile phone and rang Frank. It was answered immediately. "Mm, I miss you too, but I'll have to be quick," she said to him, after his affections and concerns about her had been proclaimed. "Look, Doug needs to talk to you. I think we'll have to go, sort of, native, and use Sir Digby Crichton. Doug contacted him directly a few days ago but nothing seems to have happened, so now we'll have to be more forceful. I think it's the only way out of the situation. Here he is - he'll explain." She handed her mobile to him and let them discuss what they had decided.

What they had talked about was the fact that Doug reckoned he had possibly found an antidote to the serum but could not possibly either test it fully or make it in large enough quantities from where he was. And any attempt to escape would incur the obvious reaction. So if Frank could at last secure the help of Sir Digby, this would put them and the government - not to mention the whole of planet Earth - onside. Sir Digby would have to accept that Doug was innocent of all the things he was bound to be charged with - such as allowing the compounds to escape into the environment, the death of Mick, his own disappearance, the car salesman's death and much more - in the interests of the far greater threat to the survival of the human race. So, assuming this, the only way was to play along with Sir Digby and get the army involved, using fire, insecticide - whatever - to get them out and into a secure location where his research findings could be put into practice. Then, if successful, these could be manufactured across the world on a global, industrialised scale. They felt that the best way out was through the skylight using a helicopter, once all the natural resistance had been annihilated.

There was a pause while Frank took all this in, then he replied that he had had a similar plan himself, and would try to get Enid - whom he now knew had a hotline to Sir Digby - to put the same proposition to him. As it happened, he added, the army and police were drawing up a cordon already around his house to a radius of five miles, evacuating anyone who lived within it in anticipation of any other incident.

"Don't forget to kill everything before you try to get us out," Doug concluded, "because if the army bungles this then we're dead and so's the planet." He said he'd ring Frank back in an hour; then he hung up and switched off the phone.

Doug relayed all he had learned from Frank to Jessie.

"Enid knows Sir Digby?" Jessie asked in astonishment.

"Related."

"No wonder she hated me."

"Not any more. Hates her uncle, according to Frank. I think she was jealous of you, that's all."

"She's far too old to want to go out with Frank," Jessie snorted.

"It's only the body that ages, not the emotions," Doug admonished.

"Talking of that, you really do look younger than when I first saw you," she said.

"Really?"

"Mm. And your hair's fuller - and less grey, I'm sure. Have you been back on that stuff you mentioned before?"

"Sort of," Doug replied, going over to fetch one of the bottles that they had brought from Shepherd Scar. It had 'manganese tripuride' written on it. "As I said, I thought I probably took in some of this when I was researching with Mick. But I think too that it might also have been something to do with when those mice in the lab bit me. The missing link, so to speak, was what was in their saliva mixed with whatever we've unleashed into the environment. But I think I might have cracked it. Without boring you with the details, I think I've harnessed it to one of the other things we were researching. In short, it seems to destroy free radicals in the body without endangering tissue. And tells the brain to stop the ageing process by encouraging the re-growth of stem cells. I was getting quite close to perfecting it before... well, before all this happened." He put the bottle down with a thud. "I had aimed that it would make my fortune. Not much chance of that, now, unless we get out of here alive: I think saving the planet takes priority, somehow. Strange, though; I never thought *I'd* be the one in line to do that..."

"Or to help put it in the predicament it's in in the first place," Jessie corrected him with a wry smile.

"Yes. I think we'll skip over that one for the moment."

"So you might technically be getting younger, then?"

Doug gave an unsure 'so-so' look, adding the usual hand-movement to imply a fifty-fifty possibility. "If I start bawling, then change my nappy and give me some of that chromitic paradiosymine over there. I think that's what Mick was on. God, he looked old. Awful, too, in fact. So, not very much, please."

They smiled at each other in the gloom. Jessie suddenly shivered. They both wished there was some heat and light in the place. And more food.

"You can tell Frank hasn't got a woman in his life at the moment," she observed.

"Why's that?"

"Hardly any food in the fridge. Still, I'll go and see what I can find."

She went quietly downstairs. Outside, all seemed quiet, but this brooding silence was almost worse than the cacophony during the attack: it was impossible to anticipate anything because there was no point of audible reference. She realised that she was very frightened and felt very vulnerable. Another sniff under the door confirmed that they were still not alone and she quickly took out some cheese and salad from the now-warm fridge, and some stale bread from its bin. Then she went upstairs again. Half-way up, she heard a hushed voice and realised that Doug was using her phone again.

"You'll give me *how* much?" he was saying quietly but animatedly as she entered. "No, that's not enough. If I'm going to get you out of this then you're going to have to give me immunity - and a safe place to work with all the materials that I ask for. And a limitless budget for the research - and definitely more money for me."

She knew then that he was talking to Sir Digby Crichton.

Enid had not wanted to talk aside to Frank whilst she was on the phone with Sir Digby for fear of the latter thinking it was a conspiracy. Then she and Frank had talked about what she had concocted with her uncle: they discussed all the options and how best to help their own needs as well as keeping him on-side. Then, she called him back and briefed him that a call from Doug was imminent. Doug, who was supposed to wait until he had called Frank back, could wait no longer to call Sir Digby and had decided to go ahead anyway. Doug could tell immediately that Sir Digby was being cagey and hiding something: but the urgency of the situation precluded any peripheral discussion and he just weighed in with what was important. He brusquely told him to accede to his demands and send a signed PDF confirmation on government-headed notepaper to Frank and Enid: when he knew that had been done then he would expect to be airlifted out with Jessie sooner rather than later.

In his office, Sir Digby listened to all this with rising concern. He could authorise the money, the attack, the airlift and the research facilities: but it would be harder to keep Doug onside, especially with all the clandestine stuff he had been authorising secretly at Shepherd Scar without anyone's knowledge save Mick. It was a benefit to him that Mick was dead - that was one person he may not have to silence. But if any one of the others - particularly Frank or Jessie - got wind of what he was doing or where he was about to depart for and why, his subterfuge would be exposed and he would be in disgrace - and the government with him. He could take that; but not the collapse of the deal that he had been creating all these years. Nor was it easy for him to face the fact that although he would somehow have to play along with Doug for a while, he would either have to buy him off or eradicate him in due course. And Enid. In fact, it would be better for him if Jessie and Frank were silenced too, now he came to think of it...

All these thoughts had been going through his mind as he talked to Doug. He had no choice but to agree to his demands, though: of course, he could organise for all of them to have nasty accidents, but where would that leave his business proposition? Or the antidote, which he would definitely be in need of, too? He had no choice: realising this, he grumpily acceded to everything Doug demanded. He was reluctant - but he had to do it and hope that Doug kept his side of the bargain - silence. At least for the time being... Soon, this would, hopefully, make little difference.

Having agreed, he put the phone down with a bad grace and reflected for a moment. Then he drew a deep breath and picked it up again.

"Everything is go," he stated when the other party answered. "But wait a couple of hours." Putting the phone down again, he then hand-wrote a letter on his headed government notepaper and did what he had been asked. Then he signed it and emailed a signed PDF to Enid at the Hickley & District News. Having done that, he went to his computer and authorised all the things that he had already set up: finally, he went into the website of his private bank and transferred a large sum of money from his account to Doug's. He sighed after he had pressed 'Enter' and then took a large draught of whisky from his drinks cabinet as he waited for the phone to ring again.

When it did, it was, as he had expected, a call from Enid. "It's all authorised," he said simply. "And tell Doug Sprake that there's a quarter of a million now sitting in his account."

"I've received it," she replied. "Is Doug's money for research or to buy him?"

There was a pause. "A bit of both. But there'll be more: there'll have to be."

"I see." There was another pause, then: "Where are you going to take them so that Doug can finish his research?"

"The pilot knows where to go."

"So you're not going to tell me." There was yet another pause. "Uncle Digby; if you don't tell me I don't think I can keep the lid on this. Frank and Jessie have to know everything or they won't be able to write and say things to keep the heat off you. They're well-known now - people listen to what they say: you've got to let them in on this." This was met by a silence, so she added pointedly: "Unless, of course, there's more to all this than meets the eye."

Sir Digby squirmed in his seat and a sweat had broken on his brow. Testily, he just said, "No, there is not. Now, let's get this all sorted out, shall we? Just do your best to keep the media off me when they start asking questions. At least until I'm in you-know-where."

"All right. Just one last thing: when will you airlift them out?"

"Just tell them to be ready. Within twenty-four hours."

"All right." And they both put their phones down.

"He's definitely up to something," Enid said to Frank. "And I think it stinks."

Chapter 23

The gloom was like a suffocating blanket wrapping itself around them when Jessie's phone rang again, a little square of luminescent light in a black void. She could see the battery was very low now and inwardly cursed Doug for forgetting to switch it off. She hoped that it would last long enough: long enough for what, though, she was unsure. They were back in the loft now as, being at the top of the house, the chill lower down had not yet set in. Jessie handed her phone to Doug and Enid recounted all that had been agreed, confirming that the fax had been received with all the authorisations and that there was a first payment of a quarter million pounds in Doug's bank account. Doug asked Enid if she trusted Sir Digby.

"Not usually," she replied. "But if he hasn't done what you've asked I think he'll be in deeper trouble later on than he's already in now. Frank and I know everything. At least, I think we do."

"Do you think he's going to try and kill us, then, when the attack is made?" Doug asked quietly. This sent a chill down Jessie's spine: she had not thought of that.

"I don't think it's in his interests," Enid answered at length. "He's more likely to get an antidote out of you and then kill you - not before."

"Mm; that makes me feel a lot better," Doug returned.

"Do you want me to check your bank account? See if the money really is there?"

"Might be an idea," he said to Enid, and gave her his bank details. "I'll call you back in an hour. We need to save the battery." Then he put the phone off and handed it back to Jessie.

"Thank God for internet banking," he murmured. He then quietly told her the contents of his conversation with Enid. Then: "Oh, by the way - we can expect an attack, apparently, within twenty-four hours."

"Great," Jessie replied sarcastically. "So much for military precision."

Then they heard it: not the approach of helicopters or soldiers or vehicles but an instant raising of the level of the natural sounds outside - a scampering across the roof, a buzzing and flapping, sniffing and other assorted noises of a suddenly alerted natural world.

"Shit!" Doug blurted.

"What - what do you mean?"

He dragged her halfway down the stairs then leaned very close to her ear and whispered frantically right into it.

"There must have been birds, or mice or something, just a few feet away above my head. I keep forgetting that their instincts... feelings... are attuned to mine... Especially when they're only a few inches away."

"You mean... they know what's going to happen?"

Doug nodded. "Yeah. Well, not specifically: but they can sense danger."

Even in the now almost total blackness, Doug could see that Jessie's face had gone white with fear. Instantly, she grabbed her phone and switched it on. After it had taken what seemed like ages to log on and during which time the movements outside had increased fourfold, she rang Enid.

"The money's in the account," Enid answered immediately, but was then cut short by Jessie screaming in a hoarse whisper: "Tell them to attack now. Attack now or we're dead. Please, please, please..." As she tailed off, Enid cut her off and said, "OK, OK - but make sure every window's closed very tight. You'll see why." After she knew Jessie had comprehended that, she cut her off and instantly rang another number.

In fact, the soldiers were already close but had been ordered to stay silent in the dark; all lights had been extinguished and all humanity within a five-mile zone around Frank's house moved out, giving an added intensity to what already seemed like a primeval blackness. All farm animals and pets had been left behind under strict order. A cordon of soldiers was slowly closing in and, as any animals were encountered, they were immediately slaughtered by silenced pistols or cut throats - whichever despatched them more noiselessly and quickly - before they could run or make a sound. They were all left where they fell, different-sized humps of still-warm flesh resembling a rockscape in the noiseless night. The soldiers knew that some animals must have been infected and that the birds above were capable of alerting others of their movements but were hoping that the dark would mean most of the latter were sleeping wherever they had made a home. The battalion moved fast and silently across fields, through the emptied housing estates and village centres: they were all wearing respirators and all-enclosing NBC suits which would offer protection during the coming assault. The first wave were spraying the ground with a deadly, cyanide-based poison as they progressed across ditches, streams, fences and hedges. The only sound was of a subdued hissing and the 'plup, plup' of the silenced firearms. If the shooting failed, the poison would take over - but it was primarily for insects and rodents.

When the soldiers got to within four hundred yards of the house, they all stopped. Nothing was said - their GPS units told them exactly where they were - and nightsight goggles meant they could see without being seen. Their all-enclosing NBC suits made their human scent all but imperceptible. They lay motionless for a minute or two; then they began to hear the helicopters, coming from north, east, south and west, converging on the house, all encumbered with huge tanks hanging underneath and containing more of the lethal liquid. The brigadier, lying on the ground, looked at his luminescent watch, pressed a button on his transmitter and whispered, "Now!"

Immediately, an SAS Sabre squadron of over a hundred men rose up as one at intervals around the entire cordon and moved towards the house, swift, deadly and inexorable, their smoothed shapes and oversized masked heads resembling a scene akin to an alien invasion. Then the helicopters were overhead and dispensing their poison onto the heaving mass of animals below them, causing a chaos of alarm and fear as the deadly liquid dropped from the sky. Then the cordon of soldiers rose up and moved in too, fifty yards behind the SAS units and with their rifles raised. There was now no need for silence now, and nothing would get away...

Having heard the approaching helicopters, Jessie and Doug realised that the moment had come and moved quietly up to the attic again, covering their eyes, mouths and noses with any form of material they had been able to find: Enid had stipulated that they do this in the last frantic call, when she had also told them that the rescue was imminent and just to hold out a little longer. The movement above and below them had not - as they had expected - become greater; it was as if the animals were instead assessing the scale of the new threat on their growing influence and power rather than avenging their beleaguered captives.

Jessie covered her head and ears with her arms as the mechanical crescendo of noise intensified, while Doug looked heavenwards through the skylight, peeping out from behind an old curtain. As well as ensuring again that all windows were tightly shut, as instructed, they had taken the precaution of closing as many doors as possible: it was imperative that, although some smaller animals might get under them, the larger ones would not - at least for a while. Any delay would be useful, if not vital. As the helicopters suddenly converged above - there were eight of them - the animals now reacted more noisily again: the tumult was deafening. Then Jessie and Doug heard the sound of what sounded like a tropical rainstorm: but the accompanying pungent acidic smell told them that it was not rain that was drenching the roof and surroundings but a toxic liquid, which was then complemented by the thudding of birds falling out of the sky as it took effect. Below, they could hear yelps, squeals and baying as the soldiers moved through the sea of bodies, some dying, some dead; a few soldiers were bitten and butted before the liquid took effect, puncturing their suits and requiring them to retire immediately for treatment and isolation - although it would be luck whether they survived or not. It seemed to be taking ages, when, through the din of the slashing rotors, the attendant sound seemed to subside. Then the noise of soldiers shooting, breaking through doors and running up the stairs was heard; the attic door flew open as if discharged from a gun and three soldiers stood there, a sea of dead rodents, cats, dogs, foxes and others which had tried in vain to stop them ascending the attic stairs dying at their feet. One of the soldiers then turned and stood at the top of the stairs and just kept spraying liquid upwards, downwards and sideways as if this was his sole mission in life and that moment had just been realised. Meanwhile, the second soldier threw a respirator each to Jessie and Doug, and two bags, each of which contained NBC suits like theirs. Unable to talk normally, he gesticulated violently to put them on as fast as possible and helped them do so while the third soldier was then smashing through the skylight with a sharp hammer as the shards of glass and torrents of the stinking liquid fell about the room, a cascade of dead and dying rodents and birds falling in with it all onto the attic floor. Then a metal wire was coming through the open space with a closed hook on the end. A man was then swinging into the room in a harness, a spare one in his other hand, which he threw at Doug. He needed no prompting and had it on with a dexterity that surprised all of them. Then, clutching a travel bag he had found in Frank's bedroom, which contained his bottles and notes, he was being winched up, still pulling on his mask, as he dangled in the darkness, humanity's hope hanging by a thread...

The soldier looked apologetic that Jessie had not gone first and shrugged his shoulders as if to imply that chivalry had to take second place to expedience at this moment. In that instant, Jessie realised that she was more dispensable than Doug, which momentarily hurt her, but she also realised that it was the right decision: she was only a journalist, he possibly had the fate of the whole human race in that little bag. A moment or two later, though, and she, too, was being winched up into the night sky towards a clattering machine, her senses numbed by the tight suit and the mask she was wearing. Then she was inside the machine and hugging Doug as the helicopter swung away with another on each side, one above and another below. She did not realise the importance of this until after a few moments when a flock of all types of birds appeared from all around them out of the dark and flew straight at their helicopter, only to receive a barrage of small-arms fire and a monsoon of poison from the other aircraft. As they fell out the sky, she wondered how much longer this could go on...

The scene resembled a depiction of hell, but without the fire. But then, as if to complete the nightmare, she was suddenly aware of a huge flash of white light behind and below them and realised that Frank's house had been blown up: an area a hundred or so yards all around it was being torched. As a woman, her first thought was to feel so sorry for Frank: in so many ways she felt that this was so much to do with her. Yet the main reason sat next to her, dispassionately looking out over the events unfolding below. But she also knew that inside he, too, was desperately concerned that it had come to this. And frightened about the potential work he had to do and its possible consequences - both for the human world and the natural one.

As they swung away towards their unknown destination, they both knew that the future would be very dangerous. And completely unpredictable.

BOOK THREE

The Beginning Of The End

Chapter 24

The events that followed were to have even more of a profound effect on the planet. Occasionally, where there had been less concentrated levels of the compound, the animals in some cases showed a reluctance to join in: but with the herd instinct suddenly sharpened due to the severity of the attack on Frank's house, the animal world had become much more aggressive. The seeds had been sown for a huge confrontation - one that by definition would mean a messy and bloody outcome as nature exacted revenge on its hitherto dominant species; but like any infiltration, the enemy was in amongst the hosts.

The only difference was that, ecologically, life on Earth could thrive without humans, but not the other way around.

As the helicopter containing Doug and Jessie left, it had swung with the escort and continued with it for about half an hour. Then the others had left it alone, humankind's tiny crucible of hope in a vast and dark empty sky. The navigator had offered Doug and Jessie a mug of hot soup each, which they accepted gratefully. The pilot had turned to them after this and said, "I should try to get some sleep if you can - we're going quite a long way."

Jessie had nodded and, despite the noise, they both found themselves falling into a deep slumber; as she drifted away, though, she was aware of a sudden feeling of unease nagging at her conscience. Then tiredness swept over her and she was dead to the world...

Sir Digby Crichton sat back into the executive limousine that had greeted him and looked pensively at his surroundings as they sped silently by outside this hushed, air-conditioned luxury. He hoped that his plan had gone well and was keen to get back into contact with his colleagues, although, for security reasons, this would have to wait until he was back in the office. The sky seemed less bright than usual but this was probably more to do with the tinted windows than atmospheric conditions.

Soon, he was passing through the imposing security gates and gliding along a driveway between the beautifully-manicured lawns and plants that he knew so well, an oasis of beauty and calm in a vulgar, oppressive world. Then he was stepping out into the bright sunlight and up the marble steps into an opulent domed hallway, lit by the sunlight but dappled by a myriad of coloured stained-glass lenses. He was presented with a cooling drink - his favourite - and the servant then melted back into the sumptuous splendour of the surroundings. A peacock croaked in the distance and then all was quiet again. He sank back into an ornate chair, the comfort of which engulfed him. He smiled to himself and mused that this was the life he loved. And suddenly, it all seemed much closer than before, despite the awkwardness of the other situation. Then someone in a sharp suit was approaching him, his hand outstretched, and Sir Digby stood to greet him. They embraced and exchanged brief pleasantries, then the other said to him, “Come, we have much business to do,” and they both disappeared into a back office the size of a large English suburban garden, but which looked out over a vastly bigger and more immaculate one.

The doors closed, and silence descended once more over this bejewelled shrine to wealth and power.

The room Doug found himself in was small and enclosed, yet quite brightly-lit with fluorescent lights. There were no windows. Some gaudy pictures hung on the walls, depicting English hunting scenes. ‘How appropriate’, he thought. He wondered where he was, then started to think back on events as he remembered them. The last thing was drinking that soup... Then, nothing. But why, when the helicopter landed, had he still been asleep? And why was he already in this room without having woken up, and now lying on this bed? He felt for his pocket but then realised he was in his vest and pants, and his jacket and trousers were hanging behind the door: of the NBC suits or goggles there was no sign, although the bag he had grasped as he was winched to safety was beside the bed. He got up but was surprised to find that he felt a little unstable on his feet and was then aware of a dull headache. However, he managed to get to his jacket and was grateful to find the memory stick containing his latest research in his top pocket, where he had last put it before being winched to safety. The only thing that was missing was his watch. Perhaps it had been knocked off his wrist in the escape... The thought then dawned on him that he must start his research as soon as he could. After all, that was why he had been brought here. Wasn't it?

He went to the door and was almost surprised to find it was unlocked. He pulled it open and found himself looking into a vast room with benches, electronic equipment, computers and all manner of research equipment stretching out before him. The room was full of people, too, many in white lab coats, although the first thing he noticed was the diversity of races present and that, like his room, there were no windows. At that moment, he was aware that they had all stopped what they were doing and were looking towards him: they all smiled and applauded him, although he found some of them looking down at his trousers and then realised that we was not wearing any. Somewhat embarrassed, he withdrew into his room and re-emerged a few moments later fully clothed.

An attractive Asian girl approached him, wearing a white coat, and looking very much the researcher. "Hello, I'm Ishrani," she said, proffering a beautiful and slender nail-varnished hand. Doug's heart melted without even having said a word and he mumbled his name. "Oh, we all know <u>your</u> name," she affirmed with a giggle. "You're famous!"

"Erm, where's Jessie?" he ventured.

"Oh, she'll be along in a minute. She's just coming to."

Doug wondered at the point of this comment: had they been drugged? He thought as much, but felt he had to ask.

"Of course you were drugged," she replied jauntily. "If you'd fallen into the wrong hands we'd have had to despatch you and you'd rather not have known about that, would you?" Doug concurred. "And also, you cannot know yet where you are. Security."

She then led him to an office at the far end of the laboratory where a computer was whirring and he saw instantly that his research notes were already on the screen.

"We took the liberty of downloading what was on your memory stick when we brought you in," she remarked casually. Doug wanted to protest but her disarming smile and apparently sweet nature were compensation enough, and he resisted. "And now, you have a lot to do and not much time to do it," she added off-handedly. "Anything you want, just let us know. We're all here for you. I've arranged for you to address us all in ten minutes so that you can tell us all what stage you've reached in your research so that we can best apply our resources to what you need."

"I want Jessie here, first," Doug stated somewhat harshly.

"No problem," she replied sweetly, turning to leave; then she turned straight back to him, saying, "In fact, here she comes now."

Doug was delighted to see that it was true and Jessie was, indeed, coming purposefully towards him in the office.

Ishrani introduced herself to Jessie and then announced her departure. "See you in ten minutes," she said as the door closed behind her. Through the glass and the window that overlooked the area, he saw her slim figure disappearing half-way up the expanse of technology that was now his to use at whim, her dark, shiny hair dancing across her shoulders. But his reverie was cut short by Jessie.

"Doug - where the hell are we?"

"Erm, I don't know," he said feebly.

"Well, haven't you asked?"

"Well, no. She - Ishrani - said that they couldn't tell us yet. Security."

"Security - my arse," said Jessie unpoetically. "I enquired, too, and was told only that we were here until the job was done and that we couldn't leave. If that's co-operation, then we're being compromised."

"Compromised by whom?"

"The government, probably. Sir Digby? Some drugs

company? A foreign power? I don't know. But I want some answers - I'm a journalist, for God's sake. I never accept what's supposedly in front of me."

"OK, OK. Look, there's a phone there. Let's see if we can ring Enid. Or Frank."

"Good idea. What happens if we're abroad, though?"

"Abroad? Why should we be abroad?"

"We were drugged, Doug. Come on, wake up... I know you're in love with that girl already but that's probably all part of the plan." Doug gave a weak look of protest but she continued: "We were out for a long time - hours, possibly. If we're in Britain, then domestic numbers will work. If not, we'll have to make international calls, and that might not be possible from these phones. It was always impossible whenever I worked in government buildings."

Suddenly concerned, Doug went to his computer and sent an e-mail to Jessie. "Right, see if that gets to you while I ring Enid," he said, with a sudden return of purpose that surprised even Jessie. Go on - log on: that computer over there." Jessie did as she was told and Doug rang the Hickley & District News. It rang a long time. Just as his fears were mounting, it was answered by a gruff voice. He asked to be put through to Enid. "She's not here at the moment."

"Really? When will she be there?"

"When the office opens in the morning, I suppose," said the voice, sleepily.

"Oh. What time is it now?"

"Five-thirty in the morning."

"Right, thanks." Doug put the phone down. "It's five-thirty in the morning."

"I've got your e-mail," said Jessie, almost unhappily. Then she realised what he had said and, looking at the people outside the office, said quietly: "So if it's five-thirty in the morning, what are all these people doing here now if we're in Britain? If it's a government department, then bloody Health and Safety will go bananas. If not, then who have we ended up with?"

Doug took all this in. "Perhaps, due to the magnitude of the situation, they've given us a twenty-four hour operation?" He did not sound too sure of himself, but Jessie seemed a fraction more receptive to that.

"Mm. I'm going to ring Frank." She went to the phone and dialled his mobile number. She had to wait a few seconds, then heard a metallic voice saying, 'This call is being diverted.' Not expecting this, she was then relieved when it was answered: but it was not Frank. Surprised, she asked if she could speak to him. She then heard the receiver being plonked onto a table, but a few moments later Frank answered.

"Frank - it's me."

"Thank God for that. Whatever you do, don't tell me where you are."

She was surprised at his harsh tone. "Er, I wish I *knew* where I was," she said, "They haven't told us." She knew Frank well enough to know that he must mean her to stay quiet about detail, so, unsure what to ask next, she found herself asking him what the time was. But his answer only confused her further.

"It's half-past midnight."

She paused. "Then why did the security guy at the paper say that it was five-thirty in the morning?"

"Erm, I don't know. What I do know, though, is that the paper's been shut down. The government came in and sealed it off last night."

"Well, where are you, then? You can't be at home - it doesn't exist any more."

"I know that. No, I'm, er... I'm with a friend. I don't want to say where, though."

She wanted to say, "Why not, Frank? It's me, Jessie. Surely you can tell *me*," but kept quiet. He continued: "I think it's better I don't." The disappointment down the line was palpable. "Just trust me, Jessie. There's a very good reason, which I'll tell you when I see you - but not until."

In a state of unease, Jessie kept talking to him about anything she could think of rather than their respective situations. Frank was being very cagey, which was so unlike him. He was picking his words carefully, as if he did not want to be misinterpreted. All he did say was, "All I've heard is that there's a heightened level of security and anyone seeing animals congregating are to alert the authorities. And there's been some sort of a dam disaster in India, near Bangalore, I think: some elephants somehow managed to ram it over a period of a few days without anyone noticing and they caused a crack to appear. By the time the authorities were alerted, the dam was about to go. The elephants were drowned, of course, but it seems they did it with the intention of destroying it."

"Bloody hell. It's all beginning to happen, isn't it?"

Frank agreed. And something's happened in France, too, although details are sketchy: something to do with a nuclear reactor in Normandy, but I know no more. God, I hate not being at work with all my newsfeeds - I feel naked without them."

Jessie almost smiled, despite being miffed at his not telling her where he was and whom he was with.

"Oh, and with all that going on, I nearly forgot to tell you the hot news: Shepherd Scar has suffered the same fate as my house. Millions of animals killed..."

"The government?"

"Of course."

"And is it in the news?"

"Of course not."

'Security'?" she asked sarcastically.

"Huh! Of course."

"Well, I'm sorry for the animals in a way. Or I would have been once. But at least it's one eyesore less."

"Yes... but there were a lot of things there that could have indicted the government, so I suspect it was for that sort of security rather than the animal one."

"I bet, too."

With that, Jessie noticed that Ishrani had entered the room and was talking to Doug. "Must go," Jessie said. "Let's talk later."

"Better not." Jessie felt put down again. "Trust me, Jessie."

They rang off, and Jessie turned her attention to Ishrani, who faced her and said: "Ready for our briefing?" She nodded and she and Doug went out into the vast arena that was now Doug's domain, where all the people were waiting expectantly. But Jessie was far from happy and she was determined not to give anything more away than she had to; she would try to ensure Doug did the same, too.

As she looked around, all eyes were on Doug, and she felt more like a prisoner than a revered guest who might assist the course of humankind's history. A prisoner of whom, though, she was not yet sure.

Chapter 25

"So how's it going?" asked the man, in a thick accent. "A few problems, I hear."

"Not that can't be surmounted, Abu," Sir Digby replied. "After all, I have the man you want."

"And a situation I don't."

"That's almost par for the course at this level," Sir Digby replied, a trifle spikily. "After all, we do have the fate of the planet in our hands, so one must expect a little turbulence here and there. I think, considering the risks, it's gone remarkably smoothly. We've just reached the tricky part, that's all."

The man nodded in an acquiescent manner. "And the man - Sprake - is that his name?" Crichton nodded. "What are we doing about him?"

"Everything's under control. He's working for me and the British government - ostensibly - in a safe location in Scotland."

"And you're still working for me."

"Precisely. Nothing's changed."

"So you'll be wanting some more funds, then."

"That would certainly help. The research will cost millions."

"But it will be worth it for me and our... 'project'... sooner rather than later, then."

"Exactly so."

"Good."

There was a delay in the conversation as each pondered their own thoughts. Then Abu looked at him and said, "What happened to the other man who was working for you?"

"Deakin... Ah, he, er, died of his own research."

"I see. Pity."

Not wanting to elaborate, Sir Digby changed the subject by enquiring: "Might I ask how my house is doing?"

"Nearly completed. I'll take you along for a look this afternoon. There were a few problems with a licence for the pool, but that's been taken care of." Sir Digby raised his eyebrows. "No, no, we didn't kill him, if that's what you're asking. No, he just lost a relative, that's all." A cold smile crossed Abu's face as he said this.

"I wish we could do business your way in Britain," Sir Digby commented.

"You should soon be able to," came the reply.

The meeting was over, and Jessie was following Doug around as he took in what resources he had and assessed what further ones he would need. But whatever they were offered in terms of help and experience, research, materials, compounds and even funds, the one thing that nobody would answer was where, in fact, they were. They all just smiled and evaded the point. It was not just the ones whose English might not be perfect, either: it was everyone. And still the call to the Hickley & District News haunted her: why had someone told her it was five-thirty in the morning when, actually, it was not? Periodically, her reservations were sidelined as details for how the new serum Doug had devised in theoretical form in the attic were discussed: they would be able to produce a trial serum within three days if all went well. Then there was the problem of how to test it. All that was divulged to them was that it would be impossible to bring research animals into this secure and isolated establishment for fear that they might bring in an infected one - or that one might escape and the location would then be under threat from the wrath of the natural world. But, without any infected animals to test the antidote on, there could be no guarantee of success - all the research would remain theoretical, and that might be too late.

Doug went back into his office and started testing some theoretical equations on his computer. Jessie wanted to help but she got the impression that Doug was like a boy with a new box of toys: he was enjoying the responsibility of being in charge and having a huge team around him, with whom and what he could do as he liked. She would have to keep him on this side of reality, she thought. She found herself wanting to talk to Enid, too, which surprised her considering their initial stand-off, but felt that she was one of the few people she could now trust, if only she could get in touch with her. She had always contacted her at the newspaper office, of course, but that was closed; she remembered though that, on one occasion, Enid had rung her and the number was unfamiliar to her - was it her home number? She looked at her mobile phone and, turning her back to the rest of the research centre, scrolled down the calls list. She got to the bottom and was relieved to see that it was the last one - another call and it would drop off the end. She scribbled it down, just in case. There was enough charge in the phone for a short call, she felt, and although there were no numbers on any of the centre's phones that she could give to Enid - and no-one would tell them what these were anyway - she just wanted to talk to her. She might even tell them where they were.

She made an excuse to find the ladies' and went in. She ensured she was alone and called the number. It took a while to be answered, and then there were Enid's tones on the other end.

"Thank goodness you've called," said Enid. "The paper's been shut down."

"I know. Frank told me."

Enid obviously had not expected that information. "You've spoken to Frank?"

"Yes."

"Where is he?"

"He won't tell me."

"I don't like the sound of that."

"Nor me."

"If he won't tell you, it's probably because he's in a nasty situation and doesn't want to worry you."

"Which only worries me more," admitted Jessie.

"Typical of men to have that point of view," she declared. Jessie was surprised at this comment but it made her feel that perhaps she was human after all. "Are you at home, Enid?"

"Yes."

"So that's why you've no numbers there?"

"Precisely. I'd left them all at work as usual but was then instructed suddenly by a phone call not to go back in."

This sent a chill down Jessie's spine: no wonder Frank had sounded offhand. "The government's clamped down on all news stories in the area," she continued, "and even the BBC's been gagged. Newspapers are baying for stories but the government's saying it's a security issue. I know the animals have become more intelligent, but I don't think they can read newspapers yet. It all stinks - sounds as though they're trying to cover their own ineptitude, if you ask me."

"I'm with you there," Jessie agreed. Then she asked if Enid knew where they were.

"Haven't they told you?" she said, surprised. Jessie confirmed that they had not and seemed to have no intention of so doing.

"Mm. Well, I have to say that I don't know myself for sure, but I think you're in Scotland. But exactly where in Scotland, I don't know."

"Why Scotland?"

"A bit like the Shepherd Scar Research Centre: remote, and the new assembly willing to do the government's bidding without too many people knowing so the current government has more chance of staying in power. There are a lot of parliamentary seats in Scotland and it would've created a lot of jobs. All secret, of course..."

"'Would have created?' 'Secret'?"; Jessie parodied Enid's words with a clipped tone. Her subtle use of the conditional allied to anything to do with secrecy made Jessie even more convinced of subterfuge. "So if you think it's Scotland, Enid... then you must have an idea. Especially after what you've just said."

"Mm, yes... Well, OK... I'd hazard a guess that you're at a new research centre in Rosyth. But it's conjecture... I just saw something a few months ago I shouldn't have done when I got a brief visit at home from my uncle... it's been built underground, so it would seem to be perfect. But I may be wrong."

"No, I think you're right: there are no windows anywhere and it all seems brand new."

"Then that must be where you are. But it wasn't me that told you."

Chapter 26

Frank had put the phone down to Jessie with an air of unease: this was hardly surprising, considering his own situation. He was essentially under house arrest - but in the home of a civil servant in Leeds. He had not wanted to say too much as even an innocent comment might endanger both of them. Yet, being both female and a journalist, he knew her imagination would be running riot and her thoughts would be that he was having an affair, or something equally imprecise.

Following the sudden closure of his paper, he had been escorted out under police guard and with what he presumed to be soldiers standing around in masks and rubber suits, spray guns in their hands and tanks of liquid on their backs. Any animals were dispatched immediately either by this means or the rifle or handgun they also had on their person around the environs of Hickley. He felt the hand of Sir Digby Crichton in all this, and yet he felt that it went deeper than that. Why were they trying to silence news which might help people? Or was it solely to avert a wider sense of panic? As usual, the government was in chaos, with different ministers saying different things with varying emphases, which only made the situation more frenetic. The prime minister - as often happened when crises occurred - had decided to leave Britain, ostensibly to see what was happening abroad: but Frank - as well as most of the country - knew that this was not the real reason.

Since his conversation with Jessie, he had had more news about Normandy, although he knew it was selective: they would only tell him the barest minimum. What had happened there, though, concerned him. After the annihilation of his house and the Shepherd Scar Research Centre, the animals had regrouped from further afield: their instinctive sense of a common cause had been sharpened by these events and birds and marine life that migrated or could travel had amassed over northern France and around the beaches, spreading the resentment. In fact, it was beginning to look as if the animals' general feeling was starting to become an instinctive reaction passed between the species, whether or not they had ever ingested the original poison at all.

The French government had decided just to observe at first; then the attack had happened. In the dawn, literally thousands of animals had appeared all around the Flamanville nuclear reactor. The cordon of creatures around the perimeter fences was over a hundred yards deep, and workers could neither get in nor out. Those that tried were swamped and trampled, bitten, butted and suffocated to death. At first, the heavier animals with boney heads such as sheep and cattle had rammed the wire fences: then the inner electrified fences were breached as wave upon wave just destroyed themselves until the holes were big enough for others to pour through. Then it was the turn of the smaller creatures to get in through the masses of piping, entering the heart of the twin-domed building, the turbine rooms and then, of course the reactor itself. By the time the army was alerted, it was too late, but some helicopters that arrived had the same fate meted out to them as in England as waves of birds flew at them and sent them crashing into the surrounding farmland and one into the reactor itself. The human element inside the buildings was swept away as the creatures surged through the control rooms, biting, scratching and engulfing whatever futile resistance there was. Then they were gnawing through the pipe casings and electrical cables, sacrificing themselves once more for the cause of this revolution of the species. Within half an hour, the entire reactor - with no controls working - started to overheat and, in a huge surge of boiling steam and gas which caused temperatures of thousands of degrees, the fission rods melted and the reactor's core collapsed, sending radiation into the atmosphere in a huge cloud of dust and debris, which settled on everything and was blown for miles in every direction on the wind.

Frank was concerned, too, about what Jessie had said about the time when she had rung his paper: how could the security guard's watch be out by five hours? It paled before the other global events but it troubled him none the less.

Sir Digby Crichton had seemed happy with his

new house and was now on his way with Abu Bhakraim into central Cairo for another set of meetings. Soon, all this sunshine, wealth and opulence would be *his* life, he mused, as they sped through the squalor of the outer city. He had changed into Arabian attire to blend in with the local people as, at the last election, the Egyptian Fraternity had won on a ticket of aggression against Israel and the West. In some ways this had made Sir Digby's mission easier - as long as he was seen in the company of Arabian people. All the diplomatic channels between Cairo and London had remained open, if curtailed, but he had managed to keep all his contacts available, even if they had been under surveillance. He was not the Under-Secretary for Home Affairs for nothing: and the new regime would ensure now that no pictures of him got back to London.

They eventually reached a tower-block with a minaret-styled cupola on the top and a sign in Arabic which translated as 'Fraternity Corporation'. Inside, he was greeted as a fellow revolutionary, the only difference being that many were dressed in sharp western suits. This was the front for Abu Bhakraim's campaign. It was outwardly a non-violent organisation, but this was not so: however, Sir Digby's covert involvement was useful to it in that it diverted suspicion away, not just because he was part of the British government but also because his dark research was clandestine also. And his participation in any future events, as well as recent ones, could easily be dismissed if he was ever found out, as all violence could now be blamed onto a supposed quirk of nature.

They ascended to the top floor, where a huge room under the cupola gave a view of the city. Abu opened the meeting.

"My friends, we have amongst us today someone who some of you know who is helping us with our mission to destroy the great Satan and its allies. We are close to crippling the west - not just through the usual means but now with the help of the natural world as well, *insh-allah*." There was a spontaneous round of applause and then Abu continued. "Sir Digby Crichton may be at the heart of the British government, yet thanks to their lax laws and feeble security, Sir Digby has managed to help us to defeat his own - a true revolutionary." More applause. "As you know, we have been making and selling all manner of drugs and arms to create an unstable situation in European and American cities - and making a great deal of money in the process. The West is more concerned with sex and pleasure than praying and for that they will be annihilated. Thanks to Sir Digby and the ineptitude of the British government, we have developed serums - under their noses - for a number of things. Truth drugs, mind-state changers and more. But the jewel in the crown - to borrow an imperial Britannic phrase - was the one that would control the natural world."

Inside, Abu Bhakraim knew that this had not been intended, but it gave a holy imprimatur to the event and played well to his audience. It also made him look more important. He continued: "However, it unexpectedly leaked out into the environment at the Shepherd Scar Research Centre in England before it was completely developed, and in a form where many of its attributes were still unclear. Since then, though, our brothers have been working on it: Sir Digby has, in his employment, a man who is at this very moment perfecting the serum that will help us annihilate the West - although he does not know it." Mocking laughter filled the room. "That man is also - along with many hand-picked people of ours in the same establishment - working on an antidote, so that our children will be spared." More applause. "Like many in the West, he has been tempted by money. Our money." He smiled and shot a look at Sir Digby, who smiled back. "Our money... Our money will bribe them into oblivion. But Sir Digby is our friend, so he will be spared any retribution, especially as he has made our final goal possible. That is why he is coming to join us in Egypt." More applause filled the room. "He has already agreed to take our faith." The applause welled again. "He is a true believer."

At the research centre, it had been established that Ishrani was in charge, even though her youthful appearance would seem to have precluded it. Jessie had watched her and Doug flirting but was still of the opinion that she was doing it to inspire him to create the antidote faster. And yet it seemed strange that she was just as keen to know the chemical make-up of the original serum as well. Of course they had to know its constituents to make the antidote, but it appeared to be of more importance to them than the cure. Surely, the original disaster was history, Jessie thought: whatever had seeped over the pool's edge at Shepherd Scar was irrelevant and the most important thing now was to develop an antidote. She was unsettled, too, by the number of researchers there who were not of obvious British descent. She was no racist but it seemed strange, even in a diverse culture, that every single one of the employees here seemed foreign. How had they got their jobs to the apparent exclusion of indigenous British nationals, especially at a government establishment in Scotland, if Enid was to be believed? Perhaps she was just out of touch... but she did not think so. As a determined journalist, she could sniff a story from anywhere. Still somewhat vexed, she decided to leave it; but she was beginning to think thoughts that she did not wish to...

Putting these aside for the moment, she realised that there seemed to be no restriction on phone calls or e-mails, perhaps because no-one was allowed out of the building at all. In fact, all the staff were boarding there and were apparently to be interned until the serum had been created, manufactured and successfully applied. That meant a long time underground and no chance of escape: she was already missing fresh air and daylight. She was sure that her e-mails would be monitored, but as long as she was careful she felt that nothing was that contentious - yet.

Doug was in a different part of the centre so she went back to the office and sent an e-mail to him, to see if it would get through to him. Then, on a hunch, she copied it to Frank and Sir Digby Crichton. It read: 'Testing. Hope you're well. Research going fine. Should be able to save the planet soon. Just cannot ascertain the final ingredient. Or should that read 'Final Solution'?' She sent it off and a moment later heard it arrive on Doug's computer.

She would be astonished at the responses she received.

Sir Digby was leaving his hosts, who were full of praise for his commitment to help their cause. Inside, he was pleased that he had managed to assuage their scepticism on the train of unexpected events, which had surprised all and certainly affected timescales: but it still troubled him that his researcher had not yet found precisely what it was that caused the animals to react in this way. He was less concerned with the antidote which, as far as he was concerned, was only there to protect himself and his paymasters some time in the future: his prime plan was to ensure that the natural world's revolution against *homo sapiens* was completed in Europe, America, Israel and Australia. Despite the fast and unexpected escalation of events, he felt that by the time that this had completely come to pass, Doug - or the people who replaced him - would be well on the way to creating a counterpoison to ensure their own survival. When they could categorically find the compound that was changing the animal instincts of several millennia, then Doug would be erased. Until then, he hoped that his instructions - that Doug and Jessie were not to be told where they were but could have all other communications lest they felt compromised - had been carried out. They must not smell a rat, he thought, especially that Jessie. What a pity that such an attractive girl was so clever: brains and beauty were a lethal mix and she would have to go, too. Sad. But he smiled as he thought once more how all this was being paid for by the British taxpayer, yet it was him who was making the money.

As he emerged into the sunlight, he took a full deep breath of the dry air. England and the pressures of governance seemed a long way away. He had still to explain his sudden disappearance from the government's inner sanctum, but he had explained away his poor attendance record before. After all, he was helping his country, wasn't he? He could easily claim that all the best research - thanks to government cuts and over-taxation that he himself had assisted to inflict - was away from Britain's shores and that all he was doing was to observe developments for the sake of his people.

As he sped away to the airport, he mused that this would probably be his last trip back to England. Then he would be here for the rest of his life. Any twinges of sadness or guilt were engulfed by the thought of his new, rich and palatial life here in the sunshine. He would close his mind to Britain soon. After all, it would soon cease to exist in any previously recognisable sense...

Arriving at the airport, he was fast-tracked onto an

executive jet. Once inside, he changed back into Western attire. The final journey to his homeland had begun...

The news was grim: on her computer, Jessie was reading the events happening in the world off a news website. She could tell by the paucity of detail that it had been heavily censored by the government, but it was sober reading anyway. The latest was that the annual pilot whale slaughter in the Faeroe Islands had suddenly become a slaughter in reverse: the pilot whales had turned on their assailants by upturning their boats and then submerging them with their weight, so killing many people. And when the islanders started to retaliate by shooting them from the beach, flocks of birds had swooped on them and injured many, blinding some.

In Australia, too, the first outbreak of revenge had happened: some young Australians, out on a 'roo-bopping expedition in the outback, had had their lives terminated when a mob of kangaroos fought back. And in Jilin province in northern China, bears caged for their gall bladder bile had managed to break out and had killed their terrified keepers.

Jessie reflected that there were probably many more similar incidents happening around the world that in normal times would have been regarded as news of global importance but which, in the current situation, went unreported. These were not normal times...

As she read this, her computer pinged and she saw

she had mail: she closed the news and looked at the responses she had received. The first was from Sir Digby Crichton's office. It was an automatic response, and merely said that he was currently out of the office and would reply when he returned. What she noticed, though, was that the time was five hours ahead of where they were - exactly the same time difference that had occurred when she rang the Hickley and District News. She looked at her web browser to ascertain what time zones were that far ahead, and found that it took in large parts of the middle east. 'Inconclusive,' she thought, 'but useful'. Were calls to the Hickley & District News being diverted there? Why? Intrigued again, she nonetheless returned to her inbox and found that the second e-mail arrested her even more. It was not sent from anyone she knew: but what it said was more than interesting. 'Receiving you loud and clear. Try this link.'

She clicked on the contained link and found herself staring at the notes again which she had found by herself a few weeks ago before all this blew up. And yet she could see that there were changes and further annotations... She scrolled to the end and saw a very positive message: 'Doug, try armephanol 5 grams per thousand. It should inhibit the chromitic paradiosymine and cause a chain reaction with the resulting compound, trichromitic phanolimine. If you follow its natural progression you should find it'll help. Unless you've gone down a different route. Whatever you do, though, keep this to yourselves.'

Jessie ran over to Doug's computer to check his

mail; but there was nothing there, only the one she had sent to him earlier. She went straight back and printed off the notes, copied them onto a memory stick, then made sure she had the e-mail address as well. Then she deleted all trace of it from her computer. She wanted no-one else to see it - unless they had done so already, of course. Then she went to find Doug.

She found him deep in discussion with several researchers who were hunched over phials, notes, cultures and pipettes. She strode right up to them and touched Doug's shoulder. When he turned, she could see he was slightly annoyed through his ever younger-looking features.

"Doug, I need to see you in the office."

"I'm busy."

"This is important," she persisted.

"Well, so's this. Can't it -"

"No."

Annoyed, Doug made his excuses and told them to carry on as he left with Jessie for his office. "This had better be good," he said gruffly. Jessie did not get angry because she knew what he was thinking, but was sure he would be grateful.

"Well, what?" he barked as the door closed behind them.

"Take a look at this." She put the memory stick into the computer and showed him the file. "I've just received this in an e-mail; but you didn't," she explained.

Doug started. "But these are Mick's notes - I've seen them before."

"Keep reading. Amendments and suggestions have been made."

Doug sat down and started looking at them, fiddling with the keys and scrolling. "You're right," he said at length.

"Look at the end," she suggested. He did so.

"Hell's teeth... where did these come from?"

"I'm not altogether sure. But I have an e-mail address."

"But who...? I mean, Mick's dead. Who knows what he was up to more than I did?"

"I sent an e-mail to Sir Digby."

"You what?"

"I got an automated reply from him. Then that."

"You think someone's intercepting his mail?"

She shrugged. Then: "I think we should keep this to ourselves."

"Well, I'll share it with the team, and then -"

"No. Doug, I think we may not be working for whom we think we are. Let's try and keep this as close to us as possible."

"But I've got a whole research team out there."

"I know. But I don't think that they're all working on the same agenda." Doug looked shocked, as if all his new toys had been taken away. "You remember what Enid said about Sir Digby? Well, I've spoken to her. She thinks that we're in Scotland - possibly Rosyth. But I think some of these people might be working directly for him, not us."

"But he works for the British government."

"And, perhaps, another government... movement,

faction. I don't know what, but - "

"But he's supplied all this - and the money to save us from our animal enemies."

"I know, I know. That's how it seems. Except to me. Look, you've trusted my hunches before. Now trust me for a little longer. Please. Just do what the new notes say but keep it from the others for a bit."

"That's going to be impossible."

"The impossible takes time: so treat it like creating a miracle - it'll just take that bit longer."

"Time is the one thing we don't have much of."

Jessie just looked at him intently. He looked down, then back at her: she could tell that she had got through by his expression. "OK," he sighed eventually. "I'll do my best." He stood up, then added, "You'd better hide those, then."

Jessie closed the file and pulled the memory stick from the computer, hiding it in her brassiere. She then added another thought that had crossed her mind and said to Doug, "I think, too, that calls to the Hickley & District News are being diverted to the middle east."

Doug looked astonished. "Why?"

"It's got a five-hour time difference and I think that's where all this is being masterminded from. Despite obvious appearances."

Doug left the office and rejoined his assistants. His step was less positive than before.

Since the appropriation of the Hickley & District News, Enid's time at home had been spent setting up as much equipment as she could in her living-room. Going out was becoming dangerous, as nobody knew which, if any, animals would attack. Government guidelines were that no animal should be approached and none intimidated, out of fear of possible retribution; yet attacks were becoming more regular, especially if a large number of congregating animals had been sighted and then destroyed. In fact, only that morning, a quartet of soldiers had been attacked after they had decimated a herd of deer in a forest nearby. They had killed some does, which a pair of bucks had taken exception to.

Enid's husband was on his hands and knees and getting in her way as he tried to set up an internet connection. She was frustrated with his progress and had not been able to e-mail her uncle, Sir Digby. So instead, she rang his office, the number of which was firmly and fortunately imprinted on her brain. She knew where he was, of course: she had arranged it. But she did not know when he was coming back, if at all. His behaviour was becoming truly odd, in her view. His assistant, Sandra, answered the phone.

"No, I haven't seen him for a couple of days. Nobody knows where he is, although you can be assured that it is government business."

"Yes, I'm sure," Enid responded: that was the formal excuse. "So you don't know when he'll be back."

"No."

"Can you ask him to call his niece at home when he returns?" The assistant assented and Enid gave her details. 'Some chance,' she thought, as they rang off.

The fact that he was away was both a blessing and a hindrance: his absence meant that she could probably circumvent officialdom without the knowledge of her uncle and find things out - possibly even help Jessie and Doug. That they were in Rosyth she was now sure and, for the purposes of her research, she would have to presume that.

A few minutes later, her husband informed her that a dial-up connection was now ready - not perfect but better than nothing - and he had set up an e-mail address, which he gave to her. Her first response was to ring Jessie's mobile and tell her what this was.

Jessie was glad to hear from her. She had managed to find someone with a phone charger that fitted her phone and it was now charged. She explained what had happened and the notes she had received again. At this, she was surprised when Enid just told her sharply to say no more. "We don't know who's listening in," she said conspiratorially. "But send me an e-mail - anything that's not contentious."

"You can tell me what the weather's like outside," Jessie commented. They rang off and she sent Enid an e-mail. She just wrote: 'Testing. Message received' and also sent it to Sir Digby again and Frank. Something Enid said had given her an idea.

A few minutes later, she received a reply. But it was not from any of the people she had sent it to: it was from the unknown address which had supplied the updated notes. This is what she had wondered:

who was forwarding stuff to this person, whoever they were? So she responded: 'Good. Glad that I could help.' But she sent it only to Sir Digby. A few moments later, the reply came through - but, again, not from Sir Digby. It just said, 'OK, you've found that I've hacked into Sir Digby's e-mail address. But send the next reply to me direct.'

She did so. 'Who are you?'

The reply came back: 'I know where you are and who you're working with. But I cannot tell you who I am, except to say that I'm on your side. Let me know how Doug's getting on and of any development as soon as possible.'

She replied that she would, but still felt uneasy: she had to know who he was before she sent Doug's research results. After all, what if it was Sir Digby after all? She had only sent bland notes to him in the hope that she could find things out. But this was all very unexpected...

As she wrestled with this, Doug came back into the room, slightly excited. "I think I've cracked it," he said, still trying to stifle his exuberance lest the others some way behind him at their benches noticed. "Thanks to that e-mail. It's all academic, so I need you to run the computer model past whoever this happens to be. Tell them that it should work but I need confirmation. Just say: try it with an added milligram per thousand of ..." He tailed off, then went to her computer and typed it in. "Send that," he said. She read it: 'Try it with an added milligram per thousand of anthicin: this should inhibit the trichromitic phanolimine, resulting in reduced volatility. In principle, we've cracked it. If you can test it, then I don't need to.'

"What if it's really Sir Digby and we're stooges?" Jessie asked flatly after a brief discussion.

"It's a risk we'll have to take."

She looked at him for confirmation. "Well, it's not quite finalised," he added.

With that, she pasted it into an e-mail and sent it direct to the single address.

The response took ages to come back: three hours. In that time, Doug had left his research so many times to return to his office that he felt his colleagues might suspect something. "I've sent them on a wild goose chase," he confirmed under his breath the fifth time he returned. "Still no news?" Jessie shook her head.

"I've got to have a break soon: I can't go on like this. Having no windows makes you unaware of what the time is, but we've been going for hours."

"Take a 'break' when we hear back," she suggested.

"Good idea." With that, he turned and went back to his pretty new colleague and her less attractive helpers.

As soon as he left, of course, she received an e-mail from the unknown person. She opened it and read the contents with fervour. All it said, though, was: 'Congratulations! You've done it! I'm still at the academic stage, too, but in principle it must work. So how will you test it? And get it made? Let's talk - I'm closer than you think.'

Jessie was confused: if this person was that close, were they in the building? If they were going to talk, he or she would have to be. Was it Ishrani? While she waited to surreptitiously attract Doug's attention, she e-mailed back: 'Don't know where we are and cannot get out anyway. Virtually under house arrest. Don't even really know what the time is. You'll have to come to us.'

The reply surprised her. It read: 'I can meet Doug - and only Doug - in two hours' time. You keep everyone off his scent. Tell him to go to the Boulevard. It's an in-house shopping mall where you are, but they probably haven't told you about it yet - they don't want you to stop work on the project. Go to a shop called Insight which sells things people can personalise their dungeons with while they work long contracts there! Ask for John and he'll take you to me. Make sure no-one follows you or we'll all be dead.'

A few minutes later, Doug was reading it. "This is bizarre," he commented in an exasperated way. "We're in here, and yet this person seems to be as well... yet why aren't they on the project? And if they are, then why are they asking if we can get the product made? It makes no sense." The answers would have to wait. And suddenly, two hours seemed a long time ahead.

After Enid put the phone down to Jessie, she pondered her next move for a moment. So uncle Digby was out of the country but had not told anyone where he was. She felt that, because she had a good idea of at least his general location, it might be worth stirring things up a bit. So she decided to send a letter by e-mail to all the major newspapers who, although they were being gagged by the government, were keen for any news from the public; they especially, too, wanted to publish letters - real, or fabricated - that they felt would circumnavigate the new draconian laws on freedom of speech. Her note was short and concise and read:

'Sir,

We live in dangerous times. With the prime minister out of the country, would it not at least be desirable that our Home Affairs ministers were here directing responses against our insurgency? I refer, in this, to the fact that one of them is currently out of the country on non-government business in a middle-eastern country which has recently espoused aggression to the West subsequent to its recent elections. I have grounds to believe that the two may be acting in concert. Surely, at this unsure time, we should be having open discussion.

Yours sincerely, Enid Courtfield., the Hickley & District News. (Closed down by government edict).'

Within the hour, she had had five responses, all wanting to know who she was and why she felt that there was a huge story here. She weighed her options, then decided to go through one paper only - at least for the time being. Her price for exposing her uncle's probable involvement was not money but to ensure that the editor in question would do all he could to lean on the government to get Frank out of house arrest; thus, he would be able to contribute his first-hand experience for the benefit of humanity.

A few minutes later, she was on the phone to the editor. She told him everything she knew about her uncle, including where she felt he was now and what she was sure he was doing there. The other part of the story - concerning Doug and Jessie - she kept quiet for now. She wanted to see what a hornet's nest she would stir up with these revelations first...

At the appointed hour, Doug made his excuses and said he was going for a walk. Some of the others had already gone for a break so not many eyebrows were raised. After all, he was human, like them. He had asked Jessie to go and find the Boulevard and tell him where it was, something which had not been easily ascertained as no-one seemed to want to tell her. Eventually, though, a cleaning-lady directed her. What had surprised her was the size of the place, which only became apparent after leaving the research centre area. It had been built, the cleaning-lady said, behind the naval base in a hole in the ground that had once been a vast quarry. Now roofed in and grassed over, it had been billed as a top secret military enclave so that it was impregnable, bomb-proof and secure. Jessie also learned that there was only one entrance, so that it would be virtually impossible for security to be breached.

Once Jessie had found the shop, she retraced her

steps and then drew the route out for Doug so that he would not be too conspicuous asking all and sundry for directions.

So now Doug found himself in the Boulevard and was looking for the shop called Insight. He found it quickly and slipped inside, looking as if he was interested in buying something he had seen in the window. Actually, the stock was ghastly. An anaemic man with thinning hair and dandruff and wearing a polyester suit which matched the merchandise confronted him.

"Are you John?" Doug asked.

The man looked slightly surprised, then, without saying anything, led him to the side of the shop. He pulled aside a display for drab materials to reveal a door. The man intimated that he should go in and moved away. Doug took a deep breath and went in as the display fell back into place behind him.

He was in a small room lit by a solitary uncovered bulb. On the walls were racks of materials and unopened packages; these were full of fabrics with exotic names that contrasted violently with the dour surroundings. Boxes of varying sizes were everywhere. He closed the door: a fibrous, dusty smell assailed his nostrils which immediately made him feel thirsty. His eyes were still adjusting to the gloominess at the far end of the long, narrow room when a voice addressed him from behind.

"You haven't changed a bit. Except you look younger."

He recognised the voice immediately, but it was at

odds with his expectations: he spun round, his eyes peering into the dullness, and in an instant he felt slightly queasy.

"Well, say something," said the voice, with a chuckle.

Doug still stood there, astonished, rooted to the spot. "Mick?" he eventually emitted, hoarsely. "I thought you were ..."

"Dead," rejoined Mick, approaching him into the sparse light and holding out a hand. "But as you can see, I'm not." He was obviously relishing this moment of utter disbelief on the face of his former colleague.

"But I saw your body... your car... I - I saw your briefcase." Then, indignantly: "How come you look so well now?"

"This and that. And drugs."

"What sort of drugs?"

"Ones I was creating. That's why I had to kill myself. Or they'd never have got off my back. Because it was all bound up with secret research - and bloody Sir Digby Crichton's own agenda, which I'd been forced into helping him with."

Doug sat heavily back into a chair which fortunately happened to be there, as he had not looked first. He wanted to know about all this but the question he really wanted to ask just had to be answered.

"But the body - it was you. I was up close to you -"

"Him."

"Him? Who?"

"My twin brother, Sam. He died of cancer four days before. That's why he looked so rough. I'd been looking after him for over a year but nobody knew because he was housebound. I told them he'd died years ago. It was my insurance policy. In case. Went through all the funeral stuff. Paid my doctor for a death certificate. Actually buried my dog."

Doug was speechless. As he was incapable of saying anything, Mick continued. "I knew that bloody Sir Digby Crichton knew I knew too much. Poor old Fouracres knew nothing, of course. What an idiot running such a secret operation... Still, it worked for me, didn't it?"

Doug suddenly found a question to articulate amongst the thousands more that were crowding his mind. "But you... I mean, you told me to meet you. So how did you get the car there?"

"I knew I could trust you. So I put my brother's body in the back seat - covered up, of course - and towed the car to where you saw it. I'd bought a four-wheel drive with the humungously large advance given me by the company that's bought my research. Not Digby Crichton's stuff, of course - I'm saving that side of things for another day. Probably soon, though."

Inside, Doug was seething. That had been his idea all along. And now Mick had done it first. The bastard. "But how did you know I'd found the body?"

"I was watching you."

Doug had run out of facial expressions, but still one more - of incredulity - managed to convey itself. Then he uttered, "You were watching me?"

"Yeah. Towed the car, like I said, unhitched it, put Sam in the driving-seat, drove behind North Crag and waited for you. It was a close thing, though; you got there quicker than I expected. When I asked you to meet me at the labs I knew they'd know about it because they'd been tapping my phone. So I rang you to make it all seem real - me looking awful, and all that - because then they'd think it was because my research had gone wrong. It was a gamble, but it worked: it was my disappearing act. You - and they - thought I'd died on the way to work. Or been killed."

Doug was getting more annoyed by the second: Mick had had the cheek to presume he was gullible in order to advance his subterfuge, and Doug hated being taken advantage of. Especially as he had originally thought of using Mick in a similar way. It was that which really irked him. Seeing his glowering countenance, Mick continued: "But if you remember, I called you twice. The first was on my home phone, so they'd hear; the second was on my brand-new pay-as-you-go mobile." He held it up as he said this. "So you were the only person who would know how to access my notes."

"So they didn't know I had your notes?"

"No, not specifically. Mind you, when you did a runner they might have suspected."

"I wasn't running from you, though. I was running from the animals."

Mick looked surprised. "Blimey - did that start then?"

"Yes. Well, soon after. When all the compounds

leaked out of the pools... Then the animals wrecked the place. Did you know that?"

"Well, I heard something... I was out of the loop for a while after I got away. It was only through keeping up with Crichton's e-mails later on that I began to catch up with what was going on. Slimy bastard. So tell me your version of what happened."

Doug told him everything.

"Jesus," Mick said when he had finished, "You're in this deeper than I thought. No wonder that my research suggestions were of use to you."

"So it was you who put your notes onto the internet?"

"Of course. That put the wind up a few people."

"Including me. I knew it couldn't be you because I'd seen you dead. It never crossed my mind that you were still alive..."

"The notes were shut down pretty quickly. But whether it was Crichton or the government I really don't know. Same thing, though, I suppose."

"Not really," Doug commented. "Jessie thinks he's doing his own agenda, and now you've just confirmed it. I wasn't sure at first, though."

Mick nodded. "Someone's funding him from the middle east. That's why I got out - I couldn't do what he wanted to do to his own country, whatever the financial rewards. So I concocted something else while he wasn't looking but based on the filth I was doing for him. When I'd created it I approached another company and got out. But I knew too much, so I had to kill myself."

"So why did you post your notes up there?" Doug added.

"I had to. If Sir Digby'd found me, he'd have had me really killed. So although I went off the radar by appearing to have died, I still had to ensure that he wouldn't get away with it. But thanks to the Freedom of Information Act I could make sure that the government - or Sir Digby - couldn't get away with burying my revelations. Fortunately, you saw my notes on the internet."

"No, it wasn't me: I had them already. It was Jessie. It was her that started all this off." Mick nodded again, although he seemed more reflective than before.

"Ah, the lovely Jessie," he commented.

"You've seen her?"

"Only on TV. I enjoyed her slagging off Crichton. And that other guy was good, too."

"Frank."

"Yeah. Frank. He did well."

A pause descended as they both sank into their own thoughts and tried to piece things together after events had prised them apart. Doug eventually broke the silence by asking Mick how he had managed to hack into Sir Digby Crichton's e-mail address.

"Oh, I did that ages ago. That's how I knew what he was doing and that I had to run. I mean... how can someone in that position of trust do what he's doing for a foreign government...?" He tailed off, with a disdainful sneer. Then he looked Doug in the eye and said, "Mind you, so am I now. But it's good stuff, not bad."

"Which one?"

"It's a big German chemical company, but it does a lot of state work. And they know that this has to be secret - even from the British government, which I think they're quite enjoying, actually."

"Do you still call yourself Mick?"

"No, of course not. I've changed my name, identity, everything."

"So what's your name now, then?"

"I'll tell you another time. Just in case," he added evasively, after a slight hesitation.

"Do you work here, then?"

"Sometimes. 'Freelance'." He smiled as he articulated this word, then continued: "When I need something I can't get in Germany... Not often, mind you. What's good is that I have contacts here - people trying to get out like I was. They tell me things I can't find in Germany and I pay them for it. It's useful."

"So how do you get in and out? This can't be official, in any sense of the word."

"Of course not. They say there's only one entrance, but I know another one. I told the person who built it that I worked for the government. Which I do, in a way. I gave him a lot of money, too, of course. You can do anything with money."

"I thought there must be more than one way in and out."

"Of course. Did you honestly think that bloody Health & Safety would allow only one escape route, even in a place like this?" He laughed. "It's supposedly secret, but it's there." Doug could tell that he was enjoying this new freedom, this release... and, of course, the subterfuge and the cash.

Doug broached the question that he needed most answering: "So how are we going to make some of this stuff and then test it, now we think we've got the formula?"

"The company I work for in Germany. They'll soon be making so much money out of the anti-ageing compound I created on the back of Crichton's research at Shepherd Scar that they'll fall over themselves to make this."

Doug was annoyed again. That was what he was working on. "Manganese tripuride?" he asked.

Mick looked surprised. "Yeah. That's right. Why, were you onto that as well?" Doug nodded, then said: "I thought you were using chromitic paradiosymine."

"Nah - that's an ageing compound. That's what I was using for Crichton's stuff." So that was where their research had both crossed and diverged.

"I didn't realise that you were two-timing him," Doug said after a moment.

"Of course you didn't. But I knew you were."

Doug was surprised at this. "How did you know?" he asked indignantly.

"Why else would you have asked about my research with the dogs? I knew you were up to something; I'd have asked you what it was but for the fact that it was just the moment I had to make my exit."

Doug was annoyed and deflated. He thought he was the only one who knew. "I wasn't working for

Crichton, though," he blurted.

"No. He didn't think he could trust you," Mick retorted airily. At that, Doug felt even more annoyed. "So he picked the wrong bloke, didn't he?" Mick added with a reassuring laugh, and patted him on the back. "Anyway, now that we might have cracked this together, I'll make sure that you're rewarded for it. I couldn't do it myself, you know - there was something that I just couldn't work out. But you did it for me. It was like a light going on. It was part my research, part yours: the anthicin was what mainly did it. You were obviously using it for your tests as I was mine. But the amounts were dissimilar, and we were approaching the same problem from different directions. That's when I got back in touch. We'll both be multi-millionaires. Well, I am already - at least on paper."

"If we ever get out of here."

"Oh, you will. And Jessie. Leave it to me. When you've got money and influence - and a stonking huge drugs company behind you - it's amazing what can be done."

"But if the animals find me, I won't last a minute. They've only spared me this long because instinctively they believed that I could make more of the stuff for them. But they don't need me now - it seems to have taken off genetically. I'm redundant."

"Not to the human race you're not - you're their saviour. If you can wait a few more days - and not let anyone here know we've cracked it - I guarantee you'll be out of this place within the week. If they find out, you're right - you're dead." He looked furtively around and then added: "Mind you, so am I if they find me here."

"You mean, Crichton's running this as well?"

"Of course he is. Who else would have bankrolled your escape? You're working for him." Doug's heart sank: he had hoped that he and Jessie were rid of him.

Mick continued: "The only difference is that this time the government knows just a little about it. But I doubt if they know it all: as usual, he's doing this for himself. And, as I said, someone in the middle east; but we don't know who."

"I do," said Doug simply. "At least, I think I do."

"Who?"

He paused as a thought entered his mind: "I'll tell you when we're both safely out of here and the compound's being produced."

Mick hesitated. "OK," he replied, "Seems fair."

"It's also my insurance policy."

"Snap," he replied, shooting Doug a wry look.

"Right, then. Back to work."

Mick nodded. Doug suddenly felt very tired, not just because of the weight of research on his shoulders, recent events and lack of sleep, but also because of the subterfuge and the expectation that was being placed upon him. And he still had to escape, with Jessie. Pity he would not be able to take Ishrani.

He then asked the last question that he wanted to know of Mick: "So... after you knew I'd seen your brother's body and saw me go up to the labs at Shepherd Scar... how did you get rid of the car and your brother so quickly?"

Mick's smiling face changed on the instant and drained of blood. "I didn't," he said faintly.

Chapter 28

As Sir Digby Crichton's executive jet touched down for re-fuelling, he was dimly aware of a blue flashing light that swept in a circular motion across the small plane's interior, refracted by the rain on the few windows. He had no reason to leave the plane as the refuelling would only take a few minutes before he would resume his onward journey to London. So he was somewhat surprised when his Arab pilot came into the passenger area and told him that the police here in Frankfurt wanted to see him. Annoyed and slightly concerned, he straightened his tie and, as the door was opened, stepped out and down the steps. He was instantly cold and his nostrils were assailed by the smell of jet fuel as he pulled his flapping jacket around him. He was close to the terminal building but the police car was at the bottom of the steps and he was courteously but firmly assisted into the back of it.

"What's this all about?" he asked testily, "I'm a British government minister with diplomatic immunity so this had better be good."

"Oh, it's fery good, Mr. Digby Crichton." The voice, from the front of the vehicle, had a thick German accent and was from what he assumed to be a detective as he was in plain clothes.

"*Sir* Digby," he corrected.

"I don't sink zis vill make much difference from now on," came the reply.

"Where are you taking me?"

"To ze British Embassy, of course," came the reply. "Someone vants to speak to you. Someone important. I can say no more for ze moment." With that, he turned away as the car sped through the rainy night, sirens blazing, his consorts, two overweight policemen, hemming him in.

Mick and Doug parted company, both uneasy about things that had been said. For his part, Doug wanted to have the drug tested sooner than Mick said was possible, so he could get out of this stifling place; for Mick, he could not understand how his brother's body and car had miraculously disappeared off Shepherd Scar. He felt it must be Sir Digby's doing, but could not understand how he had managed it so quickly: perhaps he had been closer to him than he realised. It made him shudder, which was not helped by his emerging into the cold blast of a North Sea wind off the Firth of Forth.

He closed the heavy steel door, which lay flush with the heather at an angle, and heard John bolt it from the inside. Then he covered the door with a fake curtain of plastic heather - which had been designed to keep all but the most discerning eyes away from it - and pegged the bottom down. Having finally placed a couple of small boulders for good effect, he looked about; then he turned away from the sea and went inland to his car which was parked a hundred yards away and out of sight from where he had just emerged.

He opened the door and saw his lovely young German assistant still sitting there at the wheel.

"OK, Heidi," he murmured, "let's go. I've seen him. We've got to get on and make the drug as fast as possible. There's far more to this than I realised and all sorts of things are beginning to happen. And I don't like most of them."

"Frankfurt, then?"

"Mm. I think we can get the next plane from Edinburgh, although it might be tight." As Heidi bumped the large four-wheel-drive car over the uneven ground, he wondered how quickly all this could be done. He did not think Doug could keep it from his nominal colleagues for long: he had been so close to a result before that they would soon realise he was stalling. Yet if it got into the hands of the British government first - or, more correctly, Sir Digby Crichton - then their whole plan would be compromised. Then, the government would be bypassed or held to ransom, or the animals would take over by stealth and lack of counterpoison.

Twenty minutes later they were entering the airport perimeter. Heidi parked the car while Mick went to buy the tickets. Having done so, he put his mobile on and accessed his e-mails. Nothing of much importance, although he had been alerted to an unconfirmed report from a colleague that Sir Digby Crichton had been taken in for questioning by the Frankfurt police. This intrigued him: why on earth was Crichton in Frankfurt? Had he uncovered Mick's subterfuge, knew that he was based there now and had been trying to find him? Or was someone else now pulling the strings? His answers would have to wait. Yet he wondered whether a visit to the police there might be useful: after all, he knew more about Sir Digby than the German police could ever know and circumstance had unexpectedly delivered the man into the same city that he was returning to. Perhaps this was the moment...

An hour later, he and Heidi were both in the air and on their way back to Frankfurt. But still his dead brother's disappearance troubled him.

It appeared that Enid's ruse was working. No sooner had she talked to the editor at length than he had written an article headed 'Secret Britain' which articulated all she had said and dropped a huge hint that the paper had sources claiming to know of shady goings-on in the Ministry for Home Affairs in general and Sir Digby Crichton in particular. And that the government was unaware of much that was going on under its nose and was even funding programmes that it knew nothing about. Her name was kept secret, of course: and the worried government officials who were onto the editor for his source were met with a cold response. So when his paper was threatened with closure under the hastily-drafted 'Offences Against the State Act', he could say with assurance that they would have to shut down all the newspapers and TV stations if that was the case, because his source was in touch with them all: and the government did not want the spectre of controlling the press to be so blatant, even though they had been doing so for years. They had hushed up one local paper's closure anyway and its editor was under house arrest: a national shutdown would damage their pleadings of democracy and free speech forever. TV closure was out of the question, too, of course; especially as it was their favourite conduit for propaganda.

Enid read all this with a smile of satisfaction. She and the editor had decided to turn the screw slowly for maximum effect: soon she was sure that Frank would be released and the Hickley & District News would be reopened. Then she received an e-mail from the editor to say that Sir Digby had been arrested in Frankfurt, taken off a private jet whose flight had originated in Egypt. She scanned the article, then added the news about Sir Digby: then she e-mailed it all to Jessie.

Doug, who was desperately trying to keep his new findings away from his colleagues, was having a hard time. He was wary of straying too far away from his research because that would appear too obvious: yet he was terrified that one of his colleagues would create a computer model - or grow a culture that would suddenly replicate the initial devastating compound. From then on, a counter-compound could very quickly be created and soon in the wrong hands. He was pleased, then, when Jessie appeared and told him she had something to discuss in the office.

Sitting him down and giving him a cup of tea, she

showed him what Enid had sent her. His heartbeat rose a little as he read it.

"Excellent," he said as he finished. "But don't forget to delete it." Jessie replied that she always did. "I don't know how long I can hold out like this," he said. "And Ishrani's made it clear that she fancies me; although I'm sure she doesn't really."

"Mm, if she thinks she can get round you then we'd all be stuffed," Jessie agreed with a cautionary tone. "Do you think you can hold out?"

"I'll try," he said. "But she's so sweet and beautiful - and just my type."

"That's why she's been put here, I'm sure," Jessie proclaimed baldly.

"That's what I keep telling myself. But after so long..."

"It won't be for that much longer."

"Hope so. Jessie, you've got to help keep her away from me. After this is all over, perhaps I'll try to ask her out, but..."

"That's a good idea. And anyway, we've got more important things to think of. I miss Frank, too, you know."

"I know." With that, he sighed and stood up. "Back to temptation," he said under his breath, just loud enough for Jessie to hear.

"We'll soon be out of here. And then you can do what you like," she said lightly.

"Animal retribution permitting," he declared heavily.

"That and the government."

"God, how did we get into all this?"

"You wanted to be rich and kick the government and get a girl like Ishrani," she said. "And if you hold your nerve you're not far off achieving all of it."

"That's the big problem."

He picked himself up, forced a smile at her and said, "Thanks for everything, Jessie. You've given me a life - if this is ever resolved." He waved a hand around vaguely. "And it'll all be thanks to you. So in case anything happens to me, I just want you to know that I appreciate it." He went over and gave her a huge hug, and she could see there were tears in his eyes.

A few benches away, in the middle of the research centre, Ishrani observed the embrace through the office window and was not a little annoyed...

Sir Digby Crichton stared at the police chief with incredulity. "You're accusing me of <u>what</u>?" he spat.

A man in the corner, discreet by stature and even more so in manner, coughed politely to draw attention to himself, and stood up. "I'll answer that one," he said, in a thin voice with an English accent. His drab overcoat matched the room, which was gaunt, grey and badly-lit, with bars over a skylight in the roof. Sir Digby Crichton felt that the world was closing in on him and this stifling metallic claustrophobia was far from where he had planned to be at this stage in his life.

"My name is Smythe. Nigel Smythe. I represent Her Majesty's government, Sir Digby. I understand that you've just been to Egypt," he stated, waving his hand wearily in the direction of that country.

"May I remind you that I'm a member of HMG, too," Crichton responded tartly.

"Just so. However, there are a number of irregularities that we've uncovered. I'm hoping you'll be able to help me fathom them out."

"I'll do my best," he replied curtly, with not much conviction and a touch of disdain.

The man continued. "You're well acquainted with the Shepherd Scar Research Centre, of course. Now, as you know, several things have happened there over the past few months, including the death of Dennis Fouracres -"

"Nothing to do with me."

The man closed his eyes for an instant, as if brushing aside the intrusion, and continued: "- and not to mention the creation of drugs that through, shall we say, neglect, got out into the environment and have started to cause problems." Sir Digby Crichton knew the man was a British government agent with that: understatement was their calling-card.

"I know all about everything that happened there," he blurted. "What am I here for?"

"I'm coming to that. Did you at any time run any research that was not of a government-funded nature?"

"No."

"So what were you doing in Egypt then, when your office didn't know where you were?"

"Private business."

"Just so," he said again. "And could you tell me what sort of business that was?"

"I don't have to tell you that. It was a private trip. And I might remind you that I have diplomatic immunity and that this is nothing to do with you."

"Ah, but that is where we beg to differ. We have some evidence - sketchy, but evidence nonetheless - that you have been dealing with Abu Bhakraim, supposedly of the Fraternity Corporation, based in Cairo." Sir Digby tried to resist the temptation to shift uneasily. "You have also been bankrolling some research that would appear to be contradictory to your position," he continued, "and not only do we believe it is funded by this said Abu Bhakraim but also that the research is based on that which you did without government knowledge at the Shepherd Scar Research Centre." Sir Digby Crichton could feel his neck itching and despite the cold room a sweat was breaking on his brow.

"That's rubbish. Prove it."

"We have lots of proof," Smythe replied. "What we want to know is what you were doing it for."

There was a silence as all eyes in the room bored in on him. "I want a lawyer," was all he could think of saying.

"I am a lawyer. And I believe you were too, once, which should make things a lot easier." This he said with a snide, twisted smile.

"I have nothing to say."

"Then let me say it for you. We in HMG believe that you have been conducting research into drugs that were not part of any government remit which you were running without government knowledge to create drugs and compounds that were in breach of international and UN guidelines. This we believe was being funded by a movement of people unsympathetic to western values. To be precise, the terrorist movement known as the Fraternity. At this moment, we are unsure where your main researcher is as you managed to remove him and his assistant from government cover. So my next question is, 'Where is Doug Sprake ?'"

"I have no idea. Who is Doug Sprake, anyway?"

"OK. What about Mick Deakin?"

"Who's that?"

"Oh, come, come, Sir Digby. He was the one doing all your dirty work at Shepherd Scar."

"Ah, him. He's dead. But he wasn't doing any dirty work for me."

"Just so. So you did know him, then?"

"Well, yes, now you mention him. He was working for Dennis Fouracres. Nerve serums, truth drugs, I think. It was all well documented: but it was top secret because it was being done for the government."

"Ostensibly."

Smythe's understatement was beginning to annoy Sir Digby. "Well, either it was or it wasn't," he retorted. "I didn't know everything. Fouracres was in charge."

"Again, ostensibly." There was a pause. "But of course, now he's dead..."

"Nothing to do with me," Crichton snapped again, wondering if they were implying that he had ordered his death.

"I didn't say it was," Smythe pronounced unctuously and full of implied menace.

Sir Digby could feel his chest tightening. "May I have some water?" he asked.

"Of course." A plastic tumbler was put in front of him, its 'clup' noise echoing round the room as it was placed on the table. Smythe poured the liquid from a glass jug. As the water flowed out, it reminded Crichton of the swimming-pool that he had just reviewed in his new home near Cairo. It suddenly seemed a long, long way away.

He took a long draught, then put down the cup and looked at it, twirling it in his fingers, waiting for the next assault and unsure within himself how much to admit and how much to deny.

"Haf you heard about ze nuclear disaster in norzern France?" the police officer intervened. Sir Digby shook his head slowly. "Zen you vill not know a large area is devastated by radiation."

"So what's that got to do with me?" Crichton asked without emotion. The police officer raised an eyebrow and looked back at Smythe.

"We believe it's all part of your overall plan," said Smythe.

"What overall plan?" Now he was beginning to get angry. They could not blame him for that, even if it was all part of his strategy. But it was not supposed to be happening yet, not until all the compounds had been manufactured: so it was definitely nothing to do with him, and he said so.

Smythe just looked at him, with a slightly pathetic

look. “But, Sir Digby; we know all about it.”

“What? Look, if you have something to say then just say it. Or let me go.” There was a pause, while Smythe studied his fingernails. Sir Digby wondered how much they really knew and how much was speculation. Getting no reply, he found himself thinking back to the morning he had heard that Deakin was dead. He had ordered Deakin’s death only if he would not agree to continue working for him. He had thought Deakin would comply but was expendable by that time if he did not; but having heard of his death, he had never checked up on who had actually killed him. He had just heard that it had been done. Had someone in the intelligence services told the authorities? When he got back he would find out who it was... Then he realised that, perhaps, he would not be going back; at least, not in a position of authority. He suddenly felt a pang of guilt. But all that was too late.

Smythe looked up from studying his hands and just said to the police inspector, “Bring him in the moment he arrives.” Then he turned to Crichton and said, “I’d get some sleep if I were you,” intimating a bench in the corner on which was a thin foam mattress.

Then they left the room and the door was locked from the outside. Sir Digby had never felt so alone in his life.

Frank was sitting on the bed in his enforced incarceration in Leeds, looking out over the back garden. Although it was dark, the yellow path lights picked out a squirrel bounding about in its jerky yet sublimely fluent way. It seemed to be an allegory for his own situation, and yet he wondered whether it would attack him, with hundreds of others, if it smelt him. He instinctively stood up and moved a few paces back into the room. The squirrel seemed so benign... It was still difficult to believe all that had happened, and he hoped that Doug was managing to find an antidote. It was all the more urgent now due to the fallout from the reactor in France, as the animals' success there was sure to be replicated elsewhere. He suddenly felt smug that he had always been against nuclear power.

His thoughts were interrupted by his gaoler entering the room. "You can leave now," he said. "And your paper's been re-opened: you can go back to that, too." With that, he threw an early edition of a national newspaper down onto the floor in front of him and left the room. The headline that faced Frank read: 'GOVERNMENT IN TURMOIL AS DRUG AND TERRORIST ACCUSATIONS TAKE HOLD.'

He instinctively thought that Doug must have succeeded. When he got back to the Hickley & District News offices he would phone Jessie and find out. He picked up his meagre belongings, but when he got downstairs noticed that the police car in the drive at the front of the house was no longer there. His gaoler had vanished, too. So who would protect him, and who would drive him to Hickley?

He wondered if he was being set up.

Chapter 29

Doug had told his team that he needed sleep, which was mainly a means to buy some time. So when, a few hours later, there was a knock on his door and Ishrani was standing there, he was unprepared for what she would say to him.

She stood in the doorway, the light in the corridor framing her slim young figure. "Doug - I think we've cracked it," she said excitedly as she put the light on. "Asghar has suddenly found a link. Can you come and see what you think?"

He was awake in an instant, despite a deadening tiredness that pervaded every part of his body. He noted that Ishrani was not wearing her white coat but stood there in tight jeans and a crimson top that complemented her dark skin, long black hair and huge, beautiful brown eyes. The top button of her blouse was undone and as she leaned over him he could see a hint of black brassiere underneath and all his senses seemed to go into overdrive on that one instant. She smiled, her perfect teeth sparkling bright white in the bland light. He had to think quickly: was this a bluff or genuine, or was she there just to try and get round him? That was both what he dreaded and craved. But he had to make a decision on what to do there and then.

"Tell me about it first." She hesitated a moment, then came and sat next to him on the bed after pointedly closing the door. It was that action which made him think the worst: no woman of this beauty had ever found him attractive before and, although he looked better than he had ever done thanks to the drugs he had unwittingly ingested, he still did not believe he held any attraction for anyone.

She put her long, slender fingers on his shoulder and said in her soft Indian accent: "Doug, I really think we've done it. I'm so proud of you." With that, he could bear it no longer and he found himself kissing her. She did not resist but was kissing him, too, her hands caressing his neck and shoulders. At the back of his mind he was thinking that this was all buying time and that he could tell her anything she wanted and deny any advance they thought they had made. Surely, he was good enough at his job to be able to do that? Then, as his hands found themselves touching her dark, firm nipples, all thoughts of everything were subsumed by a burning desire to enjoy the moment and work out the consequences later.

They slid down the bed and soon every one of his dreams and prayers seemed to be answered all at once...

The door opened and a figure stood there, an outline in the doorway. It was difficult for him to see at first who it was but the silhouette seemed familiar. Then, recognising the person, a shudder slid down his body and he realised that he had been set up.

"My God," he said, as the man walked into the light and the door closed behind him, "I thought you were dead."

"I know you did," said Mick. "Lucky for all of us that I'm not, though."

Sir Digby could feel his heart pounding and the previously nascent sweat on his brow was now a torrent.

Smythe and the police officer, standing behind Mick, looked at each other and nodded, confident that their strategy had worked. Mick had not needed to contact them: they were waiting for him when he landed at the airport and seemed to have known who he was all along. So much for his changed identity, he had thought.

"So you know this man?" Smythe asked rhetorically, coming further into the room.

Sir Digby looked down at his expensive shoes, which seemed to have lost their lustre, and nodded. "I cannot deny I know him," he admitted, "but that does not make me guilty. I used to work with him, that's all."

"Let's stop playing, Crichton," Mick butted in. "You blackmailed me into doing your work for you. Fortunately, I was doing some of my own, too. So we've each deceived the other." He gave a forced grin at the despondent minister. "And now your government's going to be in even more of a pickle," he chuckled. "What's more, I've worked out an antidote."

"You're bluffing," Crichton spat. "How could a pipsqueak like you afford to do that without the help of the government or big business. I don't believe you."

"OK," Mick replied cockily, "but just wait and see. There's more than one government in the world, you know. And loads of big businesses who'd love to have 'saved the world' written on their CVs."

Sir Digby Crichton remained silent. He had been outmanoeuvred. He now hoped even more that his intended apocalypse would happen, whether or not he was caught up in it. He had to tell Abu to do whatever he could to enable massive production of the serum as soon as possible. "I'd like to make a phone call," he requested hopefully.

"Out of the question," said Smythe. "In fact, we're about to confiscate all your effects before extradition back to Britain. So please put all your belongings on the table in front of you, starting with the mobile phone in your pocket."

Crichton slowly did as he was told. "So how did you find out?" he asked in a pathetic, beaten tone, as they scooped his belongings into a brown paper bag.

"As soon as I realised that you were running Shepherd Scar and not Fouracres, I was on to you," obliged Mick. "Fouracres knew nothing - I couldn't believe it. Then I saw you were manipulating him - and me - and that I was doing lots of things that were nothing to do with official government work, even though a lot of that was dirty enough. Then, when you started threatening me, I knew you were on to me too and I began to get a feel for what you were trying to do. It was all part of your plan."

"And what *is* my plan?" Crichton shot at him.

"To annihilate the West by implementing your serums and poisons into water supplies and from the air, so that your paymasters could set up a militant theocracy. You sold yourself for their motives and a luxurious life in the sun while we all died a horrible death."

"You wouldn't have lasted long there, though," Smythe added pointedly. "We have it on good authority that your house in Cairo was actually destined for someone else."

Crichton went quiet for a moment: was his life's deceit so fragile? Had he really been Abu Bhakraim's stooge all along? He felt sick.

"So how did you know all this about me?" he enquired.

Mick took a moment to reply. "I hacked into your e-mails," he said eventually. "And got to know some of the people you do business with. A pretty unpleasant bunch. But they were good: we've only recently realised who and where your paymaster is."

"So who is it, then?" he glared.

"You know. Abu Bhakraim."

"Prove it."

"Oh, we will."

"So why did you run?" he sneered.

"You were after me and wanted me dead because I knew too much. You just didn't know how much. That's why I 'died'."

Crichton looked beaten, but asked, "So who was it that we saw dead in his car, then?

"My twin brother." Mick paused a second, then asked: "So who cleaned up the mess?"

Crichton shot him an indignant look. "I don't know."

Mick looked at him; for once, he felt that Crichton was telling the truth."Blimey... so Abu's men were after me as well, were they? Without your knowledge?"

"I suppose it's possible."

Mick shook his head slowly. He was enjoying this: the hunter hunted. "You were all closer than I thought, then. If it wasn't you it would have been them." He turned away, reflecting on how close he had come to being killed. And, possibly, Doug, who might just have got in the way. Then he turned back and shouted angrily, "I got out just in time, didn't I? The funny thing is, you each must have thought the other had killed me, when it was me who'd killed me all along." He started laughing. "That's really funny..."

Crichton realised he had laid a trap for himself and fallen into it. He reflected for a moment, then felt he ought to express a few truths.

"I had nothing to do with what happened with the animals and the leakages at the Shepherd Scar Research Centre," he stated.

"No, not directly," agreed Mick. "That was completely unintentional. But it almost helped you. If you could let the animals do your work instead of your followers... Very tidy. The wrath of God. Huh! And even now you're more concerned about getting the poison rather than the antidote. Trouble is, you still don't know what the exact poison is that you're trying to find the antidote for." Then he leaned into Crichton's face and said: "But I do."

His triumphant expression really angered Sir Digby. "So how and why has this all come up at this precise moment?" he enquired, stifling his resentment.

"Someone else knows without question who you're in contact with," Mick replied. He leaned behind the police officer and picked up an iPad which revealed the front page of a British newspaper. It was that morning's Hickley and District News and he placed it in front of him, pointing at the headline, which stated: 'TOP GOVERNMENT MANDARIN ACCUSED OF AIDING ANTI-BRITISH INSURRECTION'. Sir Digby's name was prominent in the first sentence.

"You should have been nicer to your niece," Mick commented with a slight sneer.

"Enid?" he said, incredulously. Mick nodded.

With that, Crichton knew the game was well and truly over.

Chapter 30

Frank had not wanted to leave his incarceration on his own, for obvious reasons. Finding the house empty and unguarded, he had used its phone to ring Enid at home; this was not to discuss anything, which might have been monitored, but to see if she could collect him - if he could find out where he was. However, he was surprised and delighted to hear a voicemail message requesting callers to phone her at the offices of the Hickley & District News, to which she had returned very early that morning. When he found himself talking to her, she informed him that she had written and printed the paper - the front page of which Sir Digby Crichton was at that moment being presented with in Frankfurt. She had exposed his connections with Abu Bhakraim and was hoping that this would have a knock-on effect. She did not want to talk in too much detail for fear that Frank's phone was being monitored, but implied that there was much more to tell. She found that she had his number on her caller display and would ring the phone company for the address. Then she would send her husband to pick him up immediately.

As he waited, he had time for reflection. So, his paper was open again: Enid had told him that the government had lost a vote in the Commons condemning their shutting down of provincial newspapers - it was deemed an assault on local democracy. With that, the national papers had stepped up their right to print what they felt was seemly and, according to Enid, were now hammering the government in revenge. He had praised Enid for her actions: after all, he could not chastise her as she was only doing what he would have done. But he nevertheless could not wait to return to edit his newspaper as soon as possible: he, too, had some scores to settle that were best done in print.

Two hours later, a huge Land-Rover was at the gates and he recognised Enid's husband at the wheel. He looked around for the possibility of hostile wildlife, ran to the car, and jumped in. He never thought he would have been so keen to see Enid's husband but his relief was palpable. Roger locked the doors and they were off.

On the journey, Roger told Frank of all that had happened over the time he had been under house arrest and filled in the details: none of them had known where Frank had been taken but thought that he had been hidden for the government's sake rather than for his own safety.

"I need to get in touch with Jessie," Frank said after a few minutes.

"Do you know where she is?" asked Roger.

"No. When I last spoke to her on her mobile she didn't seem to have a clue and I didn't want her to tell me anyway. I don't trust phones where one's under arrest. That's why I didn't ring her just now while I was waiting for you."

"Well, we think she's in a compound behind the naval base at Rosyth - a new government research centre which was set up by Sir Digby Crichton - but we're not absolutely certain. Doug's with her, though. Enid feels that they've been appropriated by Sir Digby to create the antidote - well, the poison, too, actually - and it's all being funded by his foreign contacts. Supposedly government auspices, of course. But we don't know yet if the government does know if they're there and anyway, Sir Digby's just been arrested in Germany, according to the newsfeeds. It's not that well known yet, though, so we don't know what that'll mean in the long run."

"I hope it doesn't jeopardise them," said Frank quickly. "If they're of no use to Sir Digby and the government doesn't actually know where they are... He might try to get rid of them."

"Christ - I hadn't thought of that," said Roger. Instinctively, he pressed the accelerator down further.

What they did not know was that at that moment, Sir Digby Crichton was being led away in handcuffs to another small plane that was waiting solely for the purpose of taking him back to justice in England. The pilot of the executive jet he had flown in from Egypt had been detained and was being interrogated by the police, too, but much more harshly. They had touched down just before dawn, but now the sun was bright and an easterly wind had blown away the clouds. It was cold, and Sir Digby shivered in his suit that had been manufactured for warmer climes. He was shepherded into the small plane and Smythe accompanied him, along with a detective.

The plane was nowhere as luxurious or well-appointed as his previous transport and this made him even more indignant: he was a member of the British government, even if he was about to be exposed and disgraced. He wondered what effect his actions would have on it. Actually, he felt he knew...

The pilot informed them that they would have to take a huge detour northwards to avoid the nuclear fallout over Normandy: this would take them up across the top of Scotland, down the west coast of England and thence to London. It was the only time a smile crossed his face that day, as that must mean that the plane would have to refuel somewhere remote and that would give him a chance to escape.

Abu Bhakraim was on the phone. He had just been told the news about Sir Digby Crichton and slammed the receiver down angrily. He pondered for a moment, then picked up the phone again and made a call. Then he sat back into his deep leather chair and contemplated what to do next. He had bankrolled this whole project for years and it was just starting to work, so why did Sir Digby have to get arrested now? And especially on the way back from his country. He still felt deep down that his project was salvageable but Crichton's situation made things more difficult and the stakes higher. He felt relieved knowing that he himself was in Egypt: his contacts in the new government would protect him and he would not be arrested here. Perhaps if he had made his scheduled trip to Italy he would have been, but he was safe enough in Cairo. Except for one thing: he still did not have the counterpoison. And without knowing the make-up of the original deadly serum he could not produce it anywhere. But with the British and American governments now pressurising the UN in general - and Egypt in particular - for his arraignment, he wondered how he could get his researcher out of the research centre in Scotland. That would not be a problem, except that he would have to build him a research centre and a bespoke chemical production facility from scratch here in Egypt. Although he had the money to do that, he did not have the time and soon he and his people would be at the mercy of the animal kingdom just like in the West. He had trusted Sir Digby to deliver: indeed, with his help he had appropriated the Shepherd Scar Research Centre from right under the British government's noses. But Rosyth, at least, was different: it had been built mostly with private money donated by a charitable institution - his. He and Sir Digby had been planning to switch their operations from Shepherd Scar to Rosyth anyway, but due to the unforeseen events of the leakage Rosyth had only been ready in the nick of time. Although the building itself was completed, they had subsequently been hurried into getting sympathetic staff from around Britain who would support the thrust of what he was trying to do without raising any eyebrows: he had not wanted any more whistleblowers. By and large he had succeeded and he mused that he could thank Sir Digby Crichton for that, even if the house he was building was never going to have been for him but for his own country's finance minister.

Chapter 31

Doug woke to find that Ishrani had left. He was instantly out of bed and dressed quickly whilst fondly reminiscing on the events of a few hours before. Where that put him in her eyes and those of her colleagues he was unsure. He walked out of his room and into the research centre, only to be astonished at what he saw.

It was completely empty. It had obviously been evacuated in a rush, as there were computers on, notes lying around and experiments and formulae in various stages of progress. But no-one was there.

Then he heard a loud bang of a door opening behind him: he spun round to see a soldier in full combat outfit and carrying a rifle, which he pointed at Doug; he seemed as surprised at seeing Doug as Doug was to see him.

"What are you doing here?" he asked loudly. "Why aren't you with the others?"

"Erm, I don't know," Doug replied feebly. "I was asleep. What's happening?"

"Place has been shut down by the government. Who are you, anyway?"

"I'm Doug Sprake. I'm the head researcher here."

With that, the soldier lowered his rifle. "Ah, we've been looking for you," he said. "Where the bloody hell were you? We searched the place good and proper."

"Sorry. I was extremely tired, and... and pressure of work... must have been flat out."

"You bloody must have been, the din we made. OK. Follow me."

As he followed the soldier up the stairs from whence he had come, Doug asked, "Is Jessie with the others?"

"Search me," the soldier replied, mounting the stairs purposefully.

"And Ishrani?"

The soldier stopped and turned, looking at him with an odd stare. "Dunno. He or she might be there. Depends." Then he turned back and continued on up the stairs. Eventually, they emerged into a large open space. On the right, he could see something he had not seen for days: daylight. It was the entrance to the building, which was flanked with an armed cordon of soldiers. On the left, standing and seated in a random order in what looked like a large café, was every person he had met at the research centre and many more. At that moment, two female voices shouted from opposite directions, "Doug."

He was relieved: Jessie and Ishrani were both still there. And safe.

After Sir Digby Crichton's departure, Mick spent some productive minutes with the German police officer and then joined Heidi in his car. Within the hour they were entering a large office building's car park, around which were the massive pipes and smoking towers that announced it as a vast chemical works. The complex was also surrounded by several men and women in the now familiar NBC suits and masks, their backs weighed down by tanks of liquid. They could not take any chances and feared that an attack, similar to the one in Normandy, was imminent.

Mick was well-known, even famous, within the company: they knew he had a clandestine past but nobody knew what it was. All they did know was that he was a very fine researcher. He and Heidi swept into the light, clean laboratory and he immediately walked up to a small man with a big, bald head and an even larger beer belly. This was Gunter.

Without stopping for pleasantries, Gunter said, "I think it'll work. We're just finalising the computer models now. What leaked into the environment - that did the damage - was this," and he showed Mick a screen full of chemical equations and hieroglyphics that would have vexed an optometrist but which Mick comprehended as if reading a book.

"So where's the antidote?" he asked casually, after he had taken it in.

"Here." Gunter went to another screen and showed him what he had sent him after Doug's work and observations. "Mm. Good. That's down to good old Doug. He's a better chemist than I thought. It was staring me in the face for long enough. So you think it'll work?"

"We've tested it already - on some animals we had

in the labs from before. We gave them the original stuff, then, when they showed the expected communication characteristics and hostile behaviour, we sprayed them with this." He motioned towards the screen. "It took about twenty minutes to react, but is non-reversible. Even when we applied more of the original."

"Fantastic. So when can we start making it? I think there'll be a lot of people in Egypt after this as well."

"In theory, we've started already. It's just awaiting the chairman's say-so."

"To hell with the chairman," said Mick. "Just do it. The planet's waiting on us. Go on - I'll sort the chairman out now - just get on with it." Gunter needed no further exhortation and Mick went straight to the chairman. It was agreed in seconds.

Next, he turned his mind to how he could get Doug and Jessie away from the Rosyth centre and the British government. That, he thought, would be altogether a more difficult proposition...

Doug was delighted that Ishrani bore him no ill will: it had all happened so suddenly that he was concerned that she might resent it - it had happened to him before. Jessie seemed to have realised what had taken place but she seemed pleased, if a little worried at what he might have told Ishrani in an intimate moment. So they were both trying to talk to him privately first, a situation that he was not used to at all. With that, though, a well-dressed man approached him. For a second, he reminded him of

Sir Digby as their demeanour was similar and he froze in disbelief. But the man stretched out a hand, smiling, and introduced himself.

"Doug Sprake; good day. James Brownlie. I represent the Jennings Chemical Company. I'd like to talk to you. In private, if possible."

Doug made his apologies to the ladies and went to the side of the room with Brownlie. The man did not waste a second. "We need you, and we need you fast," he said. We'll pay you whatever you want and give you unlimited funding for whatever it takes to get a vaccine, antidote, counterpoison - whatever you want to call it - into production as soon as possible. We are a British-based company with facilities in Cheshire which is, as yet, unscathed by recent events. I hope you will join us."

This was all too much for Doug. In the space of a few hours he had made love to the girl of his dreams, nearly saved humanity and also been offered instant and everlasting wealth. Was he dreaming? He was sure he was not.

"Are you anything to do with Mick Deakin?"

"No. The company he is working for is German - Hörst Industries. But we - humanity - will need as much of your product as possible: millions will need it and so we think that there should be as many installations making it as there can be. If there was another event like the one in Normandy last week, humanity would be lost. We - and Hörst - will be producing probably the same thing under a different name but franchising it around the world so that there's as much of it as needed. It's the only way to save humanity."

Doug was confused: how could this man just walk in and offer him millions? Who was he? How did he know where to find him? Nobody else did. Was it another government ploy? Or Abu Bhakraim? It seemed as if the man was reading his mind, for he started talking again with all of the answers.

"Allow me to explain. I worked for the government in Home Affairs until last month. But I left when I saw what they were doing - or not doing; how they were covering things up and getting confused over the simplest of issues rather than acting quickly and responsibly - too much infighting and vested interest. Fortunately, being in a position of influence, I had already made some soundings and managed to get onto the board at Jennings. Knowing a little about you from Dennis Fouracres -" he suddenly looked apologetic as Doug gave an astonished expression: "Sorry, but it's true; I was a good colleague in government of his. He'd been suspicious of Crichton for a while, so when we all thought Mick Deakin was dead Fouracres said you were the best man at Shepherd Scar to carry on his work. So we knew that you were the man for the job; trouble was, you suddenly disappeared and we couldn't find you. Until yesterday, when Sir Digby Crichton was arrested thanks to briefings from his niece, who happened to work for a local newspaper. She told us where she thought you were."

"Enid."

"Precisely."

Doug held up his hand, implying that this garrulous but well-intentioned man should stop for a moment. Dennis Fouracres! Had he known more than he let on? Was he, perhaps, more in the know than even Crichton believed? Could his death have been avoided? He looked back at Brownlie.

"When did you last speak to Fouracres?" he asked.

"I think it was only a day or so before he was killed," Brownlie replied. "A hit and run."

"Yes... yes, I know..." Doug murmured. "So you think he knew about Crichton?"

"We think he did; he discussed Crichton with me a couple of times but I was never sure if he realised the extent of Crichton's plans. None of us did. Mind you, we're pretty certain now that Fouracres would have been erased by Crichton if... well, if he hadn't been killed beforehand. But... well, we're still not even sure if it *was* instigated by Crichton."

Doug decided not to comment on that - best left alone. But he felt awful. Poor Fouracres. Everyone ridiculed him but perhaps he knew more than any of them realised. And he rated Doug. That was gratifying, even if it was too late to thank him. "So what's going to happen now?" he enquired.

"Well, what the people behind me don't know is that - for the moment at least - they are all under arrest."

"Not Jessie, surely?"

"Sorry, no - not Jessie. She's part of your team, isn't she?"

"Yes. But what about Ishrani?"

"Which is she?"

"That beautiful girl over there."

Brownlie turned discreetly to look, then his eyes focussed on him again. "Yes, she'll be under arrest. In fact, she's the one in charge who takes orders directly from Abu Bhakraim."

The bottom suddenly fell out of Doug's world. He had tasted paradise, and now it would be taken away from him. "Are you sure?" he said. Brownlie nodded. "She was put there to inspire you to perform better, I suspect. Nothing like a bit of feminine persuasion."

Doug could not bear to look at her. He had originally thought the same but what had happened between them had seemed so genuine... And he had not told her anything: passion had subsumed everything to a state of unimportance.

"Why are the others under arrest, though? They can't all be suspects, can they?"

"Many of the employees here have been specially recruited. Let's just say that they have a hidden agenda. Their interest is not to us but to the ideologies that motivated their paymaster, Abu Bhakraim."

"You came just in the nick of time," Doug said at length. "I'd just fallen in love with her."

"I'm not surprised. I would have done, too."

"Can you call Jessie over? I need to talk to her."

"Only when I have your word that you'll join us."

"Do you have someone who can verify who you are and who you represent? I don't think I'm very good at picking the right people, somehow."

"You can call Enid. She put me in touch with you. She knows what I look like, too: I was on TV last night, so you can describe me to her for verification."

"Right."

"You seem to pick <u>some</u> nice people: Jessie, for example."

"She is nice. Very. But she's in love with Frank."

"The editor of the Hickley & District News?"

"That's right."

"He was released from house arrest this morning. He's back at work, giving the government hell. And rightly so."

With that, he felt that this Mr. Brownlie was all right. But he still wanted a second opinion.

"I'll give you an answer to your offer only if I can have a few private minutes with Jessie," he said.

With a smile, Brownlie said, "I'll get her," and left. Doug kept his eyes away from Ishrani as he could not bear to look at her, even though he knew she was willing him to look towards her. A moment later, Jessie was sitting beside him. He told her of all the things Brownlie had said, particularly about Ishrani. Then he asked if he would be doing the right thing to accept the offer.

"I don't think we have a choice," she said. "I think we just have to hope he's telling the truth and go for it."

"I agree," he confirmed. Then: "Are you going to see Frank?"

"I hope so," she said, her cheeks flushing a little.

Sir Digby Crichton looked at Smythe in front of him in the small plane. They had been airborne for three hours and were about to land in Stornoway for refuelling. A few minutes later, they touched down. After the plane had taxied to a halt, the door was opened.

"Please feel free to stretch your legs," said Smythe. "But don't go far."

"Where are we?"

"Stornoway, Isle of Lewis."

Sir Digby shot a quick look around the cabin: the detective was with the pilot in the cockpit. He leaned towards Smythe and spoke softly.

"You could be rich, if you wanted. Very rich."

Smythe looked at him. "How's that, then?"

"I have access to all the formulae - or can get you to them. I'm done for, but if you let me go, then you could sell your knowledge to the highest bidder. Could be quite a tidy sum."

"You won't get around me," said Smythe. "I'm essentially honest. Boring, perhaps, but honest. And I don't think trying to bribe a member of HMG will improve your legal defence. It might have worked for you before, but not here."

"It could be worth millions."

Smythe looked at him again. "I said 'no'."

Sir Digby Crichton took a flash card from his pocket. "It's all on here," he said. He was lying, of course: there was nothing of value on the card at all and, even if there had been, his knowledge was now out of date; the serum was still not finalised. He was playing his last cards, though.

But Smythe knew it.

Chapter 32

Over the past few days, the animal world had become more subdued, apart from a mass shark attack on a beach in South Africa and a vast army of killer ants in Ecuador that had literally eaten through a swathe of villages until they were devastated by a circle of man-made fire. But the natural world around them had not, for once, wreaked any revenge: it was as if the animal kingdom was saving itself up for a final all-out attack over as wide an area as possible - the lull before the storm.

What was sure was that the instinct to attack humanity - initiated through the spillage at the Shepherd Scar Research Centre - had spread right across the planet and was now in the genes and very DNA of the natural world. But there seemed to be subtle shifts in its behaviour, too: whereas most animals would have killed as many as possible of their prey in a frenzied carnage, now they had been observed as being more careful and not taking more than they required. This was apparent with bears in the Canadian wilds catching only the salmon they needed for survival, and foxes not taking more than one or two chickens - where they could now find them in the wild.

To say that the human world was tense was an

understatement: with the variety of species and their distribution so vast and profound in every pocket of the earth, there was always the chance of a deadly encounter, whether it was on a small or grand scale. And no-one knew where the next attack might occur. Due to the mass killing of animals and birds which normally would have been slaughtered for food, the rise in vegetable consumption had caused huge problems. It had become essential to introduce rationing - not seen since the second world war in most countries - to control overconsumption of what had overnight become the staple diet of the Western nations. In some instances, riots had happened when people had not had their rations satisfied: and in warmer countries such as Italy, The Canaries, Israel and Spain, the incidence of stealing vegetables for the black market had become unstoppable until armies were ordered to guard the sheds and fields. Luxury fruits such as strawberries were replaced with more nutritious and filling vegetables such as potatoes and tomatoes: but still there were shortages and the insects that were their usual enemies were now viewed with even more hostility in case they were the vanguard of a possible plot against humanity.

The British government, rocked by the accusations and apparent complicity of the Sir Digby Crichton revelations, had gone into meltdown, with ministers claiming and counter-claiming against each other. The prime minister was powerless to control them and the scandal had implicated him, too. In Egypt, the new government had denied all knowledge of Abu

Bhakraim or the Fraternity Corporation. Instead, it intensified its invective and called the accusations slander. In America, the UN had tried to make all races work together to conquer the threat from the natural world; but with the usual nations pitted against each other expressing the customary entrenched views, and with the serum apparently in the hands of two European nations who, in turn, could not agree amongst themselves whether it was to be administered under EU, British, German or UN auspices, the diplomatic chaos was intense. It was beginning to look as if the natural world, having fomented this catastrophe through an error of humanity, was just standing back and observing the resultant bedlam.

Doug had safely made the journey to Cheshire without being attacked. He had noticed some birds of prey regarding him at the army heliport on departure but it did not presage any attack. Not yet, anyway. His chopper was escorted by four other army helicopters which drew attention to him but which should have been able to repel an assault. Everywhere below him he could see the rotting corpses of animals that had been killed, either by poison or gun, and swathes of land blackened or bleached by fire or chemicals. He could not help but feel that all this killing was only provoking the animal kingdom further...

He and Mick had been in constant touch, and they both agreed that they should pool as much of their research together as possible, from different locations, for security, despite the distance. After all, they were both millionaires several times over now - if they ever got a chance to spend it. The important thing was to manufacture the antidote as fast as possible. The trouble was, the animal world would soon know where they were and what they had created. And they would not just stand by and accept it.

There were others who wanted to know where Mick and Doug were, too; but had not yet located them. When they did, the weakest link would be internet security...

Sir Digby Crichton stepped out onto the airstrip. As he did so, another small plane swooped in and landed bumpily not too far away. In the fresh, crisp air that blew at him, it crossed his mind that it was strange a plane could land so quickly and so close to theirs, but did not make any connection. Then he saw people shouting and waving and in a moment it was all very apparent indeed.

The pilot was taxiing towards him now and he could see he was gesticulating wildly at him: Sir Digby suddenly realised that salvation was at hand and, without looking back, found himself running towards the plane. The door was opened and he tumbled in, grabbing at a red plastic loop handle above his head and pulling himself in. Someone slammed the door shut and fastened the latch; the plane was by then turning and bumping down the grass airstrip and, as he tried to sit in one of the luxurious seats, he realised that he recognised it: it was the plane that had taken him to Frankfurt. He managed to see out of the window and saw Smythe, the detective and the pilot running after the plane, waving and shouting madly, but then it was off the ground and soaring away, his former captors becoming tiny specks as the plane gained height.

He looked around. It was then that he saw his fellow passenger, the one who had pulled the door shut. He was a heavily-bearded man in Arab dress: but Sir Digby did not recognise him. So he smiled at him, and this was reciprocated.

Their sparse and hurried conversation revealed that the man had been at Frankfurt airport and had been instructed to pass on some information to him: however, when Sir Digby was arrested, his mission had changed.

"But you have offended Abu Bhakraim," he stated, finishing the story and still smiling.

"I had no intention of so doing," said Sir Digby, unsure at what emotion he should be expressing. "We were found out. I was betrayed."

"And now you have betrayed Abu Bhakraim."

"Er, I think not. Look, I have many other contacts. We can get this back on track if -" but the man was now hemming him in by the door. Then, he grabbed the loop on the roof of the plane to steady himself and deftly unlocked the latch, opening the door. The sudden torrent of air caused Sir Digby to stumble and he fell against the frame, grasping at anything he could hold on to, papers and plates and blankets scudding out into the slipstream. His last sight was the pilot looking around the cockpit door and, seeing him at the edge of the abyss, turning the plane suddenly sideways so that the earth was precisely below him. He shouted as his hands slipped off the leather seat and he fell out, his jacket and silver hair contorted and flapping in his downward spiral to oblivion. Then the pilot righted the plane again and the two men were turning back towards the east, their duty accomplished.

On the ground, the pilot and Smythe had been lent binoculars by the airfield staff and had watched the event as it unfolded. When the body left the plane, they had all gasped, but knew there was nothing they could do. Sir Digby Crichton was dead, his body splattered across a rocky outcrop by the sea.

"I'd better go and make out a report," said Smythe, with characteristic British understatement.

Mick sat at his desk, a restrained smile on his face; he was observing a computer screen on which there were twelve graphically represented vats. He was monitoring the levels of these remotely, for it was today that the first batches of serum were being produced. They were filling slowly as the production process started to gain momentum and it was soon possible for him to see a thin red line at the bottom of each vat. They were on the way at last.

After Gunter's initial tests, the serum had been tested on many more different species; all of these had been caught locally - at risk of vengeance from the surrounding fauna - and had shown signs of inter-species communication and group hostility towards humanity. With a military escort, they had been transported to the factory and divided into diverse groups, where they had been sprayed with the serum under controlled conditions. Every movement was monitored, recorded on disc and analysed and, in each box, air quality and inter-species reactions were observed and annotated. Mick had been delighted to see that in every case the results were the same: after twenty minutes, all aggression had disappeared and with it the ability of all these different species to communicate with one another. Mick was relieved and pleased, and e-mailed Doug in Cheshire, who was doing the same experiment under similar circumstances; the two firms had agreed to share their knowledge lest one facility was lost for whatever reason, a torrent of data passing between them across the continent via the internet. However, production at Doug's establishment, Jennings Chemicals, would commence two weeks later as their preparation had been less advanced than Hörst's; yet neither company had time on their side as, in each instance, the captured animals had conveyed their whereabouts exclusively to the surrounding wildlife before they had been returned to their benign state...

And so it was on that Sunday that a massive, unheralded and concerted attack was launched on both chemical establishments simultaneously. As backup and diversion, wherever wildlife could influence the movement of people, they did so, in an instinctive and rebellious rush; at airports, thousands of foxes, dogs, badgers and rodents criss-crossed the runways, causing several incidents where landing planes spun off the tarmac, crashing into ones awaiting take-off and resulting in passengers being engulfed in flames and smoke, killing hundreds: the animals also ran riot in the passenger halls and maintenance areas, attacking and injuring, biting and, occasionally, killing. Across motorways, deer, sheep, horses and more that had escaped culling were running - traversing the lanes and causing multiple pile-ups, carnage and death; in every country, indigenous species joined together to compound the mayhem. In addition to the global chaos at airports and motorways, other acts of revenge were being exacted: another nuclear installation was put into meltdown in China, and others in Japan. In Australia, the High Flux Australian Reactor, only just decommissioned but, like all reactors a radiation hazard for another twenty-four thousand years, was invaded and began leaking radiation into the soil and atmosphere. In continents such as Africa and India, larger animals, like elephants, rhinoceros, crocodiles, hippopotami and gorilla joined the fray; in Kashmir, a train was derailed as it collided with a herd of elephants who then charged and trumpeted their way along its length, pushing carriages over as passengers ran for their lives, only to be trampled by others and killed and chased by the speed and carnivorous instincts of hyenas, leopards and tigers and abetted by mosquitoes, termites and ants; even smaller mammals and reptiles like meerkat, gazelle, monkeys, iguana, lizards, porcupines and armadillo joined the fray in this surge of revenge against the ravages of humankind and its destruction of their habitats, lives and food chains.

Crocodiles came out of swamps and attacked villages across Africa and Australia, alligators did the same in America; in Spain, fighting bulls in Seville's *plaza de toros* managed to kick down their enclosures and ran into the ring, killing four matadors, two horses and members of the crowd before they had been overcome. Even pets attacked their doting owners and in a battery-farm outside Geneva, thousands of geese being fattened for paté had attacked a foreman and then escaped into the wild, attacking passers-by and causing an old lady to have a fatal heart-attack: across South America, millions of bats attacked any human they could find, different breeds inflicting a variety of different wounds and intensities. They all had a grudge, never before expressed so totally, so completely and with so much determination - and today they were showing their power...

At sea, too, yachts and small ferries were lifted out of the water by massive shoals of concerted and single-minded fish, with help from sea-going mammals such as seals and walrus. In the wider oceans, Japanese and Norwegian whaling-ships were targeted by the quarry they were hunting, and two ocean liners were capsized. And, as always, birds of prey finished off what other mammals and reptiles could not, swooping out of the sky like squadrons of death; even usually unaggressive birds such as thrushes and starlings swooped on people in cities, making it impossible to go outside, whereupon many were attacked within their buildings by insects, rodents and reptiles that got in through open windows, pipes, or cracks in the floors and walls.

Yet the assaults on Hörst and Jennings' chemical facilities were the most concentrated: happening at precisely the same time, there was no possibility of dialogue between the two. As at Flamanville, the animals drove at the fences and gates with selfless vigour, sweeping away in moments those who were spraying them with lethal poison and causing them to die in their own liquid. Then they were through the fences and running across the compound, birds swooping in dozens into windows to smash them whilst sheep, cattle and other bony-headed creatures rammed doors to open them. Soon they were inside the internal perimeter fences and threatening the control rooms and research centre, chemical stores and main offices from where the operation was being masterminded. They seemed to know precisely where they were going, many of them turning, swerving and attacking in unison, like shoals of fish in a clear ocean. Other, larger animals just battered away in ones and twos, patiently and objectively wrecking whatever they could in their quest to get inside and destroy the means of neutering their ambition to retake the planet: it was their final chance to go back to a time before the upstart man had arrived to subdue them.

Everywhere the din was deafening as structures collapsed and the combined cries of thousands of animals, birds and insects contributed to the maelstrom of destruction.

From his top-floor office, Mick watched this surge of creation welling up towards his inner sanctum: birds were flying at the windows but here these were thick and double-glazed, unlike lower down. Although he had been expecting some sort of attack, the venom and cohesion of it astonished even him: it was so well orchestrated, precise, focussed, deadly. Beside him, Gunter was in a wild state: "Lock the doors," he was screaming as people ran in opposing directions, not knowing where to go or what to do and all in a state of total panic. Mick was shouting at them, too: "Stay calm - do what I say and we'll repel them." But no-one was listening. So he slapped Gunter hard around the face as the noise and panic intensified and grabbed his shoulders. "Listen," he screamed, "Can you open the vats?" Gunter looked at him, uncomprehending. "Open the vats," he shouted. Suddenly, Gunter realised what he was trying to say, but it was too late. All the lights then went out and the computers stopped.

At the far end of the facility, the animals had chewed through the power lines and were now swarming over the pipes linking the actual production part of the installation to the vats, surging over and amongst them, the smaller ones gnawing and tearing, the bigger ones butting and shoving: soon, fractures appeared and fine sprays of liquid started to fan into the air; then these became bigger and soon torrents of fluid were pouring from the pipes and valves, flooding the concrete under the vats and creating a chemical stink that assailed every nostril, whether animal or human.

Mick was watching this and suddenly a ray of hope spread about him. He observed the ranks of animals below, saw the battalions of birds darkening the sky around him and the insects that crawled and bit wherever they were, but started to feel more, rather than less, optimistic. "They've punctured the vats!" he shouted, "They've punctured the vats!" Most of his staff were on the floor, crying and attempting to make phone calls to loved ones on now-defunct mobiles: the landlines had been severed in the first wave. Those who spoke English there reacted strangely to his observation and calmed down a little: those who did not continued wailing and screaming as the aerial assault continued. Birds were flying ever harder at the windows in a desperate attempt to breach them, but the panes held firm even though the frames rattled and shook with each thudding attempt to destroy them. Any insect that was found was being trampled or squashed into oblivion as the terrified humanity made a futile attempt to seek revenge. But Mick was smiling... "Twenty minutes," he said to himself over and over again; "If we can last just twenty minutes..."

Outside, most of the birds hitting the windows had become stunned and fell to the ground. Once there, they splashed into the deepening flow of liquid that was now covering every part of the concourse as the vats were emptied and more were breached. From his vantage-point, Mick noticed that the animals were revelling in the liquid and in an instant realised that they believed it to be the original, not the antidote that he and Doug had created: they were bathing in it, drinking it... Mick's spirits rose further, for he knew that by the time the attack had started every vat was at least a quarter full and increasing. And it was beginning to take effect...

At the Jennings Chemical works in Britain, Doug's firm was going through the same ordeal - with one difference. The army and air force had, in the face of governmental paralysis, decided to take command of events together without ministerial say-so if the need arose. As a result, plans had been made and defences created that would save the country's only producer of the anticipated chemical saviour should an attack occur. So as soon as the animals had appeared, they had been met with the combined wrath of several battalions surrounding the fences, all heavily armed with guns, flame-throwers, lethal poison and a test run of the very same liquid now being drained out of the vats in Germany: but the results were in stark contrast to what was happening there. The animals, although of much the same numbers, were repelled more effectively and the birds, although they did their best, were powerless to inflict the same damage. And, as in Germany, the serum was beginning to take effect...

Mick watched as the assault lost intensity: the animals who were in the mire of fluid were suddenly looking lost and bewildered, their sense of objectivity annulled and their reason for being there unknown. Many just started lumbering about aimlessly as the antidote took effect. The birds that had fallen, stunned, into the liquid were now unsure of their role and as they regained their consciousness just flew off, their mission forgotten. As the liquid was ingested, the rodents that had severed the pipes found themselves looking out at the devastation they had caused, without realising who had done it or why; soon, they were scuttling back to their nests, holes and banks. In all cases, though, they were carrying the serum back into the wild, which would return them to the state of subservience that had existed for thousands of years before.

And as the liquid seeped over the concrete surroundings into the earth, it would be carried by water-courses far and wide. The revolution of the species would soon be over...

BOOK FOUR

The Aftermath

Chapter 33

The repelling of the attack in Britain had been greeted with joy around the world, even in the middle east: and as the Jennings installation started to produce the compound, hope and expectations rose. In Frankfurt, the sudden diminution of the animals' assault had at first been taken as a sign of retreat and, despite Mick's protestations to the contrary, for several days a more virulent attack was generally expected: but as the hours and then the days passed it seemed as if the ingestion of the serum had started to take effect. Although it was realised that the return to normality might be slow, hope was high that at last the threat was fading. Within two days the perimeter fences at Hörst Chemicals had been repaired and the pipes mended. Four days later the installation had once again started to manufacture the precious serum. It was even given a name: Vida. It had become a product, rather than a hope or dream...

As Vida became more plentiful, so the armies and air forces of the world started to spray every square inch of land, starting with centres of population and then areas where there were high levels of wildlife. Homes, factories, offices, woods, estates, heathland, fields, streets, parks, farmland, transport infrastructure - all were systematically sprayed, inside and out, as were intensive arable operations and battery-farms. Even abattoirs. A hundred-mile area around the Shepherd Scar Research Centre was the first obligation of the government and its last major act for, following the scandals which had been brewing for years and caused institutionalised sleaze and ineptitude, it had crashed in on itself, destroyed by an angry public and furious backbenchers who had orchestrated its own downfall. It was annihilated at a snap election by a mood of public disgust and betrayal: as the Shepherd Scar Research Centre had been destroyed by a mood of fear and reaction, so their respective claims as crucibles of influence were now the stuff of history. The first would never be rebuilt: the second would never recover...

As the stocks of Vida rose, and outbreaks of animal violence lessened on land, it became possible to apply vast quantities of it into the seas as well, where there had been further attacks. At river mouths and estuaries, sprays were initiated, and in the oceans, where fish stocks were plentiful, huge drums of Vida were dropped into them, the currents and thermal vents ensuring that its effects were disseminated around the globe. As marine attacks lessened - as they had on land and in the air - so people became more confident and life started to return to normal, both for humankind and the natural world. It would take time, though: the Earth would soon be functioning as it had done for millennia, but humankind had at last learned that the natural world was one that must be respected and integrated, not destroyed or confronted. Or would do so at least until homo sapiens became arrogant once more...

After the attacks at the respective chemical facilities, Frank had been approached by a national newspaper and offered the post of editor; this was done as a gesture of gratitude to delight the populace as much as for recognising his integrity and vision. He stipulated, though, that Jessie must join him as assistant, which was readily accepted: she had become not just a well-known face and contributor to television and newspaper articles but an icon of resistance against terror and bad government. She was also paid a huge advance to write the story of the Shepherd Scar Research Centre, which would become a global best-seller. She and Frank had also become inseparable: when they had re-met back at the Hickley & District News, Enid had not seen them for hours. They just melted into one another and then disappeared, allowing their relief, love and mutual respect to blossom and to administer itself in the most humanly natural way possible. That two souls were meant for one another was never questioned by anybody.

It was not so easy for Doug. He had fallen for Ishrani but had not seen her since he avoided her eye at Rosyth and been forced to tear himself away. Unknown to her, though, he had followed her trial and even put in some emollient words to her prosecutors. She had been accused - with the others recruited at Rosyth - of incitement to racial hatred, contravening the Official Secrets Act, and aiding and abetting a foreign power to destabilise the country. They were hefty charges, and each would carry a long prison sentence if she was found guilty. In her defence, she claimed at her trial not to know that she was in the pay of a foreign power, believing that she was working for the British government, which had been what she was told: it was not her fault that Sir Digby Crichton was a traitor and had misinformed her. And the fact that all the recruits appeared to be descended from foreign backgrounds she dismissed as something that she had not even noticed, given the diverse cultural mix that was modern Scotland. As for the racial hatred, she professed to having none for anyone, and Doug had been touched when he had heard that she told the jury of her admiration and affection for him; as she, of course, was of a different faith to his, where was the racial hatred? Some time later, when the authorities had asked Doug's views on this, Doug had presumed the positive, although he could not honestly verify it; only that they had spent some intimate time together. He resisted the plea to go to court either to accuse or defend her, citing his business at getting the serum out into the world. He mused, though, whether it really had been to gain his trust to further the aims of a foreign power or whether her affection was genuine and unassociated: that truly was the sticking-point. As such, this accusation spilt over into whether it was a contravention of the Official Secrets Act: it was this which would be the tricky one. She admitted to have willingly colluded with Abu Bhakraim when she had met him once briefly at her job interview but maintained that she thought he was working for the British government: what she would not admit to was that she was implicated in research to help his cause and his corporation. She stated her belief that it had been to create the counterpoison to revert the supremacy of the human race back to its dominant position, and that was her driving motive. Nothing else was on her mind and she had had no intention of conspiring against her countrymen, whatever their colour, faith, persuasion or politics.

It seemed to be working; and when Doug received a message from her asking for a visit in prison, he found it difficult to refuse. However, having agonised over his feelings, he decided to await the verdict, and sent a message to say that he would meet her after that. He was somewhat surprised, though, when all charges against her were dropped; he felt sure that she would at least have been required to serve a few token years in prison, if only to appease a fractious public. Whether he would have waited for her was debatable: with his money, new house, fame and apparent youth - helped by the age compounds he and Mick had both stumbled over at different stages and degrees - he was not now short of feminine interest. Indeed, the new compound - called Aegis - was now a joint product between Jennings and Hörst and selling worldwide in vast amounts - particularly in France and America. He and Mick both reflected on how the twists and turns of events at Shepherd Scar had played with their lives and then dealt them both a wonderful, winning hand...

That Doug still had a soft spot for Ishrani was obvious; Mick had discussed her with him on many occasions whilst his relationship with Heidi had faltered - she did not want to be 'in the spotlight'. He had tried to make her change her decision and promised a lot of time away from work: after all, he could afford it now several times over. Yet she was not to be dissuaded. As for Doug, he was so attracted to Ishrani that it made discussion difficult: but the fact that she had been cautioned and told she would be 'under surveillance' for the foreseeable future disturbed him. She was also prohibited from working for any government institution or chemical facility. So how could he talk to her of his work while these restrictions applied? And was she lucky to be innocent and free, or guilty but very, very persuasive?

He weighed up his feelings and decided to risk seeing her. If she really wanted to get to know him better, it would be apparent. At least, he hoped it would be. He decided that, whatever happened, he would definitely tell her he could not marry her and, if they lived together, he would sever relations before they were deemed to be a common-law couple. And if she was not the girl he secretly hoped she really was, then he was not going to sacrifice his wealth and work - or his country - for someone who was not in concert with his interests.

When he saw her, though, he was entranced anew. It was only then that he noticed a mild Scottish burr in her otherwise Asian voice: perhaps he had been blinded before by the quality of her research, her beauty and the fact he was tired, stressed and over-worked. But now he could assess her again, away from the pressures that had divided them; and now that she was exonerated, it would be impossible to walk away from her again. Within a few weeks she had moved in with him, even though the government would caution him against giving her any sensitive information. This he agreed to gladly: he loved his country as well as his new life. He just wanted to grow old with the woman he loved...

It was perhaps fitting that, during this time, the mystery of Mick's missing brother was resolved: but as is so often the case, it threw up another question. The army, having previously destroyed the Shepherd Scar Research Centre, nonetheless frequently made reconnaissance flights to ensure that nothing had begun to stir again. On one occasion, they had noticed something strange in Bracken Mere and had flown closer for a better look. They had then alerted troops on the ground who had subsequently found it to be a silver car, immersed under the surface. But inside it was not one body, but two: Mick's brother, Sam, and a man of obvious middle-eastern extraction. With the latter was one piece of incriminating evidence - a document with a picture of Mick and details of where he worked. And the letterhead was 'Fraternity Corporation'. But whoever had executed this man - or why - would remain a mystery forever...

The full details and chemical processes that created Vida for the benefit of humankind had only been given to selected governments: after the Crichton debacle, many were sensitive about where the information ended up. This threw up a bitter resentment, for a number of middle eastern countries, perceived to have a possibly hostile agenda against the West, were excluded; bitterness and a sense of missed opportunity to overthrow years of what was seen as oppression and insult in the Arab world started to become prevalent. Indeed, it had come to believe that the animal kingdom was their potential saviour and had been chosen by their faith as an agent for a rebalancing of not just the geopolitical order but that of theology, too. After all, as the deity had created the Earth, so the animals had been created as well; they were both divine and indivisible...

Once Vida had passed a critical point in its production volumes, Mick and Doug had laboured to understand the reasons for the outbreak: they were perplexed by the fact that, on their own, the chemicals would have had little impact on the environment, except locally. So when they had eventually concluded that the leaking chemicals had interacted with the type of soil found at Shepherd Scar and that one if its components, a loam rich in phosphorous, was the elusive catalyst that had tipped the events into the cataclysm which had followed, these findings were disseminated across the world in minutes.

Everything now seemed to be getting back to normal, a huge progression from the utter despair of only a few weeks before. But as with all progress, there was an Achilles' heel: once the lines of electronic communication had been fully restored, franchise operations to allow chemical companies to make the serum available globally had been initiated across the web, albeit in encrypted format but to authorised recipients only. For Mick and Doug, it was often necessary for them to travel to different locations, advising on the production of Vida around the world, and although they never travelled together for security reasons, their trips engendered a great deal of internet traffic, weblinks and discussion.

So it was no surprise when, one morning a year later at the head offices of the national newspaper group that Enid, Frank and Jessie were so influential in that they found themselves looking at a newsfeed which disturbed them. It was information intercepted from the middle east, where a company called Fraternity had spent millions of dollars researching the conditions and chemicals that had started the first crisis; they had now managed to make a close copy of the original serum - but with a secret, crucial difference. And they were threatening to use it.

But, this time, the antidote was known only to them. A new revolution of the species, targeted against the West, was about to begin ...

ABOUT THE AUTHOR

Simon Holder worked for most of his life in broadcast television for the BBC, Channel 4, ITV, Sky and more before turning to writing novels. His topics are wide and varied - love stories, short stories, the environment and a humorous thriller set in a TV background are his most recent. His interests include the environment, politics, music, literature and freedom of expression.

Printed in Great Britain
by Amazon

28530507R00205